ISLAN

DRE...

GW01401155

Aline P'nina Tayar

ISLAND OF DREAMS

Aline P'nina Tayar

This novel is a work of fiction. Names, characters, places and incidents are either the product of the author's imagination or are used fictionally. Any resemblance to actual persons, living or dead, or to events are entirely coincidental.

ISBN 978-0-9573783-0-8

Published by Ondina Press

CONTENTS

The Toledano Family

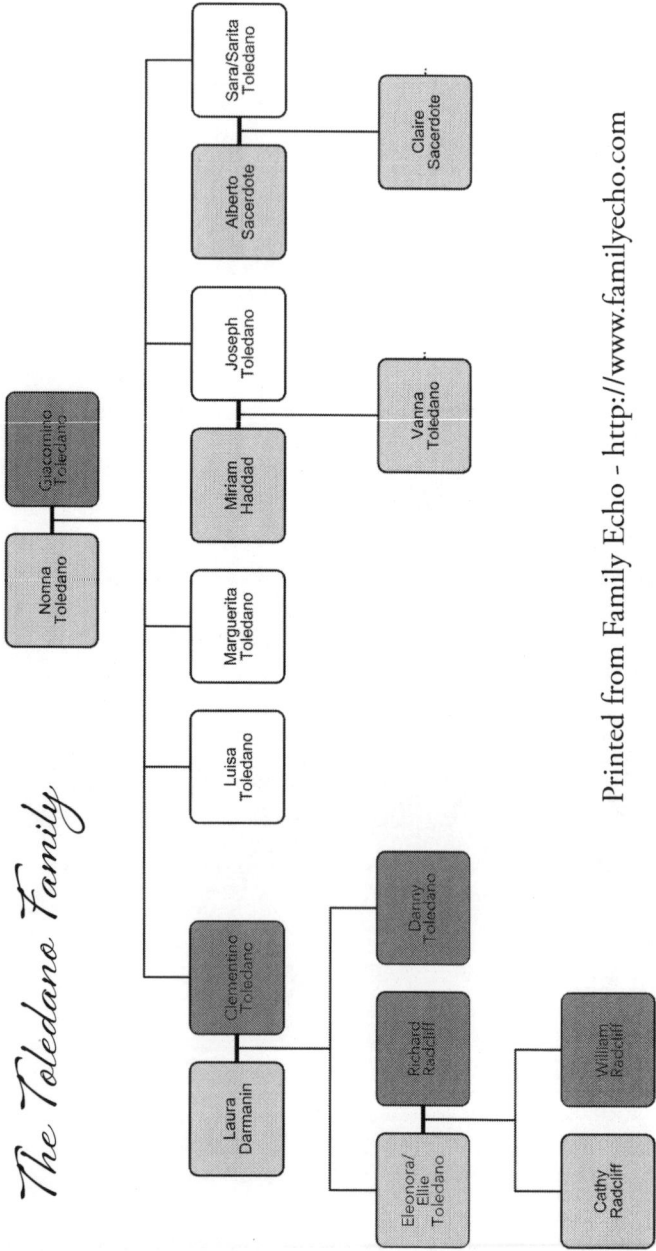

Printed from Family Echo – http://www.familyecho.com

Claire

1 The Heron in the Park

Two days ago, in the Parc Léopold, I saw Yves with the boy. Turn on your heels and flee, a voice in my head yelled. Get out of the park! Make a detour round the front of the Dinosaur Museum. It won't take you that far out of your way.

For two years I had lived in fear of such a chance encounter with my estranged husband, and now there he was walking through the park holding a child by the hand. Without him as my reference point, I had felt bereft. My home in Brussels had never truly been his, and when we were married he always said he did not want to live permanently here. Nonetheless, he has chosen Brussels to live with another woman and their child. Seeing him again was bound to cause me pain.

Charlotte Brontë named Brussels 'Villette' – Small Town – and her account of an emotional collapse caused by rejection and extreme loneliness has rarely been bettered in English literature. It's a novel I have read over and over. Sometimes, when showing visitors from abroad around Brussels, I take them to the place where there's a small remnant of the wall of the *pensionnat* where Brontë taught for a year. The rest is buried under a roadway.

If Brussels is Small Town, then the quarter where the European institutions are located is a tiny village. Not only on my way to work but also at weekends, when winds whistle around the imperial buildings and sweep through deserted squares, I bump into one or two people I know in this quarter. Yves lives here so there has always been a risk that one day our paths would cross.

Just two days ago in the Parc Léopold, my curiosity was greater than my anxieties. In the twenty-five years I had known him, I'd never seen Yves chatting with ease to a child. He had not shown any interest in the offspring of our friends and had rejected the idea of fathering children himself. We had been a very modern couple, living in two separate households. He worked in Rome; my work was in Brussels. Where would we bring up children? On the overnight Wagons-Lit via Milan, Yves would joke. Even when they abolished that sleeper service, years ago, he remained amused by his own *bon mot*.

I quickened my pace so as not to lose sight of him and the boy. My husband is fair whereas the child by his side had blue–black, dye-straight hair. This had to be the son by his Chinese lover, the brilliant geneticist from Hong Kong, the gifted amateur pianist, the future Nobel laureate. Only in retrospect do I remember that in the last years of our marriage Yves had often spoken about their joint research at Leonetti Pharmaceuticals s.p.r.l., although I don't recall hearing her name. Perhaps I hadn't been paying enough attention. Lovers like repeating the name of the object of their desire. Secret lovers are strangely more prone to it. I had become too complacent. After fifteen years of marriage, I did wonder

8

why Yves had begun to speak English when talking to me about his research, but I concluded that it was to do with a change of job. As an interpreter, my working life is all about words, so I should have noticed when he came out with new terms and talked about things that were not only out of character but also outside his range of English vocabulary, particularly in matters emotional. Now I think he was reproducing the thoughts and ideas of that other woman, not just saying something he'd read in the press or a novel.

Yves did not see me hurrying down the slope behind the Dinosaur Museum, which is perhaps where he had taken the boy, the sort of thing a good father might do with an eight-year-old on a Wednesday afternoon in Brussels. I often watch men with small children and feel a pang of sadness at my childlessness. Having been brought up solely by a loving father from the age of twelve, I am moved by the sight of fathers taking their children for a walk or a swim or playing with them in the park.

My colleague Iris Elizabeth Walton used to say that Yves didn't just enter a room, he took possession of it. He is tall and, though lean, has broad shoulders. He has always been proud of his thick mane and holds his head high, tilting his chin upwards. I have always loved the way he appears so completely at ease with the world. So it was painful but touching to see the child mimicking the adult's gait, his thumbs hooked in the pockets of faded jeans exactly like the ones his father was wearing. 'Yves's cool dude look,' Iris Elizabeth dubbed it. 'It's all pretence: the French despising the Americans. They adore American films even when blasting them for their commercialism.'

By late November, the trees in the park are stripped of their leaves. I could advance no further without the risk of being seen. I posted myself by the hedge that surrounds the playground located in a corner of the park not far from the central pond. Anyone passing might have taken me for one of the mothers of the children playing in the sandpit or running around whooping as they scuffed up fallen leaves. This was the last place Yves would expect to spot me, I thought. I was safe, but it did feel humiliating to be a grown-up woman hiding in this way.

From the playground I had a clear view to the pond, and I saw Yves leaning forward, an ear close to the boy's mouth. My blood rushed to my stomach as he gave the child his complete attention. When he rested his hand on the boy's shoulder, I remembered the gentle, sustained pressure he'd used to coax me to his point of view. 'Let's be rational. With our way of life, kids are not an option.' I heard his words in my head. At that moment, in the middle of the playground, I could also feel the weight of his hand. The heat of it too. There was a rock in my throat and a metallic taste in my mouth as I watched him steer the boy away from the path towards the edge of the pond.

The child was already three years old by the time Yves told me he had a son. I walked around with stomach cramps for days. I realised I didn't know my husband at all, or was it that the loving things he'd said to me in the first years of our marriage had been true and that it was only much later that he'd stopped loving me?

Since the day he confessed his liaison, I pictured a chance encounter not with Yves but with his Chinese lover. In the last twelve months it has become compulsive. I stare at every oriental woman who crosses my path, sizing up her elegance and comparing her looks and her clothes to mine, especially the clothes. During my teenage years, when I might have developed an interest in what I wore, my father was in charge of me and he thought clothes were mere detail. In my first school in England, when I was just fourteen, my class had been assigned to write an essay on 'Clothes Maketh the Man'.

'What a ridiculous topic,' my father said. 'Is this what I'm paying good money for you to learn?'

Yves, on the other hand, had always paid careful attention to what women wore. I imagined the mother of his child as not only beautiful but innately elegant. These days, I have lost the appetite for clothes' shopping. Without Yves to guide me, I end up far too on edge to choose well. If in the past I deferred to him, it was because I could never muster the right degree of reverence for designer wear and luxury products. Perhaps Yves now tries to mould the tastes of the mother of his son, and she is as willing to be influenced as once I used to be.

It would be ironic if his mistress turned out to be the tall Chinese woman with the swan neck and high cheekbones whom I regularly see at *The Lunch Company* on the rue de Namur. I first noticed her and cast her in the role of Yves' mistress because of the low and husky voice she used when speaking to the waiters, so different from the musical highs and lows of Mandarin tones. We all have a template in our head of our ideal man or woman, and Yves had always said he preferred thin, fine-boned, dark women with deep husky voices.

He and I might never have met had he not heard my voice on mike at a conference and sought me out among the interpreters invited to the gala dinner.

'Ah, I've been listening to the English booth. To improve my English, of course,' he said. 'I bet if you sang, it would be contralto.'

I was so in thrall to his beauty that half an hour later I did not object when he suggested I wear my shawl in the way of Indian women, draped around my shoulders with the ends trailing at the back, rather than knotted at the front.

'Indian women have a natural elegance,' he said. 'It's so much sexier this way.'

Another woman might have told him to get lost, but I was pleased to be receiving attention from such a good-looking man. I was aware that other women in the room were looking at him with me, and I liked that.

I haven't told a soul about my obsessive interest in oriental strangers, and I certainly haven't said a thing to Laurent Bertrand, my therapist, to whom I am only just getting the hang of offering up snatches from my dreams to stop him harassing me about trusting him. What would he say if I told him that for the past year I've been lacerating myself with comparisons to strangers? I do it even when I cannot tell whether the woman is Chinese or Japanese.

৵৶

Yves and I had been lovers for only a couple of months when I first complained that I felt like a nomad, belonging nowhere, least of all Malta, where he had just suggested we go on holiday.

'Wouldn't you like to see the island again? Surely you're a little bit curious,' he said.

For me Malta was – and still is – a hostile place. In the mid-1970s, after the Medical Association of Malta had called upon the island's doctors to stop treating patients in protest against the government's health scheme reforms, my father, an anaesthetist, had remained without work for more than a year. Had not my mother been killed, however, we might not have been forced into exile, wandering from one country to another and changing homes seven times in ten years. It was inevitable, perhaps, that I should end up an interpreter.

It wasn't just that my father blamed himself for what had happened, but that he could not live with the accusations of my mother's family, spoken and unspoken. If he hadn't been on strike, he wouldn't have been targeted. The letter-bomb had been meant for him, not for my mother, although as a pharmacist she had been seen as siding with the medical profession. She had been the youngest and the brightest of all her family. Gradually my father broke off contact with the Toledanos. Once I'd had a vast family, now my family was reduced to just my father and me.

'Anyway, it's too bloody hot in August in Malta,' I said. 'As soon as you've dried yourself off after taking a shower, you have to shower all over again. And they don't have proper beaches, only rocks, which cut the soles of your feet to pieces. It's impossible not to tread on sea urchin spines, and the wounds get infected so easily. Look, the food isn't great. Timpana, the national dish, my God! Macaroni in a pastry pie. Talk about heartburn.

And though it might seem hard for you to believe this, the wine is even sweeter than kosher wine. How does that grab your tiny Frenchman's soul?'

'Okay, I'm convinced.' Yves waved the yellow marker pen, which he had been using to highlight sentences and paragraphs in travel brochures he had brought home for me. 'We'll go to Cyprus instead,' he said, 'and I'll help you shed the confusions and bad memories by turning you into a Frenchwoman. You must marry me.'

It was what I had always wanted, someone who would come to my rescue with a solution to my rootlessness. Thanks to marriage to a Frenchman, I would be able to state with confidence that I was French, and I had the passport and identity card to prove it. I would no longer have to explain my complicated origins when people asked me where I was from. At first I might have said it was Malta. For a long time after my father took me away, I missed the sun and sea of the island, the walks back from school along the promenade with my cousins Ellie and Vanna, the afternoon Russian lessons. We would drop in at my aunts' and mother's pharmacy and sometimes do our homework in a small room above the shop. My mother and I would go swimming every morning from the middle of June until the end of September. When we came out of the water, treading carefully to avoid the *rizzi* – I didn't know the English word, sea urchins, until much later – we sat on the rocks together, like best friends, picnicking on thick slices of Maltese bread.

In the years my father and I lived in Scotland, I never felt truly warm, not even in summer. After we left, I missed the spare beauty of the Scottish countryside and

14

even the rain. Just as I still miss the hills and vales of England now that I live in Belgium with its flat landscape and low skies. I seem to define myself more easily by the places I no longer live in than by the place in which I find myself; that was already the case when I first met Yves.

While he made his proposal, he rested one hand on my shoulder. With the other, he tilted my chin and, looking deep into my eyes, he suggested we go shopping, which is when I learned that aubergine was a colour that made me look ill by accentuating my pallor. Even though I liked navy, my father's favourite colour on me, Yves insisted it didn't suit my dark brown hair. Grey, black, beige, camel and cream denoted sophistication, he said. And a woman who is short should wear narrow trousers or, as he put it, 'Risk looking like a walking *champignon*'.

In retrospect, I hear a hint of insult in those words, an implied criticism of my lack of taste, and feel a touch of injury. But if I were to dissect every word my husband said to me, even the memories of our good times together would turn to ash.

It becomes harder and harder, however, to hold to the moments of shared pleasure and laughter, such as those Saturday mornings when we would take the train to Bruges, Antwerp or Ghent and stroll around antique shops and flea markets. One Sunday morning in Brussels, Yves found a copy of the memoir by Brand Whitlock, the American Ambassador to Belgium at the beginning of the First World War. Apart from having an avenue named after him, no one much remembers who Whitlock was, but he had access to the houses of the nobility and knew everyone it was important to know. The spine of the memoir was broken and pages were missing, but Yves meticulously restored the book.

It was my idea to visit the places mentioned in Whitlock's account of his posting in Belgium on the weekends Yves came to me in Brussels. We would make it a twice-monthly pilgrimage. I would write in advance to the owners of the grand houses that Whitlock described, asking them for access, and more often than not access was granted. Once a minor member of the Belgian royal family invited us to lunch at which six courses were served with a different wine for each. Though I already knew Yves was a gourmand, I hadn't until that day known how learned he could sound when discussing vintages and provenances. He was always surprising me, and that kept me interested throughout our marriage. Until, that is, the final surprise.

After the luncheon, we came home slightly tipsy and made love sleepily on the sitting room floor and, by then, wide-awake, we moved to the kitchen table before withdrawing to the bedroom and making love again.

Now I cannot help wondering if the Chinese geneticist has also undergone a transformation and, whether, once Yves has re-modelled her, he will again get bored with his new invention.

৩৵৹

When people ask me why I married Yves, I usually tell them it was because he had perfect taste. But more than that, I add, he had perfect table manners. I am not being wholly flippant, though I realise people must sometimes think I'm trying to hide the hurt by being funny.

Yves and I first met in Rome when he had just begun working for Leonetti s.p.r.l. The morning after our first night as lovers, I woke up to the smell of coffee and toast. Yves had got up before me and set his low Japanese dining table with beautiful minimalism: square white plates and lotus-shaped celadon tea bowls as translucent as eggshell. In the centre he had placed an emerald green vase with a single yellow rose. I watched him from the doorway in his thick bathrobe as he put the finishing touches, moving with a grace I found deeply arousing and unexpectedly so because I still had not discovered what could act as a trigger to my own sensuality.

Yves had spent part of his childhood in Japan where his father had been the French Cultural Attaché so although he is a tall man he has no difficulty sitting cross-legged on the floor to eat, whereas after a few minutes in that posture, my knee joints and back started to ache. But I would not have broken the spell of that first breakfast together by admitting my discomfort. It was mesmerising to watch Yves eat his toast. Not a single crumb fell on his lap while I, on the other hand, created a disaster zone of spilled crumbs all around me. Before using his knife to help himself to another pat of butter, Yves slid the blade into the side of the toast and pulled it out dishwasher-clean. Not having seen anyone do that before, I was curious. What was this show of delicacy all about?'

'It's something I learned from my commanding officer when I was doing national service in Toulon,' Yves said. 'This way, you clean the knife thoroughly and leave no crumbs on the butter.'

One day, I might tell Laurent Bertrand how that knife sliding into the toast had aroused my desire. It was the delicacy of the gesture, its surgical precision. I immediately had a mental picture of Yves and me making love the night before. I had at first been unable to relax and had had to ask him to stop. Getting out of bed, I put on his bathrobe and padded to the window where I stood hugging myself, feeling cold and miserable. At ease in his nakedness, Yves came up behind me and, without saying a word, put an arm round my shoulders and gently stroked my hair. Across the courtyard, on the first floor, there was a light on behind one of the tall and narrow windows. Through the frosted glass, we saw the silhouette of a woman. She was getting undressed in a leisurely way.

'Ah, Veronica, she's been trying to get me to notice her ever since she moved in.' Yves sounded amused as he nuzzled his face in my neck. 'Don't worry, she and I have never been lovers.'

The woman moved closer to the window and opened it. When she stood with her arms spread wide, I had no doubt that she was being deliberately provocative.

Yves took my hand and led me back to bed. The unexpected effect of seeing him through the prism of another woman's desire now stoked my own. I let him slide the robe off my shoulders and toss it on the floor. As he eased me down on my back, I opened my arms out, like the woman at the window. At that moment, the game, which both of us understood without speaking, was to make love without hardly any part of our bodies touching, swiftly and focused on just one thing. A few minutes later, Yves rolled over and I lay on top of him. This time we moved with exquisite slowness. A knife cutting through butter, that's what I thought of then. I was aware of Yves looking over my shoulder at the window across the yard, but I didn't mind. Picturing Veronica spying on us doubled my pleasure. In the morning, as we sat down to breakfast, I saw that her window was still open. I got up and crossed to the other side of the Japanese table. Sitting astride Yves, I was the one who took the initiative. This time the necessary balance in good sex between controlled violence and tenderness was perfect. Later, I think we became too familiar with each other and were no longer able to reproduce that finely balanced mix. Perhaps this happens to all married couples. When there's no element of fresh risk, where does the excitement come from?

For a long time, however, Yves went on surprising me in different ways. Three months after we'd first met, for instance, I discovered he was a talented amateur viola player. More astonishing was that he was in a team of expat rugby players. Since he was remarkably good-looking that might have made other men aggressive towards him, but he seemed very popular with his rugby pals. He also drew very well, but I only discovered that a couple of years into our marriage when we went on holiday to India and instead of a camera he brought a sketchbook with him. That book was one of the things he took from my place here in Brussels shortly before leaving me.

'What else don't I know about you?' I said, feeling pleased with myself for being the wife of such a multi-faceted man. Of course I'd have exiled myself to a desert island with him, but I cannot deny there was a side of me that wanted people to acknowledge that he was bound to me.

A few weeks after we'd become lovers, Yves began supervising workmen to demolish partitions and create a large, open-plan space in my apartment in Brussels, keeping a close eye on builders, plumbers, electricians and plasterers. Details that were sloppily executed had to be re-worked and re-worked. For the structural changes, he imported from Italy the same architect who had helped him do up his duplex in Rome.

My father hadn't taught me much about keeping a house tidy. As long as things were reasonably clean and he knew where what he needed was, the rest was unimportant. We had left Malta with two suitcases between us. In the houses we lived in after abandoning our home on the island, all our furniture had been functional, and in our many moves we had accumulated very little in the way of paintings, ornaments and souvenirs. Apart from my early childhood, when my mother was alive, I had only ever lived in flats and houses that had been decorated by previous owners and which, though never ugly, could not be said to have been beautiful either.

On first entering Yves' apartment on the via di Ripetta, I was intimidated by the perfect décor – every precious object and painting had been carefully placed to create a studied, dramatic effect, which was enhanced by the lighting. Having only seen such staged interiors in home-interiors magazines, I did not feel comfortable with such perfection. When removing my clothes in the bathroom, I found nowhere to hang them, which made me panic, and I scrunched them up and stored them in a cupboard under the sink. After showering, I wiped the splashes off the screen with my towel, so that it was soaked when I began to dry myself. There was no question of my disturbing the neat pile of white towels stacked high on the glass shelf above the sink.

I was as eager as a child to learn from Yves and please him, so I went along with anything he planned for me – and for the two of us. The design of my Brussels bedroom – a glass cube suspended from the ceiling high above the living area – was his stroke of genius, although he left it to the Italian architect to work out the engineering.

'*Ci penso io*,' was the architect's refrain – 'I'll see to it. No worries.'

Yves and I laughed in complicity at the flurry of busyness the architect liked to create around himself.

'It would be cruel,' Yves said, 'for the man to realise he was not the one in charge.'

I dared to believe that our shared laughter augured well for us as a couple, and though we both made fun of the architect, nicknaming him 'Signor Cipensoio', Yves had great respect for Cipensoio as an artist if not as a man and was patient when he failed to meet deadlines.

'You should learn to be less anxious and impatient, *ma chère*. Admit I know a thing or two about art and design. The result will be stunning. Trust me.'

It was Yves's decision to have everything in my apartment painted white, including the floor, just like the floor in his Rome apartment. On his insistence, visitors had to remove their shoes at the front door, which is an oriental custom I like, something we always did in Malta when I was a child, but which I have felt unable to enforce among my visitors. When Iris Elizabeth, my colleague and oldest friend in Brussels, refused to walk indoors barefoot on a cold day, Yves hinted that I should not invite her again. So when he was around I never did, and she, quite naturally, accused me of thinking more of the state of my floors than I did of her, remaining angry with me for years.

I can see now how the weakening of my friendship with Irish Elizabeth left me with one less point of reference in my life, and, God knows, I had few. She and I had been through the tortures of an interpreters school in Paris together and had survived the humiliations seen there as a necessary part of ensuring success in our careers. Apart from my work, all I had to define myself was my connection to Yves, my French husband. I got rid of all my old furniture and bought low armchairs upholstered in white. The cost of the lighting came to tens of thousands of old Belgian francs, but my husband convinced me it was worth it. Apart from the paintings, the only other colour in the living area came from the low, burnt-orange lacquer dining table, which Yves bought from an oriental furniture importer on the Avenue Louise. It looked exactly like the table in his apartment in Rome although not an antique.

Marriage did not mean that Yves and I lived together. He went on working in Italy where he had a large team of researchers and generous funding. I never knew what he did on his evenings in Rome. I supposed he worked overtime a great deal so that when he came to Brussels he could leave early on Friday night to catch a plane and stay on until Monday morning when he caught the first flight back. I should have asked him more questions, shown an interest in his working week, but it seemed to me that he didn't speak about it because he thought it would bore me. He didn't say anything about going to the theatre or cinema, so I assumed he only did that when he was with me. And though he knew much about modern and contemporary art and could expound at length on the fake emotions of Picasso's Blue Period, he didn't mention attending art exhibitions either. 'I pride myself,' he once said, 'on being able to identify false notes in any work of art.' I can see now I should have asked him then and there precisely what he meant when he spoke of fake emotions in a painting or a sculpture. How does one go about identifying them? Now I can't help wondering if the critique of Picasso was something that had come from his lover and that he would not have been able to explain. I took it for granted that when he was alone he ate out a great deal especially since at the weekends when it was my turn to travel to Rome we ate out all the time and it was clear that he was well known in the city's best restaurants.

A few years after we got married, a chance came up for me to work in Rome as a translator. It was Yves who pointed out that I would find translating boring because it required precision and orderliness which was not part of my nature. I had to admit it was true.

'Besides which,' Yves said, 'doesn't living apart make for a more exciting marriage? We need never fall into the humdrum.'

Ah, humdrum, another word I hadn't known he knew. Anyway, I did not give up my clients in Brussels or my single-woman's way of life. If I hadn't been able to see my husband every weekend, I would have been unhappy coming home to an empty place. But during the week, when I was by myself, I tended to gobble my food, standing up at the kitchen counter, then get into my dressing gown and read and watch films and not worry about washing up dishes or putting away my clothes. I was able to loll about and not feel I had to be perfectly groomed. Only when Yves was in Brussels did I pay attention to the way I looked and to what and how fast I ate. Together he and I would take our time over food shopping and cooking. We always ate at the Japanese table, making every meal, even breakfast, formal.

There is almost nothing in this home of mine that is of my own choosing. This thought occurred to me ten days ago, triggered by the realisation that for the first time in forty years I had woken up and not immediately remembered my mother on the anniversary of her death. It was the phone call from my cousin Vanna, imploring me to return to Malta, which had jolted my memory. Though I do not believe in an afterlife and think it is sheer arrogance on the part of people who do believe, I suddenly felt I needed to make amends to my mother's spirit. Hence my decision to have the only photograph I own of her and her siblings as children framed and put up on the sitting-room wall.

When I came across Yves and his son in the Parc Léopold, I had been on my way to *Artiges* to choose a picture frame for that old photograph taken in a studio in Valletta in 1936. In it, the children are lined up, tallest to shortest, going from right to left, all dressed in sailor suits. The girls, Luisa, Marguerita and Sarita – who was to become my mother – have big bows in their hair, whereas my uncles, Clementino and Joseph, are wearing matelot caps. Standing at right angles to the camera, the children look beguilingly over their shoulder at the photographer. My mother, however, must have moved just as the picture was taken for she's not quite looking at the viewer and her face is blurred. At the risk of sounding dramatic, it seems to me that the blurring was some sort of premonition of my mother's early death and this is why the picture speaks to me more than any other photograph I have of her.

∾≈

'Bravo, this is very good.' Laurent Bertrand had welcomed my plan to take down one of Yves' massive paintings and put up the family photograph in its place.

'Perhaps you're beginning to come out of this long somnambulist phase. Maybe you'll soon be able to reclaim a little of your territory and hence of yourself by erasing some of your husband's imprint from your surroundings.'

No doubt the larger painting will have left a shadow, I thought, and I will have to paint the whole wall before putting up the smaller picture.

I was definitely in a trance in the Parc Léopold as I watched Yves and the boy draw nearer the pond. That small piece of water is all that is left above ground of the Maelbeek, the stream that used to run by the old Berlaymont Palace. Like many watercourses in Brussels, the Maelbeek had already been buried some time last century, but now and again, when it rains heavily, the river bursts through and floods not only the building sites but also the nearby Metro station, and we are reminded of the forces that lie hidden under our feet.

'A strange habit, covering over your waterways,' Yves said once. 'They did precisely the same with part of the Senne, which used to flow through the city. This is why Brussels lacks a focal point. Oh, forget the *Grand' Place*. A true city has to have water at its heart. Humans are made up ninety per cent of water. To feel alive we must live by the sea or a river.'

When people asked Yves why he refused to make Brussels his home, he would say that the depredations of the developers in this city more than in any other depressed him.

'Not that I was ever a great fan of the Art Nouveau which used to abound in Brussels. Art Deco is my thing. All those tangled vines and that *foisonnement* of curlicues in Art Nouveau decorations and friezes, what's that all about if not suppressed sexuality?' Yves would add. 'And now with all this demolition and re-building, even the suppressed sexuality has been suppressed.'

Some people dismissed his broad generalisations and tactless sniping about Brussels as typical Parisian arrogance. Others felt deeply offended. For many years, however, I admired his outspokenness, seeing him as courageous, ready to challenge all received wisdoms. At the time, I also believed that tact was just another form of hypocrisy. It was something I had learned from my father during the years he kept up the battle with the Maltese authorities to hunt down my mother's killers. For two decades after we'd left the island, he would assault the editors of the Maltese newspapers with letters accusing the island's government of blatant corruption and damning not only Mintoff, the Prime Minister, but all the benighted people of Malta who lived under the thumb of thugs and the Church.

So I was used to Bolshie men and therefore willing to accept Yves' sense of embattlement, thinking his negative view of Brussels perfectly sound, a good reason for his not wanting to live here permanently. We would go on arranging our life as a couple living one thousand miles apart, which is what made it so painful to find that Yves had followed the mother of his son from Rome and set up home in the city he claimed to so hate.

అం

On top of the hill in the Parc Léopold stands a high school. At lunchtime, when the pupils spill out of their classrooms, the park turns into something that most closely resembles a colony of seals. The din is deafening. You have to dodge the schoolchildren playing tag and throwing frisbees. I was glad, however, to be in a crowd of noisy children. It gave me cover as I got closer.

What struck me was that my husband – for we are still not divorced – had shrunk a little in the year that had passed since he told me about his son. His shoulders seemed to have grown narrower and his taut leanness had turned scrawny. I watched him step cautiously down the grassy slope towards the edge of the pond then reach out to take the boy's hand and help him down. In his other hand, he was clutching a box to his chest. Crouching down so that the top of his head was level with the child's, he held out the box to the boy who took something out and hurled it into the pond. A moorhen dipped its head into the water and kept it there for a long time, looking as if it had been decapitated. This made the child laugh.

So this is Nathaniel, I said to myself.

I once told Laurent Bertrand that if I had had a daughter I would have called her Clemency. To me clemency, more than faith or hope or charity, is the greatest of the virtues.

'And if you'd had a son?' Laurent had asked.

'If I'd had a son, I'd have chosen Nathaniel. Natan. Given. Third person masculine, past singular in Hebrew. El. The name of God that cannot be spoken. Nathaniel. Gift of God.'

'Did your husband know that?'

'No. He's not a linguist. He doesn't know any Hebrew.'

'That's not what I meant.'

The truth is that once we had agreed not to have children, Yves and I never spoke of children again, let alone of names. Probably it was just a coincidence that he'd called his son Nathaniel.

Laurent Bertrand fixed his gaze so steadily on me that I had to glance away. We both knew I had been making excuses for Yves ever since our sessions together had begun.

৩৵৶

Yves first told me about his lover and their son on one of his weekend visits to Brussels. He was sitting in my apartment, on the other side of the Japanese table, leaning forward, legs crossed, with his elbows on his knees and his hands clenched. Now and again as he spoke he tapped his knuckles against the sides of his forehead. Not once did he look me straight in the eye. It seemed that his voice came from somewhere very far away. I remember clutching my belly and, overcome by pain, rocking backwards and forwards. I do not remember curling up on the floor. But I do recall kicking my legs at Yves like a hysterical child when he tried to pull me onto my feet. I screamed at him to get out. My words seemed to be coming from somewhere far away. The sound from the back of my throat was the sound from those recurring childhood nightmares in which my mother tried to drag me underwater with her. The day after she died, I had overheard one of the grown-ups in the family say that she had drowned in her own blood. She had suffered terrible injuries in the bombing, but in the end her own body fluid had filled her lungs and choked her to death. For the first year after she was killed, she would come into my room every night, rouse me out of my sleep and take me by the hand to the rocks at the spot near Spinola from which she and I would go swimming in summer. She would dive in first then, splashing about and calling out to me. I would dive in too, but when I came up for air I could not see her. I would shout frantically until she bobbed up again behind me, making me burst out laughing with relief. Then she would grab my long hair and try to pull me under with her. That feeling of drowning, of being pulled under, and the gurgling sound as my lungs filled with water are what snapped me out of sleep. This is the sound I heard as Yves tried to force me onto a chair to calm me down as I kicked his legs and punched his chest.

If you had asked me only moments before about the state of our marriage I would have said that he and I were perfectly matched. Though he is secure in his French persona, Yves had had as much of an itinerant childhood as I'd had. We are both that contradiction in terms, Jewish non-believers, even if his family are mostly Ashkenaz, from Poland on his father's side, from Hungary on his mother's, and mine are wholly Sephardic from all over the Mediterranean. We both like to read. Yves has never once given me a present of a book that I did not enjoy. We both love opera and only disagree about which is Mozart's greatest work, and about Wagner whom Yves loves but whose music always sounds like pea soup to me. One evening when listening to Beethoven's 'Emperor', the two of us looked up and laughed, realising that we had simultaneously discovered a passage of humour in the music.

In the spring of the sixth year of our marriage Yves and I were staying at Claridge's in London. I love staying in five-star hotels, don't get me wrong, so I'm not being churlish when I say the sheets in such places are sometimes over-starched. Even when you aren't putting a lot of energy into love-making your skin can end up red and raw. That was another thing Yves and I would joke about together. Most couples have secret words and phrases that become a private code, a sign of complicity between them. Pack the Savlon! was Yves's catchphrase when he called me to say that he had booked a weekend for us somewhere luxurious.

After we had made love on Claridge's stiff white sheets, Yves pulled away from me and lay on his back. '*Quarante-cinq*,' he said.

'Forty-five what,' I murmured, on the edge of sleep.

When Yves and I made love he spoke to me in French, the language that of course came most spontaneously to him and behind which he could not hide in the way people often do when speaking a foreign language. I had always felt the intimacies spoken in his mother-tongue were proof that he was not only physically but also mentally laying himself bare to me.

'This is the forty-fifth time since we got married that we've fucked in a five-star hotel,' he said, again in French.

'*Putain de merde,* I hadn't realised you were notching up your conquests.' I sat up with a start, feeling cold and grabbing the top bed-sheet to cover my breasts.

Yves was grinning at me, but I was not in the mood for joking now. It felt as if he had reduced our weekends to statistics and thus diminished them. Meaning to cause him pain, I hit him on his shoulder and shouted, 'Shit!' Was this all that our marriage amounted to, a list of fucks in luxury hotels which Yves ticked off as we visited one capital city after another.

'Don't be so prudish.' He caught hold of my hand and squeezed it until I loosened my grasp of the sheet.

'*Merde! Merde! Putain de merde*! Why are you keeping count?'

'I love it when you become aggressive, and especially when you swear in French.' He pushed me back until the top half my body was suspended over the edge of the bed. 'You're not playful enough. Come on, relax! I'm not going to let you fall.'

Standing on his knees, he eased me down further, then holding my waist with one hand, he pushed my legs

31

apart with the other. Catching myself in the bedroom mirror suspended upside down with my head and shoulders now touching the floor, I couldn't help laughing.

'*Mais arrête! S'il te plaît, mon amour.* Stop laughing or it will make this position unworkable.' Yves too was trying to contain his laughter.

'And now you're going to tell me it's the forty-sixth time.'

I still feel a stitch in the corner of my heart when I think of Yves's physical beauty especially when he was a young man. I loved the smell of his body, the softness of his hair. Soon after he left, I was in a perfumery on the rue de Tongres and found myself standing next to a man who was buying Vétiver, the after shave that Yves preferred. I thought I would burst into tears there and then. In a haze of misery, I bought a bottle of that aftershave and went straight home to my apartment where I stripped completely and splashed myself with Yves' scent. Having lowered the blinds, I went to bed and surrendered to sensuality by rubbing myself against a pillow, which is when the tears finally came, leaving me with a sense of desolation at such a sterile act.

As I walked towards the pond in the middle of the Parc Léopold I thought of the way Yves used to walk naked round a room, like a panther. He was walking that way now and the boy following him seemed to have the same ease and gracefulness as his father, the same way of 'taking possession' of his surroundings. Once, I had hoped that some of that ease and gracefulness would rub off on me, some of Yves' certainties too. He might be Jewish but he was first and foremost French. His father had escaped during the Occupation but returned with de Gaulle and joined the French diplomatic corps. His mother's family had sat out the Second World War in New York but had never doubted that one day they would live in Paris again. I was born in Malta to a Jewish family which, on that Catholic island, made me an outsider from the second of my birth, and then my mother had died horribly. What was that other than absolute proof that we did not belong? Yves was never troubled by issues of identity. He had never doubted his taste or his considerable intellectual abilities. For years he had convinced me that he and I were truly free. If we'd had children, we would have been tied down and soon grown bored. Now, he is certain he wants to be with his son and live in the same place as the boy's mother. All that is left to me is the certain knowledge that he no longer needs or wants me to be with him.

ക∾ഏ

'So, what's in the tupperware box?' Although it could not have taken me more than a minute to reach the pond, it felt as if I had been moving for hours through treacle that stuck to the soles of my feet and clogged up my nose and throat. I only breathed again after I had spoken.

Yves did not swerve around. Nor did his back and shoulders appear to tense up as they might have had I taken him by surprise.

'Just some fresh sardines from Le Cap du Vivier d'Oie,' he said placing his hand on the child's shoulder again as the boy twisted around to look at me and squinted against the sunlight which was unusually bright for an autumn day in Brussels.

My oesophagus was burning as I noted how, despite the darker colouring, the boy resembled his father even more from close-up. I had not been married to a geneticist for almost two decades without understanding something about gene-centred evolution. I had heard that lecture dozens of times on how we are neither driven by conscious motives nor by what we imagine is free will, but are governed by our genes. And these will always tend towards an evolutionarily stable strategy. I can speak as ponderously as any scientist on how genes serve their own explicit purpose. In the end this is how the partners we mate with are selected. Looking at Yves's son now, I could not help wondering whether, had I had children with him, they would have turned out as fine-featured and beautiful. Perhaps in the end Yves' gene pool had never been destined to combine with mine, and so only blind biology was to blame for what had happened.

Closing my eyes did not help blot out the sudden flash I had of my husband with his ear pressed to the round belly of his pregnant lover. I saw her running her long, fingers through his silky hair. All year I had been imagining them listening to The Marriage of Figaro while talking about the forthcoming birth of their son and of their new life in Brussels, a father, a mother and a child planning to set up home in a beautiful Art Deco house not far from the Parc Léopold

'So the ducks and geese in this park are too fussy to eat breadcrumbs. They'll only accept sardines bought from the poshest fishmonger's in town.' I had to step sideways down the slope to get right down to the edge of the pond without slipping. The ground was muddy from the previous night's rain.

'The sardines aren't for them.' Yves still did not turn round to look at me.

Of course, he was not going to ask me how long I had been watching him and the boy. He could have, I suppose, accused me of spying on him. On the other hand, by asking me what I was doing in the park or even simply how I was, or any other question, he would have risked eliciting more of a reply than he was probably interested in hearing.

'If we keep our voices down,' he continued, still with his back turned to me, 'we might catch a glimpse of the heron. The sardines are for him. Nathaniel, throw another one, *s'il te plaît, mon ange.*'

'Ah yes, I see,' I said. 'I see the heron now. That's him peeking round that bush on the island in the middle of the pond.'

Without asking Yves' permission and still wearing my knitted gloves, I took one sardine from the plastic box with my right hand, another sardine with my left and threw the first and then the second into the water. Instead of falling at the heron's feet, they hit the pond with a splash. The startled heron pulled its head back out of sight.

'He doesn't appear to know he's supposed to dive for his lunch,' I said, making the boy grin. He looked happy to have me join in the game.

As I moved a step nearer I could see that the muscles of Yves's clenched jaws were twitching.

'You know something' – I ignored his jitteriness and addressed the boy – 'I don't think that bird has a clue that he's supposed to eat fish. I guess he's been eating nothing but Parc Léopold garbage for years.'

Nathaniel laughed but Yves frowned then threw another sardine towards the heron. This one also fell short, landing on a small wooden platform that stood a few feet away from the central island, which triggered a flock of scruffy pigeons to swoop down on it.

'*Quel con*! Damned stupid heron!' Yves picked up the lid of the container, which he had set on the ground, and closed it tight. 'It doesn't matter anyway.

Viens, mon grand. There's that other heron at the Etangs d'Ixelles. I think he's a bit smarter than this bird. Say goodbye to the lady.' He took hold of the boy's hand once more. '*Mais qu'est-ce que c'est que ça*? He examined the child's hand. 'You've scratched yourself on something. Come on. Let's go home and put some Savlon on it.'

For a moment I couldn't move or speak. Even the Savlon code had been hijacked. What else was Yves going to surprise me with? As if he hadn't already taken everything from me.

When he turned away again, I noticed pigeon droppings on the back of his expensive leather jacket. My calling out to warn him was reflexive, but I realise I should not have also offered to wipe off the mess. My gloves stank of fish, but I suspect what really irritated Yves was revealing in front of his son how flustered he had become by the dirt on his back. Perhaps he thought I was deliberately trying to show him up, turning him into a bit of an old fusspot. So I handed him a packet of wipes from my bag and, clutching the envelope containing the photograph of my mother and her siblings to my chest, I continued on my way to Artiges.

Ellie

2 Breaking Through the Clouds

The camera swivels from Ellie's face to an aerial view of Malta projected on a giant studio screen behind the anchorman. From high above, it swoops over and shaves past the curtain-walls of Valletta. In free fall, it plummets to Grand Harbour, then, streaking out to sea, homes in on a trawler towing a wide circular net. On the blue-black surface, the net looks for an instant like the milky bloom of a giant medusa unfurling.

Standing in the doorway between the hall and sitting room, arms crossed and his eyes fixed on the television, Richard Radcliff recalls his first sight of Valletta. Wasn't it Michelangelo who said that the task of a sculptor is to set free the figures lying dormant inside quarried marble? More than twenty years ago, as the plane carrying Richard and Ellie broke through the clouds, it struck Richard that the Knights of Malta had not built their capital in the usual way, from the foundations up. Rather, they had gouged into the coralline limestone to reveal the grid of streets and the solid fortifications trapped whole within it. In the late afternoon, the flat-roofed houses and church domes rose, pink and gold, out of the geometry of deep shadows below.

Ellie had told Richard a lot about the island, but though she spoke nostalgically now and again, she had never called it beautiful. The topography she described was, on the contrary, hostile, the soil thin, the vegetation sparse, people poor and superstitious. It was not just a barren rock, it was a moonscape with one occupier after another.

'Three hundred and fifty years of rule by the Knights of the Order of St John and the Maltese word for God is still Allah,' Ellie had said. 'I guess that shows a sort of bloody-mindedness. As my dear cousins Claire and Vanna would have said, *plus catholique que les Maltais et tu meurs* – if you could find anyone more Catholic than the Maltese, he or she would be bloody well dead from it.'

Before the Knights, Malta had for centuries been governed by the Arabs whose capital had been Mdina, perched on a rock in the middle of the island, a city of the East, with narrow streets and buildings that huddle together against the pounding Mediterranean sun. The Knights had decided that they would rule from a brand new Christian city overlooking the sea and had turned Valletta, with its symmetrical lay-out, grand palaces and churches, into one of the wonders of western baroque.

With the plane now beginning its descent, Richard had leaned over Ellie to get a better view of the rock rising out of the sea. In Grand Harbour, large container ships were surrounded by swarms of small fishing boats painted in blue, green, red and yellow. The colours were so sharp that they might have been painted by the great Caravaggio, who had been a prisoner on the island at one time.

'I think, my love, you're getting a bit carried away with your artistic comparisons.' Ellie had turned her gaze away from the window and kissed Richard on the tip of his nose. He may have talked her into returning to Malta, but she was not going to lower her guard and all of a sudden find the place magical.

Over the years, her view has never changed.

৶৶

'What's that in the water, Cath?' Richard now settles down in front of the television, on the sofa next to his daughter.

'It's those guys whose boat sank.' Cathy turns up the volume.

Once more, Ellie's face fills the entire screen. With her mass of steel-grey curls pulled tightly backwards, the twitching at her temples is clearly visible. 'In just this single incident off the coast of Malta, forty people are known to have drowned,' she says. 'The survivors clung to the tuna pen for three whole days before they were rescued.'

Take a deep breath, Ellie. Lower the pitch of your voice, Richard wills his wife. Release the tension.

'And now the Maltese, Libyan and Spanish authorities are squabbling over who's responsible for these refugees.' Ellie's grip on the armchair begins to relax as if she has received Richard's thought-waves. 'The Maltese say it's the fault of the Libyans that boat people keep being washed up on their shores. It's true that the Libyans do a terrible job of patrolling their coastline. The Spanish are only involved because it was a Spanish trawler that finally picked up the survivors. But since what we've just seen on that clip all took place only a couple of miles off Malta and the tuna pens belonged to a Maltese fishery, I'd say the duty of care lies principally with the Maltese government.'

What makes the Australian media interested in Ellie's views on the boat people crisis in the Mediterranean is that she is a well-known human rights campaigner who was born in Malta but lives in Australia.

'Next to Dom Mintoff, your mother must be the most pugnacious Maltese in the world,' Richard jokes to his daughter. 'Actually, since these days hardly anyone outside Malta remembers The Dom, she must be top of the list by now. But hang on –' he tilts his long body sideways, picks up an empty glass from the floor and sniffs inside it – 'what's this? Let me guess. On a pit stop home this afternoon your mother noticed you lying here on the sofa. So, bingo, she prescribed her usual remedy for period pain. Whisky!'

'I didn't drink it. The smell makes me want to puke.' Cathy punches the cushion she has been hugging. Her thick dark lashes, so like her mother's, appear to weigh her eyelids down, making her look sullen. Once, when she was nine years old, her father overheard her tell a school friend that in the maternity ward the nurses had swapped her with Ellie's real baby. Kids say this sort of thing all the time, with great earnestness. In his early teens, Richard himself had felt that he could not possibly be the son of a mother who always tried to disguise the inflexibility of her views by expressing them in an apologetic tone. He hated the hypocrisy. Ellie, however, never apologised. From their first meeting, what had attracted Richard to her was that she was the opposite of all the women he had ever known. He had never, for instance, met a woman who shook hands when being introduced, just like a man. Richard saw that as part of Ellie's European exoticness. Not only was her handshake firm, she was never the first to glance away. Perhaps Cathy had disowned her mother because it is just too hard for children, who are by nature conformist, to bear the burden of a parent who stands out by speaking her mind. On the other hand, no one looking at Cathy's thicket of curls, golden eyes, long neck and lean limbs could take her for anyone other than her mother's daughter. 'The pot plant doesn't seem to have a problem with whisky.' Cathy winces, rocking gently and hugging her cushion more tightly. There are dark crescents under her eyes.

'Let me get you a couple of Nurofen.'

'No, Dad. Really, I'm fine.'

'Okay, if you say so. Can we take another look at those aerial shots of Malta?' Richard tenderly brushes the back of his hand down Cathy's cheek and she leans her face towards his shoulder.

'Jeezus, how come the two of you are holed up in here at this time of day?' William Radcliff stomps barefoot into the living room.

'We're watching that documentary. The one with Mum in it,' his sister says.

'You mean the one about the Japanese whalers, or the one where she's saving the world from melting ice caps? No, don't tell me, it's the documentary about the boat people of Malta.

41

ॐ

'I still dream of the island from time to time,' Ellie had confessed to Richard when they were planning their first trip to Europe together. 'Though I'd never go back there, not even to save my life, sometimes, in those few seconds between sleep and waking, I feel this terrible yearning, despite myself.' In the sallow light of the kitchen lamp, Ellie looked drained. 'The feeling doesn't last, thank goodness.' She reached across the table and squeezed Richard's hand. 'What a bloody stifling place it was.' She stood up and began pacing the room, waving her arms as if she were making a speech to a large audience. Richard had seen her like that before, in full flight, addressing a crowd at the students' union, trying to be heard above the shouts after she'd announced that the union had invited a group of Palestinians to the university. 'That wasn't just because my father's family were Jews in a rabidly Catholic society.' She walked over to the window and opened it. 'Us against them, that's the way my grandmother always saw it – the them including my mother, who was born Catholic, and my cousin Vanna's mother, who was Jewish. Poor Miriam had the misfortune of coming from a penniless Moroccan family that was mired in religious obscurantism, so she couldn't possibly come up to our Toledano standards. In my grandmother's eyes, we were constantly under siege – not only by Catholics, but also by Jews with more primitive attitudes. She didn't wish to be associated with those Jewish families who ended up in Malta as refugees before the war. It made her furious to see the Ovadias from Salonika trying to elbow their way to the leadership of the island's tiny Jewish community.

They were uneducated, which reflected badly on the Jews already established in Malta. Our family came from a long line of entrepreneurs and doctors.

Then, the doctors' strike happened. Who'd have thought it would drag on for ten years. It tore our family apart, though, even without the strike, sooner or later our family would have splintered. What happened to my cousin Claire's mother just speeded up the process. Jeezus, there were bits of her splattered all over the wall of my Uncle Joseph's house. For days afterwards, they kept finding skin and blood and hair in the nooks and crannies of the room where the letter-bomb went off. Which is why'– Ellie pulled out a stool and sat down again – 'Malta is definitely not going to be on our itinerary.'

While driving through Sicily, one late afternoon, however, Richard and Ellie had pulled into a rocky cove. 'Don't you just love the way at sunset skin glistens like polished wood?' Ellie licked the back of Richard's neck after they had come out of the water. 'This place reminds me so much of the places where we swam when I was a child in Malta.'

'Ha! Admit it. You are curious to see what the place is like now.' Richard turned over to face her. 'Come on. We're so close. Let's drive on to Palermo tonight. There's bound to be a flight we can get on tomorrow.'

Ellie heaved herself up and, hobbling barefoot over the sharp rocks, posted herself at the water's edge. The stagnant pools around Richard swarmed with sea lice. He could smell the iodine in the air but also a slight odour of putrefaction. Another word from him and he knew Ellie would have said no. She must not feel pushed into making a decision. As the waves slip-slapped against the shore, Ellie let out a deep sigh.

∽∾

Peering out of the ground-floor window, her mouth puckering and un-puckering, Ellie's grandmother called out to her daughter, Luisa, not to let strangers in at the door. Who are those gypsies – *chi sono quegli zingari* – Nonna Rosa kept asking even after Ellie had identified herself as the daughter of Clementino, her eldest son. That was not enough to get them inside the house, but Rosa did order Luisa to serve them coffee and almond biscuits outside on the front parapet. The biscuits had a strong petrol after-taste and were soggy. Ellie set them aside, whispering to Richard not to feel obliged to eat them merely out of some 'Anglo' sense of politeness. 'This is not the Radcliff Mansion in Vaucluse. It's the Casa Rosa Toledano in San Giulian,' she said.

It was Marguerita, Ellie's elder spinster aunt, who rang a family acquaintance to ask if there was room available in her B & B in Sliema.

'It's not just because we're not married that my granny won't let us stay here,' Ellie said. 'She would never allow any stranger to sleep in their house. Why do you think she never asked my mother to come back to Malta after my father had left us?'

'Think positive, Ellie. In a B & B, we'll be free to come and go as we please,' Richard said.

On their first full day on the island, Ellie took him to see the block of flats in Valletta where her mother, Laura, had lived as a girl.

44

'You can see for yourself just how close the Arch-bishop's Palace was. Nonna Rosa got it into her head that my mother had had Danny and me baptised secretly with the help of her two uncles, of course, who were priests. I feel sick when I think of the accusations and counter-accusations that flew around in the family.'

But Ellie could not dampen Richard's enthusiasm for the island, the stone that changed from blanched yellow to rose as the light changed, the green wooden balconies, the narrow streets in deep shadow. Through open front doors, he caught glimpses of dark inner courtyards, felt the cool blast of air as he and Ellie trudged past. They visited Mdina hunkered down against the leaching sun. The silence in the old capital hummed at siesta time. In the deserted piazzas, their footsteps echoed.

'Don't you like this feeling that we might be the only people left alive in the world?' Richard asked as, on their second evening, they sat picnicking on the rocks opposite their B & B.

Ellie remained silent, but after Mdina she seemed less tense, as if she too had been moved by the beauty of the old city.

On their third day, however, someone reported seeing a tall woman 'with African hair' swimming naked at sunset below the coastal watchtower in Sliema. Ellie was arrested. Although the police held her for only two hours, the next morning she and Richard were on a plane to Rome.

'There's at least one thing I can thank my father for. He took us as far away as possible from that godforsaken rock. I never want to set eyes on the fucking place again. Not ever.'

45

༷

'It's a worldwide problem, and it's not going to get any better.' As Ellie interrupts the tv anchorman, a twist of curls springs loose, but she is impervious to it for now she is in full throttle. 'Over the last couple of years, the Maltese have seen a huge increase in the number of boat people blown off course onto their coast. Of course, all that these refugees want is to get to Italy. I doubt any of them have even heard of Malta. You know, some of them have survived journeys of thousands of miles after fleeing wars and famine in the heart of Africa. In the last six months alone, more than a thousand have been picked up off Malta. While they're waiting for their applications to be processed, they're detained for months, even years, in overcrowded, unsanitary places. I know, I know. This sounds terribly familiar, doesn't it?'

'Mum's off,' William says. 'No prizes for guessing what comes next.'

'Shush,' his father and sister hiss in unison.

'The only difference between Malta and Australia is that the Maltese don't have a vast desert or some off-shore dependency into which to herd their asylum-seekers,' Ellie says.

After more than thirty years of living in Australia, Ellie still speaks of Australians in the third person. But she speaks of the Maltese in the third person too. Once Richard had pointed out that she was doing exactly as her grandmother had done, but Ellie had retorted that it wasn't at all the same, not one bit. Her grandmother had been born in Malta whereas she had come to Australia as a child.

'Does that mean you feel you belong nowhere,' Richard had asked.

'Not at all, on the contrary, I belong everywhere.'

'Isn't everywhere nowhere?' Richard had argued, feeling dismayed by her response. What he would have liked her to say was that she belonged to the family she and he had created together.

'In this next bit of footage, you'll see a Somali woman being winched off the Xavier Roquero, who had just gone into labour. From the trawler, she was taken to a Maltese hospital and after the birth she was sent to a detention centre with the baby.'

'Isn't this cool?' William slumps on the sofa, between his father and sister. 'I mean, a woman giving birth while dangling from a helicopter. It's even better than that woman in the Mozambique floods giving birth on top of a tree. Remember how worked up Mum got about that?' He pulls his long legs up on the settee and, resting his chin on his knees, starts picking skin off the side of his right foot. Pulling off a scab with exquisite slowness, William draws blood. It's a nervous tic, but his mother's threats to fine him two dollars each time he picked a scab have not had any effect.

'God, you're gross.' Cathy digs her elbow into her brother's side and thumps him on the arm.

'William, take your filthy hooves off the sofa.'

'A little bit of shush.' William snatches the control from Cathy's hand.

'Yes, William,' Cathy says, 'let's hear what Mum has to say.'

❧

It is not just the plight of boat people in the Mediterranean that has placed Malta at the centre of Ellie's warroom map again. A month ago, Ellie's Aunt Marguerita had fallen and broken her hip and right shoulder. She had been on the floor for two days and nights before her sister, Luisa, wandering out in the street in her dressing gown, was stopped by a passer-by who managed to extract from her that a strange woman was lying on her sitting room floor, refusing to get up. In the emergency, Ellie's first cousin Vanna had rushed from Israel to Malta.

'Has it ever occurred to you,' Ellie said to Richard a few days after Vanna had begun her daily, long-distance progress reports, 'that martyr and mater sound almost the same? Vanna can't resist reminding me of all the times she's rushed to Malta in a crisis. And, just in case I wasn't aware of it, she does also happen to have a life of her own, quote, unquote. No one appreciates – *oy vey*, *oy vey* – that each time she goes back to Malta it requires major strategic planning at home. Her three eldest children are in the army, so she has to call on her neighbours to look after the little ones. There are probably half a dozen of them but – *baruch ha'shem* – in the settlement there is a true community spirit. Vanna may not have been the favourite niece, but that has never deterred her from making all these sacrifices. Bla-de-bla-de-bloody-bla!'

'Dad, I forgot to tell you.' William drops his feet to the floor. 'Mum's cousin Wanda …'

'Vanna.'

'Wanda. Vanna. Whatever. She called again just after you left for work. She wants Mum to call her back, like yesterday.'

'Do you by any chance know where your mother is?'

'She did say she was going to see Nonna Laura tonight. Oh shit!' William hits his forehead with the heel of his palm. 'It's full moon.' And then he howls like a wolf.

৵৵

'If we are going to go on seeing each other, and I'm sure we will,' Ellie said to Richard when they had known each other just forty-eight hours, 'there are three important things you should know about me.'

They were sitting in the university canteen. Leaning back in her chair, Ellie stretched her arms above her head, making the dozens of bracelets and multicoloured bangles on her forearms clink. When she pushed her hair up from the back of her neck, it was an unconscious gesture, but it drew Richard's gaze to the strength and beauty of her long hands. He was also aroused by the curve of the line that ran from her earlobe down the side of her long neck and across her shoulder. As Ellie fanned herself furiously with the menu, he wanted to reach out and touch her, to help ease her tension.

In the branches pressing against the windows, the cicadas started to screech. 'Don't you wonder how they start up like that so suddenly, and then just as suddenly stop as if there's some invisible conductor up there, in the trees, tapping his baton.'

'God?'

'Of course not. Don't tell me you believe that because I for one don't.'

'So, Eleonora Toledano, you're an atheist. This is the first important thing you think I need to know about you.'

'No. Number one is that only people who don't really know me call me Eleonora. Five syllables for a first name is a ridiculous number to be lumbered with, especially coupled with another four syllables in Toledano. My father, who has spent all his life trying to compose operas and get them performed, thought it sounded operatic. It was a pity I grew up tone deaf.'

'Fact number two.'

Ellie frowned. 'Oh no, number two isn't that I can't hold a note, though I can't. It's that when I graduate I've got no intention of practising law. I'm going to work for a development agency or an environmental lobby.'

'You're a crusader. I'm not daunted. I mean, if that's what worries you. So what's number three?'

'Well, my mother is what my paternal ancestors would have called *una loca* before they were expelled from Spain by the Inquisition. I'm not kidding. She once fed a dog we owned rat poison and buried him under the floor of the garden shed. If you're interested, I could even show you where this murder took place. The shed is still there. If anyone ever asked me to write an account of the hardships of my childhood, I would only be able to produce a black farce.'

৽৵

Nowadays Ellie leaves it to Richard to recount the Tale of the Death of Max the Black Labrador. Because he is detached from the events, he does a much better job of it.

Ellie may still tease him about his 'Anglo-Saxon cool', but she recognises that a story has to be told with compassion, a feeling that is hard for her to muster after years of trying not to let her mother's depressions make her feel as if she too were going mad. If she told the story, there was always a risk she might not be able to weed out the self-pity.

Richard always starts with Ellie, aged fourteen, waking up with a heavy sensation in her chest. Sick with worry, she has not slept enough. Her eyes feel gritty. Half the buttons on her pyjama top are missing. But, as Cathy and William know, their mother is someone who has prided herself on never having learned to thread a needle. At school she had cried through her one and only sewing class. One of her father's final fatherly acts had been to go to her high school and ask for her to be put in the music class instead.

Where does this terrible feeling of oppression come from? Ellie asks herself. Her chest feels tight. Air is being squeezed out of her lungs. She never cries, but at this moment she feels like giving in to tears. Then she remembers. In the last few days her mother has stopped babbling about her latest moneymaking scheme. The storm is over. But that is precisely the trouble. In a world turned back to front after Clementino abandoned them, it is not the storm but the lull that follows that makes Ellie feel sick. How many times have they been through this before?

First, there had been the baby-pink slippers with pompons, which Laura had planned to sell from home. She had bought twenty-five boxes from an Italian importer/wholesaler in Leichhardt. Twenty-four and a half of these boxes still cluttered her bedroom. Then there had been the electric whisks. After an initial sale of half a dozen, Laura had given up. The last Grand Scheme was the rain capes. Seeing their mother so optimistic again, Ellie and Danny had been happy to help her in the evenings and at weekends fold the capes into tight two-inch squares to be packed into plastic bags in matching colours. In the last few days, however, Laura has given up on the Rain Cape Scheme too, coming home silent, lethargic and with dark crescents and goosy skin under her eyes. With the slippers and the whisks, the capes now stand in cardboard boxes that block Danny's and Ellie's rooms and also the hallway.

Heaving herself out of bed, Ellie shuffles barefoot to the window. Below, the neighbour's magpie is whistling the first eight notes of the 'Colonel Bogey March'. A morning just like any other. Splitting open the slats of the Venetian blinds, Ellie spots the bird davaning dementedly on the grass. In a wave of drunken viciousness, Mr George had clipped his pet's wings. In a tsunami of remorse, he had taught the mutilated, flightless bird to whistle the old army marching tune. Ellie hates Mr George for his cruelty. Isn't it typical of the Higher Force, which of course she does not believe in, to have given her family a neighbour like Mr George? The bird always wakes Ellie up too early. No doubt this is meant to test her reserves of empathy for helpless, mutilated creatures.

'Piss off,' she says. 'Get lost!' She rattles the blinds.

The bird remains unperturbed. Tottering a few feet away from the window, it fixes its drill-hole eyes on her and goes on staring.

On the bay, small boats lie becalmed. The drone of an outboard can be heard in the distance. Ellie is about to fall back into bed when she sees the dark shape in the water at the pointed end of the perfect white 'V' forming its wake.

'Shit!' She gets down on all fours and rummages under the bed for her rubber thongs. Not finding them there, she opens the bedside cabinet from which half a dozen pairs of baby pink slippers with pompons quivering like dandelions come tumbling out. 'Shit!' She pads barefoot down the hallway. 'Danny, Max has got out again. Wake up! He's swimming across the bay. We've got to catch him.' Without waiting for her brother to emerge from his room, Ellie rushes out into the front garden.

'Max! Maxi!' She starts down the steep path that leads from the house to the water's edge. With his snout high in the air, like the figurehead of a caravel, Max swims on.

Ellie breaks into a run. 'Come back!' she yells.

The only thing to do is to get to the other side of the bay and grab Max as he reaches dry land, before he has a chance to run across the road into Mrs Sparrow's front yard. Otherwise he's a goner.

Mrs Sparrow has already threatened to call the police if the Toledanos (she pronounces the last syllable 'danos' to rhyme with 'dagoes') don't manage to keep their dog under control. Unmoved by Ellie's precociously brilliant defence of Max's affectionate nature and superior intelligence, she stands on their doorstep again, accusing the Labrador of being a beast, as sinisterly savage as the Hound of the Baskervilles, a rabid threat to the peace and quiet of the whole neighbourhood.

'Your mongrel is leading my Hexy astray,' Mrs Sparrow says. She berates Laura and Ellie on their own front verandah as Laura holds open the wire-screen door and mosquito bites bloom all over Ellie's bare legs. 'Until my Hexy met him, she didn't even know dogs could swim.'

It's true. Max has discovered that the shortest route from home to the Sparrows' is through the water of the bay that separates him from Hexy. And he has taught the Sparrows' dog to paddle to his side of the shore. 'If you people don't care about your dog getting ripped to pieces by sharks, I just do happen to care about mine.'

Ellie has sometimes heard people say that Mrs Sparrow has such lovely big grey eyes, but she can see from close up that without the carefully applied make-up the Sparrow eyes are as tiny as a weasel's.

'I daresay there's no tradition in your part of the world of keeping pets. Perhaps you should go back to where you came from.' Mrs Sparrow pulls out her last weapon, 'The Weapon of the Racist Scoundrel', Richard calls it.

'Don't worry, we'll keep him under control.' Laura grips Ellie's shoulders. Ellie can feel her mother's hands trembling. 'You don't need to phone the police.' Laura speaks softly, almost inaudibly. As a young woman in Malta, she had been known for her beautiful singing voice. On one occasion she had performed at the President's Palace before a gathering of foreign dignitaries. Now, she no longer sings and when she is sad her voice fades into a cracked whisper and her hands begin to shake.

Ellie knows the signs. Still, she hopes that somehow she is mistaken and that her mother will not get sick again. The important thing is to stop Mrs Sparrow from being so angry. If the police get involved, Danny and Ellie might be split up again. It has happened twice already, and Ellie has promised Danny she would never let it happen again. The observant Presbyterian families she and her brother had been sent to had been scrupulous about their keeping up the practices of a Jewish faith they knew nothing about. At the Temple Emmanuel in Chatswood, the other children had taunted them. 'If you're only pretending you don't know the holy festivals and Hebrew prayers, then obviously you're ashamed of being Jewish.' This was followed by the usual corny jokes about Maltesers.

'We'll keep Max tied up during the day in the back garden, Mrs Sparrow.' Ellie steps in front of her mother. 'He won't be any trouble.'

'No, he won't be any trouble.' Laura's echo comes from somewhere at the bottom of a deep ravine.

Still, Max does not all of a sudden turn into a compliant animal. Left at first to roam inside the house while Laura and the children are out during the day, he tears open the cardboard boxes at the bottom of the stacks, the ones containing the plastic slippers, and vomits a meal of several pairs. When Ellie ties him to the clothes line instead, he strains so hard on the thick rope that it looks as if he'll end up choking himself. When Ellie and Danny take him for a walk, he pulls even harder at his leash. His howling during the night is chilling. Everyone in Battersea Street is unnerved. At two or three o'clock in the morning, neighbours come round and rattle the wire-screen door, threatening to call the dog pound and the police. Even Mr George has the cheek to accuse the Toledanos of cruelty to dumb animals.

Then one afternoon Ellie and Danny come home to find the front door unlocked. The long, windowless hallway that runs the length of the three bedrooms and down to the living room and kitchen at the back is dark. Usually as soon as they step into the front garden, Max starts to bark. But as Ellie and Danny hurry down the hall, there's no sound from the back yard.

'No, don't!' Their mother's hoarse voice startles the children.

Too late, Danny has already switched on the light. Laura is sitting at the table, her forearms resting on top, her glazed eyes staring into a distant horizon far beyond her children's shoulders.

'Where's Max?' Danny throws his satchel on the floor. 'Mum, where's Max?'

Ellie can see that he's working out all the possibilities. Within seconds, he is out of the back door and into the yard from where he goes on shouting for Max, his call soon a wail.

As she rushes to the window, Ellie's glance falls on Max's collar lying on top of the sideboard.

'Mama? Mama, listen to me. Listen. Where is he?' She kneels on the floor in front of her mother and grips Laura's wrists. 'Where's Max? Tell me! Where is he?

Her mother had never liked the dog. She had fed him and even taken him for a walk. But Max had been a present from Clementino. During a rare visit from Brisbane where he had found work as a clarinettist, he had turned up in Sydney with the puppy on Danny's tenth birthday. Laura had been too stunned to protest and anyway as soon as Danny had set eyes on Max, she realised she could not ask Clementino to take him back.

'Mama? Mama, what's happened to Max?' Ellie shakes Laura.

'I had to do it. I'm sorry, I had to.'

'Had to do what, Mama? What did you have to do?'

'I had to put him down. Mrs Sparrow was furious. This time she was definitely going to call the police, and our landlord too. We could be evicted. Don't be upset. He thought I was going to take him out for a walk. He didn't suffer.' Laura rocks in agitation. 'I'm certain he didn't suffer.' She goes on rocking after Ellie has let go of her wrists.

'Where is he?'

'I buried him in the garden under the floor of the shed. Don't be upset. I was respectful. I said a prayer.' With that, her mother's hands flutter across her breast, and she makes the sign of the cross. It is a reflex action, a hangover from her childhood.

These days, Ellie is still unsure what upset her more, the murder of the dog or that automatic fluttering of hands. Had her grandmother been right when they were in Malta and she had accused Laura of clinging to her Catholic faith? Ellie remembers feeling drained, her legs weak, a flow of lava running from her throat to her stomach. Here, in Australia, they had never had anything to do with Catholics. The Jews did not like them. Her father's family no longer wrote. Who was there to turn to at such moments?

'My mother must have known what she was intending to do that morning after she had seen Danny and me off to school.' Ellie sometimes interrupts Richard's account. 'I can imagine it all. In the silent house, she boils up a pot of old bread and leftover meat with carrots and celery and even a sprig of coriander in it to conceal the taste of the poison. Then she sets the dog bowl in front of Max. Looking back all these years later, I'm certain that before Danny and I had left for school, Max had been strangely subdued. He knew. He was such a smart dog. He bloody well knew. After that, I knew I had to take charge of everything, that from then on I was head of the family.'

❧

'I should be more patient with my mother, I know.' Ellie prowls around the bedroom. 'But she always manages to press the wrong button. Now I feel bad for having yelled at her again this evening. Really, you can never win with her. Either she's curled up and unreachable or she's spinning, unreachable in outer space.'

Having come home late from her visit to Laura's, Ellie wolfs down the meal Richard has prepared, carrying the plate around with her while one by one she sheds her clothes, leaving a trail on the floor. She sets the plate down on the bedside table, half the food left uneaten.

'Anyway, hat do you think I should do about that message from Vanna? It's not as if I can drop everything here and just go. On the other hand, I can't let Vanna cart off two confused old ladies to Israel. If Luisa were in her right mind, she would object fiercely to being set down in occupied territory, and I don't remember Marguerita being much of a Zionist either.'

Ellie sits down on the edge of the bed. 'Claire refuses to get involved. Who can blame her for not wanting to go back to Malta? She does live in Europe, whereas I have to schlep half way across the world.' Ellie parts the top sheet and lies naked on her back, staring at the ceiling. 'What a fucking mess – the aunts, the boat people, the tuna pens.'

'Ellie, it's almost two o'clock.' Richard pats her arm.

'Oh, please don't fall asleep. Did you look at the DVD, by the way? What did you think of the anchorman? That bastard used to work for Fox News.'

'I think you came across as if you cared more for the tuna than for the boat people.' Richard grins and Ellie pulls her hand from his. 'Look, I'm not going to give you a post-mortem at this hour.' He yawns so hard his jaws click. 'It was bloody lucky the boat people had the tuna pens to cling to.'

'Shit, Richard, it's not funny. Caging up tuna is like caging up elephants, and it makes no economic sense. To produce one kilo of farmed tuna, you have to feed them ten kilos of some other fish. Once they're herded into pens, they become disoriented. You know what's so bloody sad?'

'What?' Richard closes his eyelids more tightly.

'If a tuna escapes into the wild again, it ends up with withdrawal symptoms and hangs around the nets – as bad as a drug addict.' For a moment, Ellie falls silent. 'You can't have forgotten about the fish farm in Scotland.'

'That was salmon.' Richard turns on his side to face her. He has not forgotten. A wall of jellyfish, ten miles square and reaching down to a depth of thirty-five feet, had one day appeared on a Scottish river. Within hours, billions of Mauve Stingers that had drifted from the warm waters of the Mediterranean killed a hundred thousand salmon. Rescuers tried to reach the salmon pens, but the jellyfish were so densely packed it was impossible to get the salmon out. Ellie, at a conference in the UK, had flown to Scotland on behalf of Greenpeace.

'It was sci-fi horrendous.' Ellie's voice rises.

Richard sits up slowly. 'Actually, what it makes me think of is Phil Spector and his famous Wall of Sound.'

'Oh for God's sake, be serious.' Ellie wriggles her legs and pulls the sheet across the top of them.

'I guess what you're trying to tell me is that you're going back to Malta.' Richard runs his fingers down her bony spine. 'You've resisted for more than two decades. A dozen phone calls from Vanna couldn't make you change your mind, but tuna pens and boat people have done the trick.'

'It's not as if I'm suddenly going to fall in love with the place. You know how I feel about it, but if Claire won't go, someone has to stop Vanna from carrying out her crazy plan. Besides which, it'll give me a chance to see first hand what's going on with boat people there. Maybe there's something I can do, some expertise I can provide.'

Ellie rolls on to her side. 'It's quite special, isn't it?' She burrows her face into Richard's shoulder. 'That moment when the plane breaks through the clouds and there is the island shimmering gold in the middle of the blue-black sea.'

Vanna

3 War Zones

Now that she has worked out a strategy, Vanna would say things are more or less under control again.

Each night before she goes to bed, she sprinkles DDT powder all over the kitchen floor, then scrunches up sheets of old newspaper and seals the crack at the foot of the door between the kitchen and the dining room. Inside the kitchen, the old water well is covered by a wooden board, but the cockroaches still escape through the gap between the well's rim and cover. What was it her dead father used to say? A roach's life is nothing but a constant nosing for food. Vanna understands hunger. As a child she was always ravenous. Her cousins made fun of her never refusing second or third helpings and munching constantly between meals. But the night she pulled the top sheet down while climbing into bed and came face to face with a boot-brown cockroach twitching its antennae at her she swore she would never again take biscuits and cake to bed.

Cockroaches are not going to take possession of their aunts' house. No use Eleonora – or Ellie, as she insists on calling herself these days – preaching against the use of insecticides. 'Surely you understand they're a hazard to human health as well as to the environment. Don't you realise you're poisoning us too?'

Ellie may be determined to ban DDT from the house, but Vanna will not be pushed around, as she was when they were children. She has never forgotten the terrible day when, only eight, she wet herself in the middle of the promenade in Sliema. Trotting behind her cousin, Vanna had already warned her several times she was about to burst, but Ellie strode on. 'Come on, we're almost at my place,' she said. 'Don't waddle.' Vanna recalls the huge relief of suddenly letting go, the warm trickle down her legs and then, just as suddenly, the hot shame. Anyone with an ounce of empathy would have felt concern for her. 'Oh, stop that stupid crying,' Ellie said as she prodded her into the house and upstairs to the bathroom. Vanna's sobs had turned to hiccups and it felt as if someone had put weights in her shoes. Exasperated, Ellie lifted her up and dumped her in the bathtub, clothes, shoes and all, and turned on the tap. The shock of the jet of cold water stopped her hiccuping at once.

As with so many other events of their childhood, Ellie insists she has no memory of this event. 'You must be mixing me up with someone else. Anyway, I couldn't possibly have said "Don't waddle". I must have said "Don't dawdle".'

Vanna is not mistaken, and she has not invented the squelching sounds her shoes made as she walked back to her house alone. It makes her laugh the way Ellie goes on about people having no courage. She wouldn't be so brave if the cockroaches did infest the house. Already when she opens a drawer and finds just one black beetle scurrying into a corner, she yells blue murder. She even looks queasy when she comes across the ashen husk of a dead cockroach on its back with its little hollow legs sticking up in the air among the family papers.

'We need to start clearing all this old stuff out,' she says, but so far she has made no move to help Vanna put anything in order. She's out all day, busy with her new-found campaigning friends. 'I can't believe the aunts have hoarded these old share certificates from Nonno's 1920s failed investments. Just look at these packages! Studio photos of Marseilles, Livorno, Alexandria, Cairo and Tripoli. Who the hell are these bushy-bearded men in jellabahs and tarboushes and these thin-haired women with blouses buttoned to their chins? There aren't any names on the backs of the pictures.'

'Those people happen to be your ancestors and mine,' Vanna says and carries on sweeping up the cockroach corpses that lie like empty bullet cases all over the kitchen floor. She does this every morning and when that job is done she opens up the doors and shutters to let the fresh air in.

Since the uncontrolled building began along the seafront, they do not get much air through the house any more. Not like they used to when they were small children and it was the best place to be compared to anywhere. Ellie accuses Vanna of glorifying the past, but anyone who knows the island well can see how it has been ruined. Every day, historic buildings and turn-of-century villas, with their green wooden balconies, are knocked down to make way for tourist hotels that are no more than concrete boxes. The destruction had already begun when Nonna Rosa was alive. Their grandmother used to grumble all the time about bribes being paid to building planners.

'This low level of criminality is just so typical of the Maltese. Do you remember her saying that?'

'As if she herself were not Maltese,' Ellie laughs, making Vanna feel sorry she asked.

With her university education, poor Auntie Luisa was the one assigned to writing protest letters to the local Member of Parliament. By then she was in her late fifties, and who listens to the complaints of old women?

'I blame the Libyans,' Vanna says.

'Oh, for God's sake, Vanna, leave your anti-Arab sentiments out of this.'

But Ellie knows nothing about what has been go-ing on in Malta over the last forty years. She doesn't even speak Maltese properly any more. Where would she have heard about the Libyans pouring money into the island? They're so blatant about it too. Just look at the way they've taken over that lovely, huge mansion in Sliema for their embassy and planted Libyan soldiers in front of it. The Moslem cemetery, with its minaret and palm trees, now overshadows the Jewish cemetery, neglected for years. So many Toledanos lie buried there, including Vanna's father whose body she brought back from Israel – it was his dying wish – though her mother is buried in Jerusalem. One Maltese government after another, from Dom Mintoff to the present, has sucked up to Gadaffi. Even back during the doctors' strike they were shipping in doctors from Tripoli. These days, the Libyans fail to patrol their coasts, and what do the Maltese do? Let them off the hook, which means that thousands of refugees end up in Malta rather than staying where they belong – in Africa. Ellie can argue all she wants, but she can't deny that it's Libyans who've bought the row of apartment blocks directly in front of the aunts' house and illegally added four extra storeys.

With each return to Malta, Vanna has seen the old family house bit by bit encircled and dwarfed. When she and her cousins were children, they could go to the flat roof to watch the fishing boats come in and out of Spinola Bay. Now, when she hangs out the washing, she has to stand on tiptoes to glimpse the tiniest piece of blue.

To think this was the place her father kept dreaming about after they left Malta, not the modern property developers' hunting ground. The morning they set sail for Haifa, driven out by the strike, he got up before dawn and came round to his mother's, scooped up some soil into a flowerpot and planted a cutting of jasmine vine in it. Jasmines were Nonna Rosa's favourites. The flowerpot with the Maltese soil he carried all the way to Israel, and there, as his nostalgia grew, the jasmines flourished. Her mother, of course, thought all this was sentimental nonsense. She accused him of having contaminated Vanna, his only daughter, with his illusions. Mintoff had ruined his medical career, his youngest sister, Sarita, had been murdered by God knows who, the whole family had been shattered, and the splinters scattered to the four corners of the planet, but her father missed the island – and he made Vanna miss it too. He never stopped talking about going back there to live, and he never stopped hoping it would be possible. On the yearly holidays he spent with

Vanna in Malta – her mother refused ever to go back – he would plot his return, but her mother always put her foot down. For him, the only place he felt he really belonged was Malta. For her mother, the only place any Jew should ever live in was Israel. As a result Vanna, loving both her mother and her father, grew up torn between these two opposing, deeply held views.

No one was to know that the strike would continue for ten years. By the time it was over, it was too late to go back to Malta. In any case, her mother would still not have agreed to return. In her mind, her married life only began once they escaped from the island and settled in *ha'eretz*. Nonna Rosa had looked down on her. Her sisters-in-law said they could never quite get used to her adding raisins to couscous, though sweetness with saltiness is the Moroccan way. Nor has Vanna ever forgotten how one of the cousins from Florence – 'the snob-mob', her father called them – once laughed at the way her mother squashed down the backs of her shoes to make them more comfortable, 'just like an Arab'. So it's not surprising that her mother did not mind when they found themselves in a shoe-box in Rehovot where her father, once a top surgeon, could only get work as a lab technician. This ate at his morale. Her mother, on the other hand, always said she hated the island from the first time she set eyes on it as a bride of nineteen. 'There is just one thing I would ask of you, Joseph,' she is supposed to have said. 'Please, don't bury me here. Send my body back to my brothers and sisters in Tangiers, or lay me to rest on the Mount of Olives.'

Over many years Vanna has watched the old house decay because, just like Nonna Rosa, her aunties, Luisa and Marguerita, never allowed strange men into the house. Being spinsters, they were worse than Nonna. They had no male friends that Vanna ever knew of, except for Salvina Fortuna's brother, the judge, and they only invited him in because they thought he was too 'unprepossessing' to make a pass at a woman. '*Il povero castrato*', Ellie's father, Vanna's Uncle Clementino, labelled Edwin Fortuna. To this day even the grocer's boy, who is only fourteen, does not get past the vestibule where he is instructed to leave the groceries. Clementino used to call it 'No Man's Land', another of his silly jokes. After Vanna married Ephraim, the aunties did not even allow her to bring her husband to visit them. Oh, they clucked over how nice he looked in the wedding photos, how happy they were that Vanna had not married out, but to have him in the house was out of the question. Eventually, he refused to accompany her to Malta even for a one-week holiday.

The house should not have been left to fall into such disrepair. Sparks fly whenever Vanna pulls plugs out of sockets. Sheets of plaster are peeling off the walls and ceilings. None of the windows shuts properly, so that in winter the place is freezing. The worst thing, however, is not having hot water. The boiler broke down in 1972 and has never been mended.

As the place became more dilapidated, Vanna felt she had to ignore the aunties' fears and hire some workmen. She could not ask Eleonora/Ellie, far away as she was, and Claire had shown no interest in the family since her father took her from the island. So Vanna had the shutters fixed and painted and she herself whitewashed the kitchen and bathroom walls. But that was as far as Luisa and Marguerita would let her go. Already that was too much change for them.

In the last three years, however, Vanna's battle has not been with the aunts but with the aunts' Russian neighbours. Not that you could really call them neighbours. They only ever spend a week or two on the island in August and haven't been back, as far as Vanna knows, in the last couple of years. They bought the house with cash, which can only mean one thing. They belong to the Russian Mafia now flocking to resorts all round the Mediterranean. Not to mention Israel, of course, where they claim they are Jews but do not know a single Hebrew prayer. Anyway, everyone knows that for them Israel is just a stepping stone to America. They never feel at home there.

Three years ago, the Russian neighbours had injected damp-proofing chemicals into the common wall. DDT is nothing compared to this. The whole downstairs reeks of chemicals, and there's not a single thing anyone can do, whatever Ellie says – and she always has a lot to say. Vanna nonetheless thinks she is one hundred percent wrong to go down the lawyer route, though it is understandable since she is a trained lawyer herself.

The only solution is to take the aunts to Israel. Vanna's family apartment is too small for two more people, but they can put them in a retirement village and visit them every day, then rent the house in Malta to help pay for their care. It's out of the question that they should get rid of it, which is what Ellie is so keen to do.

'It's just a stinking dump,' she keeps saying.

'No, it isn't. It's stone-and-mortar proof we come from somewhere and have a history on this island.' As she speaks, Vanna hears an echo of her father's voice, not only just because there's a constriction in her throat but also because she has the same sing-song Maltese intonation, not the intonation of the Hebrew-speaker she has become.

The truth is she is the only member of the family who really cares about where they come from. Claire has dug her heels in and refuses to return to Malta, and Ellie keeps making fun of Vanna's efforts to quote 'shore up this ruin' unquote. She makes little squiggles in the air to emphasise it's a quotation in case Vanna does not know it.

They cannot delay the decision about what is to be done with their aunties for much longer. Although it breaks Vanna's heart to think of strangers living in this house, she cannot stay here and look after them.

'If they went to an old people's home in Malta,' Ellie argues, 'they would not be completely out of their "environment"' – more finger squiggles around that word. 'It would be insane to displace two frail, confused old women and plonk them in the middle of occupied territory.'

There she goes again with her 'occupied territory'. She not only tries to provoke Vanna when they're face to face but also subjects her to the same assault every night when she gets on the phone to her husband in Sydney. No one could convince Vanna that Ellie does not mean to be overheard, otherwise why would she leave the door half-open? Hamas fires rockets hourly into Israel and tries to murder Jewish children, but what does Ms Ellie Save-the-Headscarf do? She defends the Palestinians – and calls them heroic. Vanna feels sorry for Ellie's husband whom she's met only briefly, but he struck her as a gentle and patient man. To hear Ellie speechifying on the phone, anyone would think she is intending to apply for a job in the United Nations, or a senior post in the Arab League. If there is something Vanna cannot stomach it is an anti-Semitic Semite, a self-loathing Jew. Because, whatever Ellie says, she is Jewish.

'My parents and I certainly always considered you to be an integral part of the family.' Vanna hopes her words sound warm.

'So where exactly were they when my mother needed help?'

'We had no money to spare. My father wrote to tell her that.' Vanna had not meant to get dragged into this kind of argument, but Ellie has always had a capacity to make her feel like a puppy that has been slapped on its snout.

'Okay, if that's what you wish to believe.' Ellie clicks her neck. 'Let's leave it at that.'

Whatever Ellie thinks, however, neither her father nor mother took Nonna Rosa's line, which was that because Laura Darmanin was not Jewish her children, Eleonora and Daniel, were not Jewish. They had not been secretly baptised at the Archbishop's Palace in Valletta. This was just an idea Nonna Rosa got fixed in her head and from which she would never deviate. That's the way she was. Everyone was expected to keep up the pretence that her version of events was one hundred percent authentic. In her account of her favourite son's alienation from the Toledano family, Laura became the one who had pushed Clementino to migrate to Australia. He would have been much happier staying on the island, Nonna Rosa insisted, which the rest of the family knew was a fantasy. Uncle Clementino had always complained that Malta was too small for him, and far too small for his great musical genius. Nonetheless, this is how Rosa's story went. Eleonora/Ellie's parents had gone for a stroll in the Barracca Gardens on a sunny winter's day when Laura sprang her ultimatum on him. Caught off guard, he gave in and agreed to migrate to Australia.

'Such a big country,' Vanna recalls Luisa saying. She was probably not intending to sound sarcastic, but this is how it came out. Nonna Rosa never liked jokes too much. She was even impatient with Clementino when he got too funny. Her version was the one everyone was obliged to follow – as if there were only one truth ever.

God forbid that Vanna should speak ill of the dead – Nonna Rosa or Uncle Clementino. The main thing is not to let the dead poison the lives of the living. Or, for that matter, let the living poison the lives of the living. Perhaps if she said as much to Ellie, she would come round to agreeing to the aunties' departure for Israel. The truth is that Vanna is worn out by the arguing. This morning, a thought came to her that made her smile. Ellie is like that cartoon character, the Road Runner, she thought. 'Beep-beep!' He would streak down the road. 'Beep-beep!' He would run off the edge of a cliff, his little legs pumping away at a hundred miles an hour even when mid-air high above the Grand Canyon.

Since she arrived in Malta, Ellie has been beep-beeping around trying to visit refugee camps and tuna pens. God, who can tell what's going on in her head? The very first thing she did before coming to the house, was to detour via Valletta to see the Jesuits' lawyers who run some sort of advice service for refugees. What a farce to imagine she had come all the way from Australia to help the aunties. What is it they say about the shoemaker's children? They're the last to have a decent pair of shoes.

Anyway, while Ellie is out jogging in the morning and calling on her legal cronies, Vanna prepares the meals. Luisa eats nothing. Marguerita is still in the convalescence home. Remembering the big family dinners, it makes Vanna feel sad to set the table for just two. On High Holidays the family would come together. Because there were only a handful of Jews on the island, it was easy to imagine what it must have been like during the Spanish Inquisition, when tiny groups of Jews got together for secret feasts.

'There you go again with your nostalgia. Those family get-togethers were awful,' Ellie says. 'You can't have forgotten how they always ended with everyone at each other's throats.'

Vanna is tempted to remind Ellie that it was her father who was the one to start them all off, but she has promised herself not to get dragged into any more quarrels if she can help it. They will sort out this present family mess peacefully. Ellie will just have to stay in Malta until Marguerita's hip and shoulder are mended and she is able to travel to Israel. Vanna will take Luisa with her when she leaves.

'Oh, I know Luisa will put up a fight.' Just like a traffic policeman, Vanna holds up one hand in Ellie's direction to stop her from arguing again. 'It's hard enough to cope with her now.'

'Then try treating her as if she has some remnant of a will of her own.' Ellie stands up and throws her hands in the air. She doesn't want to hear any more.

Sometimes it takes a whole hour to get Luisa washed in the morning, and then she refuses to let Vanna remove her stinking pink dressing gown. Vanna does her best to get her tidied up as respectfully as possible, but Luisa has a very strong grip and for someone so tiny and fine-boned – she reminds Vanna of a humming bird – she certainly can hit hard, and she scratches. Since Vanna arrived a month ago, Luisa has not allowed her to cut toenails or fingernails, so now they are as long and curly as those of a Chinese Empress, while Vanna has the marks of dogged contests all over her arms.

'You try removing her dressing gown, washing and drying it and putting it back on her before she wakes up and lashes out at you.'

Luisa's confusion is painful to watch. There are days when Vanna could just sit down and kick her legs and howl with frustration and pity. She cannot bear it when Luisa clutches her head and rocks and chants to herself, 'I used to be so clever. I know I used to be. But now I am so stupid.'

Dr Micallef, a young locum who is caring for Luisa, says these are flashes of insight, not uncommon in dementia. How does he know that for sure?

Anyway, Vanna usually manages to calm Luisa and get her dressed. Then it's downstairs to the armchair near the courtyard door. She likes to look out from there, though what she sees Vanna has no idea. Perhaps she is remembering Nonna Rosa watering the jasmines in the big terracotta pots. Maybe images flash in the patches of her brain that have not turned one hundred percent into black holes, and she sees again Nonno Giacomino tending the lemon and pomegranate trees in the garden, or hears the voice of the Catholic doctor whom she finally did not marry. She had, after all, seen Clementino's disastrous marriage to Laura, the terrible fights between husband and wife and between them and the whole Toledano clan. Luisa knew she did not have the courage to defy her parents.

At least Luisa does seem to enjoy watching the scrawny stray cats prowling along the garden walls and has given up trying to chase them away. Vanna wishes she knew what was going on in her aunt's head. It kills her not to know what goes on in people's heads, though probably she wouldn't really like to see what is going on inside Ellie's, even assuming she understood her cousin's grand thoughts and theories. Not that Vanna is ashamed to admit there are things she will never understand. Does she need to know, for instance, why Ellie insists on going barefoot even though it is winter in this part of the world and the tiled floors are freezing? Perhaps it is a hangover from her hippie days, like the myriad tinkling Indian bracelets on her arms.

'Oh, these cheap old things,' Ellie says. 'I never take them off. Not even when I was giving birth to William and Cathy. The nurses were not amused.'

It takes a lot of willpower on Vanna's part to resist reaching over and slapping Ellie's hand when, resting her chin on her knees, she starts picking at her not so clean toenails. Vanna would kill any of her children for less than that, and God knows she loves them to bits.

ঙৌৎ

As she approaches the house, Vanna's skin is tingling. Of course, it was her idea that Ellie should come to Malta. She only has herself to blame for the feeling of dread she has been trying to shrug off ever since Eleonora/Ellie's arrival. She is constantly ravenous but, when she eats, it makes her feel slightly sick, which is unusual. Perhaps it's true what people say. The conditioning of your childhood is something you never overcome. Ellie had always dominated her, making her feel fat, slow and clumsy. She and Claire had often whispered to each other in her presence, as if Vanna did not count. Vanna knew they spent Monday, Thursday and Friday afternoons together doing homework above the family pharmacy, and no one thought of asking her to the birthday party for Danny. If it had been 'boys only', why had other girls from school been invited? Vanna remembers going into Valletta with her mother to buy her first pair of pumps, red with gold buckles. On the day of Danny's birthday, she had put them on first thing in the morning and waited for the doorbell to ring and her cousins to ask her to the party. Outside, there was bright sunshine, but she sat in the kitchen all day waiting to be called. All these years later, she still cannot eat Moroccan semolina orange cake, which is what her mother made that day to try to cheer her up.

This morning, Vanna should not have allowed herself to be chivvied into leaving Ellie in charge of Luisa. Their auntie is afraid of strangers and, to all intents and purposes, Ellie is a stranger. Even if there is a residue of cunning in Luisa, which makes her put up a good show of recognising outsiders, Vanna is one hundred percent certain that she is the only person Luisa really recognises, well, apart from Marguerita. Still, Vanna understands Luisa's needs better than anyone else. Their auntie must have a calm atmosphere around her otherwise she becomes very agitated.

The front door is not locked, the inner door of the vestibule is unlatched, and the radio is blaring out upstairs.

'Ellie, hello, I'm back.' Vanna sets the bags of groceries on the floor. 'Ellie, are you there?'

No response, only that signature tune on the radio. Lily Bolero? Lily Burlero? Lily Whatever. Vanna can't stand the jauntiness. She hates the Cheshire-cat smirk of BBC presenters' voices, especially when they describe the cruelties the Jews – they never say Israelis – have been inflicting on the inhabitants of Gaza. Anything to beat Jews over the head makes them positively gleeful.

From the bottom of the staircase, Vanna calls out again. Oh God, has Ellie gone off and left Luisa all alone in the house with the wireless on full blast? How could she be so irresponsible? 'Ellie? Luisa, *zija*?' There are fifty steps to the first-floor landing. Halfway up, Vanna has to hold the banister to catch her breath. Although it is a cold, damp day, she feels a trickle of sweat between her breasts. It's a long schlep from the supermarket in Paceville to St Julians, all up hill on pavements worn smooth and slippery. Why is the bedroom door shut? '*Zija*. Luisa.'

'It's okay,' Ellie says, looking over her shoulder as Vanna bursts in. 'No need to sound so panicky. I'm managing perfectly well.' She is spoon-feeding Luisa but, to Vanna, their aunt looks confused and cowed.

'You should have waited for me to get home. She won't take food from anyone else, especially not with all this noise around her.' Vanna marches across the room and switches off the radio.

'Actually, she's had a couple of spoonfuls of this carrot and potato purée and drunk a whole glass of apple juice.' Ellie turns back to attend to Luisa. 'Put the radio on again, would you, please.'

'She's upset. I can tell she is. It's your fault. It's bad enough for you to force me to listen to those anti-Semites on the BBC, but it's dreadful that you're now inflicting that on Luisa.'

Ellie leans over and gently daubs Luisa's mouth. Straightening her spine, she takes in a deep breath and sways her head slowly from side to side. This is how she releases the tension in her neck. Still holding the spoon in her hand, she gets up, crosses the room and switches the radio on again. 'You've been building up to this ever since I came, haven't you?' she says. 'Let's get this clear. You don't have to be a rabid anti-Semite to say out loud that injustices are being done to the Palestinians.'

'So why does Israel get all the limelight? Why doesn't your wonderful BBC bombard us with the horrors in the Congo? India builds a fence to keep out Pakistani terrorists, and what gets all the bad publicity? The wall the Israelis built to stop the suicide bombers. You can't possibly understand what it was like sending our children to school on a bus each morning not knowing whether the bus would be blown up or not.' She is red in the face now, flustered.

'Here, Vanna, *hanini*. Take this spoon. Since you insist on being in charge not just of this house but of censoring what radio programmes we should listen to inside it, I'll leave you in charge of the whole show.'

Vanna snatches the spoon and sits down on the edge of Luisa's bed. 'Open up wide,' she says, opening her own mouth wide as she used to do when her children refused to eat.

Ellie doesn't slam doors as she leaves the house, which makes Vanna hope that their little tiff is over. But it isn't. In the evening, without knowing how this has come about she's again arguing with Ellie and, of all subjects, it's about Ariel Sharon.

'Look, I know he's not everyone's cup of tea,' she says, trying to lighten up the atmosphere. 'But the last thing Israel needs is nice characters leading it nowhere. Especially not with the Arabs who would like nothing better than to sweep us all into the sea. Barak was pathetic. Olmert led us to the debacle in Southern Lebanon. I still can't help feeling more than a sneaking affection for Ariel. At least he knows how to truly fill up the space around him.'

Ellie's snort reminds Vanna of a horse sneezing. Ellie pushes her plate away, crosses her arms and juts her chin out at Vanna, who tears at the bread loaf with her hands. When Vanna is upset or worked up, she finds bread the only reliable way of stopping the churning feeling in her stomach.

They both go to bed early. Naturally Ellie is immediately on the phone to Australia. On the bedside table, Vanna has left a bar of white chocolate. If it weren't for the memory of that twitching cockroach in her bed, she'd sit up and eat it all. Instead, she lies still in the dark straining to hear what Ellie has to say to her husband.

'Sometimes, I think she and I aren't arguing about the Middle East or Zionism, but that our quarrel is over a particular perception of our childhood.' Ellie sounds exhausted too. 'I remember Luisa once complaining about how Vanna was always under everyone's feet. Slow to get out of your way. Slow to understand. Now, it's as if she's out to prove that she may have once been the least loved of the nieces, but now she is the only one who really loves the aunts.'

There is a burning sensation – indigestion again – right across Vanna's chest. It will serve Ellie right when she gets home and has to pay a huge phone bill.

෨ඁ

There is one positive thing than can be said about Ellie for all that. She has made the effort to come to Malta. She does have a husband and children, after all, and she lives ten thousand miles away. You do not grow rich working for NGOs, so the trip will have eaten into the family budget for sure, whereas everyone knows what people in Brussels earn, on top of which Claire must have inherited a small fortune from her father. Not that Vanna is at all interested in how much money other people make. If you keep comparing what others have and what you don't, it will corrode your whole life. Vanna just feels sorry for Claire. For the last month, she has called her every single day, sometimes twice. 'I plan to take Luisa with me to

Israel and we're leaving very soon. Ellie has to go back to Australia, so someone will have to be here until Marguerita is fit enough to board a plane. You must come now.' Claire, however, will not budge.

Of course, her reasons for not wanting to return are understandable. Her father took her away when she was twelve years old, just after her mother was so brutally murdered. They never did find out who was responsible for the letter bomb, and it was impossible to go on living in a place where every day you could walk down the street and suspect everybody whose path should cross yours.

Vanna has tried to sway Claire by claiming that if she were to put the aunties into a home, Luisa would die in a couple of weeks and Marguerita would not last much longer. Probably Claire has never set foot inside an old people's home. Her mother died young and her father was only in his early sixties when he died. Even Ellie doesn't have a clue. Her mother is still alive and apparently she had nothing to do with her father in his final years. Neither cousin has any idea what happens in those places. Old demented people are parked alongside other poor old people on the perimeter of a sunroom, slumped in their chairs all day, staring into space, or snoring, or mumbling in the air with the television on full blast. Here, in Malta, it's worse than that given that the other principal entertainment, apart from television, is the visit from the priest who comes to say mass twice a day. The risk is that Luisa and Marguerita will be converted.

'If they don't know about it, it won't be their fault, and God won't blame them.' Ellie is amused by Vanna's worry.

'He might forgive them, but I won't forgive myself.'

Vanna has always regretted having agreed to put Ephraim's parents in a home. Ephraim said it was too much for her to take on caring for them, that although she is sturdy and her shoulders are broad she is not capable of carrying the whole universe. Still, no one can accuse her of not doing her duty as a daughter-in-law, even if the Weinbergs did not like her. They were Ashkenazim and they thought of themselves as Israel's élite, superior to her Sephardic family, which was ridiculous really given that the Toledanos have produced doctors for several generations. In their ancestry you can even find surgeons to the court of the Bey – or was it the Dey? – of Tripolitania. Anyway, Vanna did her best for the Weinbergs, even if she will never forget Mrs Weinberg squeezing her arm so hard her fingers left an indentation. 'Ah, what nice little chubby arms you have,' she cooed, and then she laughed, which was mortifying. Vanna was so young then, only eighteen, and so timid.

In the end, however, Vanna grew not necessarily to like Magda Weinberg but at least to avoid having run-ins with her. And when the time came and she was dying, Vanna managed to convince Ephraim – before they moved to the West Bank – to have both his parents with them in their small Tolpiot apartment in Jerusalem. They got no help from Ephraim's international lawyer sister, by the way. When her parents needed her, she sent word from New York by email. Yes, she could not even pick up the phone. But she must have felt ashamed about having to say she was not coming. She would not return to Israel until it stopped being 'a militaristic state' quote unquote. The thought occurs to Vanna that perhaps she should introduce Ronit to Ellie. They would get on like a skyscraper on fire writing letters to the editor about Zionist Imperialism, but don't get her started on that again. As for Ephraim's brother, well he has not spoken to his brother and sister for twenty years already.

No one can accuse Vanna of not trying to hold her husband's family together. If she could do that then, surely she should be able to sustain her own now?

ഗav

At first, it seems as if Ellie has called a truce. At seven o'clock in the morning, she is already downstairs in the living room, sifting through the family papers and lining them up in neat little piles. Vanna is doing the sums, adding up the different amounts in the aunties' various deposit accounts.

'Poor Claire,' Vanna sighs, 'her husband has abandoned her for an oriental woman who's borne him a son. Claire is childless.'

'Oh for fuck's sake, Vanna, save your pity.' Ellie slams her palms on the table top. 'Pity is so passive. I hate it.' She gets up and walks back and forth from the window to the door. 'You shed a tear and then what? You go on bulldozing people's houses … '

'Bulldozing people's houses? How did we get to that?'

'Oh, never mind.' Ellie sits down again.

From now on, Vanna will try harder to keep her thoughts to herself. Nevertheless, she does feel pity for Claire. Though she never liked him, she is sorry about that fastidious French husband dumping her. Imagine this, you invite a man to dinner and he calls you up to ask you what is on the menu, and then informs you what wines you should buy to match each dish. 'None of that sweet, ritual Israeli wine, *s'il vous plaît*,' he once said to Ephraim, as if her husband were a complete ignoramus.

Remembering this, Vanna is reminded of the very first time Claire came to Jerusalem as an official interpreter to a European Parliamentary delegation. She and Ephraim organised a little sightseeing for her cousin. She was so happy to see her again after all those years in which their families hardly communicated. They had both suffered as a result of the doctors' strike in Malta when their fathers had been driven out. Vanna, however, was disappointed to find Claire stand-offish and cold. She never once got out of her expensive clothes and put on casual wear to go walking in the Old City of Jerusalem. It was freezing and there were flurries of snow, but she would not borrow one of Vanna's thick sweaters. Too big and shapeless for her, no doubt, though she did not say so out loud. It was the twitch at the end of her fine nose that gave her away. The money she must spend on clothing herself! But then she only has herself to spend money on, which is another major reason to feel sorry for her.

Really, it is about time Vanna stopped tiptoeing around her feelings. Of course, her suffering was the greatest, but she seems not to realise that, as a result of what happened to her mother, the rest of the family suffered too. Sarita was not just a wife and mother. She was a daughter and sister. Coming back to Malta year in year out, which neither of her cousins did, Vanna could see that, once

Sarita was gone, time stopped still for Marguerita and Luisa. Sarita was also her auntie and Ellie's and Danny's auntie too. Their families always lived within a couple of miles of each other and they were in and out of each other's houses every day of their lives. The letter bomb did not just blow Sarita up. Like all acts of unforeseen violence, it destroyed a whole family. Living in Israel where bombs go off every week, Vanna knows all about it.

She has never forgotten that her own mother also had a very difficult time after Sarita died, not only because their front room, where the bomb went off, had been turned into a war zone, but also because her mother knew everyone blamed her. They thought she was the one who should have been holding the letter when it exploded, though no one naturally said so to her face. Well, Nonna Rosa might have once or twice, but Luisa and Marguerita, for once in their lives, managed to cut their mother short by marching out of the room, taking Vanna's mother with them. The Toledanos prided themselves on how they remained polite in all circumstances. It was their British heritage, though there was not a drop of British blood in their veins only that they lived in a British colony and had had a colonial education.

But Vanna's mother always felt that everyone was thinking she was the one who should have picked up the mail which the postman had left on the windowsill. She was the one who should have been blown up. How many times had Vanna heard her grandmother and aunties terminate a conversation just as they got to 'if only' when talking about that day? The rest of the sentence hung in the air.

One day Marguerita dared to take the sentence further. 'If only it were possible to re-wind our lives like a film shown backwards. Sarita would not have dropped Claire off at Miss Sokolova's for her Russian lesson. She would not have had an hour and a half to kill. The irony of it.' Gradually, Marguerita grew bolder, taking the story back to the day when Nonna Rosa had had her brainwave about what to do if the Communists took over Malta. Because they were certainly going to do that now that Mintoff was in power again. Malta would soon become a war zone too, and someone in the family was going to have to learn Russian.

Ellie

4 Alliances

' *Isktu naqra u isimgħu*!' Keep quiet and listen!

With her sterling silver fork, Nonna Rosa clinked the Murano wine carafe. '*Zitti. Ascoltateme tutti. I have something to say to all of you.*'

Twelve faces glazed with sweat turned towards the top of the table extended so that it straddled the archway between the dining and living rooms. Ellie remembers that her grandmother had gathered the whole Maltese branch of the Toledano family around her: Uncle Joseph and her aunts Marguerita, Luisa and Sarita and Sarita's husband, Alberto Sacerdote, with their daughter, Claire, Ellie's brother, Danny, and their mother, Laura, and Miriam, Joseph's wife, and their daughter, Vanna. A long time ago she had had to draw a family tree for Richard, but now it is clear to him who everyone is.

After Nonno Giacomino's death, it was Clementino, Ellie's father and the elder son, who sat at the opposite end of the table from Nonna Rosa, on the living room side of the arch. On summer evenings, before the apartments across the road were built, the doors and windows were left open for cooling crosscurrents. To discourage the voracious mosquitoes, the lights were switched off so that Ellie could scarcely make out her great-grandmother Beatrice's face from the portrait hanging on the wall. Clementino always joked that his grandmother's sourpuss expression reflected her misery – married to someone she hardly knew and shipped off to an anonymous barren rock in the middle of the Mediterranean. She never stopped longing for Florence, where she had been born, and for what she always referred to as 'Civilisation'. Who could blame her, Clementino said?

Now, as Nonna Rosa spoke, all scraping of cutlery on crockery ceased. There was no more chinking of glasses. Ellie could just make out a spiral of houseflies hovering drowsily overhead. In the kitchen, the kerosene refrigerator, which sputtered and coughed all day, sucked in a deep breath, then it too fell silent. At that moment the only sounds in the room were Vanna's clogged-nose breathing and the tip-tap of Clementino's foot as he impatiently jigged his leg.

'Someone in this family is going to have to learn Russian,' Nonna Rosa said.

Whenever she switched from Maltese to Italian, everyone knew she meant business. In retrospect, Ellie could see that although Marguerita, Clementino, Luisa, Joseph and Sarita had been brought up speaking Italian, being a native-speaker gave their mother an edge over every one of them. In Italian, Nonna Rosa wielded her mother tongue as a weapon rather than as an instrument of negotiation. In Ellie's experience, no matter how well someone knows a second language, it is hard to avoid being browbeaten by a native-speaker. You simply don't have the same agility. Besides which, the idea that someone in the family would have to learn Russian took them all by surprise.

৵৵

Forty years later, it is the warm aroma of tomatoes and garlic cooking in olive oil that triggers Ellie's memory of the night that Nonna Rosa made her startling announcement. Vanna is preparing a simple sauce for pasta based on a recipe handed down to her by their grandmother. Ellie doesn't doubt the truth of that. Over the years, Vanna is the only grandchild to have visited Malta regularly, returning on holiday from Israel with her father each summer.

Looking around her, it seems to Ellie that nothing much has changed in the old house. Perhaps the ceiling is not as high as she had remembered it, the massive oak furniture less looming. The portrait of Beatrice has been replaced by a cheap print still life of overblown flowers. Without consulting anyone, Vanna has decided to take their great-grandmother back with her to Israel. Poor Beatrice, Ellie thinks, hauled off first to Malta and now to an even more godforsaken country. Her picture stands wrapped in bubble paper in the hallway, leaning against the hat and umbrella stand.

One thing has not changed at all. The fridge still spits and sputters, except that it is Vanna now rather than one of the aunts who gets down on her knees and packs towels tightly around its plinth to soak up the leaking water.

'Perhaps we could buy a new fridge and donate this one to the Museum of Palaeontology,' Ellie says to Vanna, trying to inject humour and warmth into her words despite her irritation with her cousin. As she pulls out a chair and sits down, she realises that she has taken the place once assigned to her mother at family dinners. Above the glass-fronted cabinet, which contains the fine china and glassware that had been part of Beatrice's trousseau shipped from Italy in 1880, the brass Chanoukia nailed to the wall now has a patina of verdigris. The *Shalom* embossed in Hebrew letters on the candlestick trunk is illegible. Ellie has not been able to muster sympathy for her mother in years. After Max's death, she had learned to distance herself from Laura's mood extremes, but as she stares at the Chanoukia, a huge wave of sympathy washes over her. She has often been bad-tempered with Laura, sometimes unkind. Her only excuse is that she has never been patient with illness, including with her own children's. Richard has always taken time off work for that. Well, it's easier for him, running his architectural practice from home. Now Ellie feels sad, understanding that it was a deliberately hostile act on Nonna Rosa's part to seat her elder daughter-in-law on this side of the table. From here, as she looked up, Laura's gaze would have been eye-level with the Chanoukia, and so at those great family gatherings she would never have been able to forget that she did not fully belong. Her promise not to have Ellie and Danny baptised had never been good enough for her mother-in-law.

Isktu naqra u isimghu! Ellie repeats her grandmother's words out loud. It is as if the whole sentence has been curled up in her head, ready to spring free. Not for the first time does she see just how much her mother had given up by marrying into the Toledano clan. It was not just her religion, her own family and eventually her

89

country. After Clementino had abandoned them, she had also given up her mother tongue. It occurs to Ellie that the sensation she has had over the years of speaking to her mother through gauze might not be wholly attributable to her mother's mental illness. When her mother gave up speaking Maltese to her children, she created a further distance between them and herself. There were no more Maltese terms of endearment, and soon the children stopped speaking the language altogether. *Mama* became Mum. *Madoffi*, bloody hell. If Vanna has also grown up outside Malta, by returning each year she has never lost her mother tongue. Ellie wonders if Claire too has kept up her first language and identity.

Since her arrival in Malta, she has, on the other hand, been pleased by just how much Maltese she actually does remember. If with strangers she pretends not to understand much, it is because it's a way of stopping them from being too inquisitive. Like Ancient Mariners, they stop her in the street or on the promenade, insisting their family had been her family's closest friends for generations. How good-hearted your people were, they say, scanning Ellie's face with glaucous eyes that make her think of dead fish and put her in a rage. 'We always went to your dear grandfather's pharmacy. Though he was a Jew, he was such a lovely, patient man. Your aunties too. We haven't seen them for ages. God bless them, and God bless your dearest mother too.'

'What drives me bananas is the fluttering of hands across the chest, that mouthing of bless you, *hanini,* as they cross themselves,' Ellie says angrily. 'Yes, Richard, I know it's my hobby-horse, but that's how I feel. At first

I thought they were mistaking me for Claire, which was why there were sorry for me. But, no, they definitely mean Laura, not Sarita. Jeezus, where were they all when my father dumped us?'

'Ellie, you were living on the other side of the world,' Richard says.

'I know, but that didn't stop them from discovering that my father was living with another woman.'

Since they never had anything to do with the Maltese community in Australia, it beats Ellie how people in Malta found out. Reigning in her fury is sometimes exhausting. It was a standing joke in St Julian's that when Ellie shrieked in her crib in the Lapsi Street clinic where she was born, she set the other babies off. That rat-bag neighbour, Marion Camilleri, who had been a midwife at the clinic, buttonholed her on the street yesterday and reminded her of that. In an apparent non sequitur, she pointed out, how unreliable her father had always been.

'You don't have to stay, Ellie.' Richard sounds tired.

'You know, I'm not in the habit of defending him, but I couldn't help agreeing with him for once. He always said Malta was suffocating.'

It wasn't just Clementino Bloody Mary had a go at. In a seamless transition from her father's good looks and talent, she reminded Ellie of the time police arrested her for swimming in the nude. She spoke in a chirrupy voice: "But we Maltese are modern people now. Everyone here can sunbake topless these days".'

'I'm surprised you're letting it get to you.'

'Oh, don't worry, I sent La Camilleri away with a flea in her ear. I told her my mother wrote to some

Catholic society on the island asking to fund our return to Malta. You should have seen how the pious old cow flapped her hands and arms when I said how very Christian of them to have never replied.'

Marion is not the only one who is keen to tell Ellie how sorry they were for her family. Everyone she meets says the same thing. So where were they when Marguerita and Luisa needed help? How come the aunts have been left to rot in their house all these years?

Ellie knows what's to be done, but she can't get Vanna to agree. The aunts need to go into a home where they can be cared for properly. There's no other solution. What Vanna is proposing – to drag a couple of frail and sickly octogenarians into a war zone – is out of the question, especially now that she's moved to some settlement in the Occupied Territories. All they've done since Ellie's arrival is quarrel.

'Ellie, you're free to catch a flight back home at any time,' Richard says.

'And let Vanna think she's won? I can't go home now. Apart from anything else, I'd like to visit one of the migrant detention centres here.'

Rosemary Vassallo, the human rights lawyer who is her contact in one of the NGOs on the island, is doing her best to get her permission. The lawyer also happens to know one of the divers who clean out the tuna pens. This man has promised to take Ellie out to see what is going on at one of the tuna farms.

'Ellie, you're not going to make it a habit to get arrested every time you go back to Malta?

౨~౨

When had the clock on the second bell tower of Our Lady of Saint Carmel stopped working, Ellie wonders on her early-morning jog? As she rounds the curve of the promenade into Balluta, she remembers swimming in the bay and liking the sense that time had stopped still. Below, she sees a man scrubbing down his carthorse with a long-handled broom. Though she cannot tell if it is the man from her childhood, when he looks up, Ellie waves to him. He does not wave back. She zigzags on the pavement to avoid the people streaming out of morning mass, remembering what the nuns who taught her at her Maltese primary school used to say: 'the Holy Trinity is a single entity working for the good of mankind'.

Funny that a trinity should have come to rule a whole civilisation, Ellie thinks, because in her experience, the dynamics of three are always negative. 'Three's a crowd,' Richard's mother would chant, and although he insisted she did it without thinking, Ellie always felt the words were directed at her. Whenever three people get together, two of them always gang up against the third, she thought. Perhaps it is natural, inevitable even. Two people can reach an agreement much more quickly than three, and sensing a weakness in the third, will go in for the kill.

Ellie must have been about eight when she first noticed how, at school, two girls would often gang up against a third, and her cousins Claire and Vanna would on occasion form a duo to remind her that she was not a 'proper Jew'.

But Ellie herself was not immune from this kind of aggression. Although her better instinct told her it was wrong, she sometimes got Claire to do things that they kept secret from Vanna. Vanna was not clever. She would only hold them back, Ellie would argue. Among their mothers, Laura, Sarita and Miriam, it was sometimes Laura, born a Catholic, who was the odd woman out. At other times it was Miriam, who had little education. Sarita might have been lifted to the rank of angel after her sudden, violent death, but Ellie remembers her sniping that Vanna's mother was a peasant.

When Ellie was eleven, Mintoff was returned to power, and all around them people ganged up against others. Really, her father had been right to describe the Maltese as a fractious people. Among their neighbours, the Brincats sided with the Camilleries, who called Mintoff the Anti-Christ, against the Grechs, who thought the man was a saint. One thing for sure, no one was indifferent to the man. Within the Toledano family, the divisions were also bad, and deepened further, after Mintoff announced he was determined to push through free medical care for all. The whole clan was polarised in a series of trinities which, Ellie now realises, went on constantly composing and re-composing. Sometimes it was Claire's father, Alberto Sacerdote, and Joseph, Vanna's father, who closed ranks against Ellie's father. Clementino liked to provoke them by saying that he admired 'Dominic Mintoff's purity of purpose'. But in the eyes of Joseph and Alberto, Clementino had no business speaking on any medical issue given that he had abandoned his medical studies to pursue a musical career that had so far come to nothing much. No staying power, the uncles said in unison. His mother's spoiled darling, they reiterated, shoulder to shoulder, two against one.

Sometimes, however, the pattern of alliances would shift so that it was Clementino and Joseph who closed ranks against Alberto. After all, Sarita's husband was only an in-law. 'Alberto is not like us,' the two brothers said, united on this point. 'Money is important to him. He's only in medicine in order to get rich.' This would inevitably pitch Sarita against her two brothers as she sprang to her husband's defence.

The most surprising alliance was formed by Uncle Alberto and his mother-in-law, Rosa, who ranged together in their loathing of Mintoff. Clementino found it amusing and liked to tease them. 'I'm surprised you dislike the Dom so much. You can't deny that he's a man who wakes up each morning with thousands of original ideas in his head.'

'*Può darsi*,' Nonna said. 'That might be – but of every thousand ideas, nine-hundred and ninety nine are bad.'

'Maybe, but if he has just one single good idea a day, at the end of the year, that makes a total of three hundred and sixty-five.' Clementino never failed to bounce back. 'Pretty good going, wouldn't you say?'

'Not if it means he's going to let Malta be taken over by the Russians. Because if he carries out the plans he's been hatching all his years in opposition, we will end up under Communist rule.'

'The Terror!' Uncle Alberto chanted. 'The Terror! This is what springs to mind when you, Clementino, talk about Mintoff's Purity of Purpose. That is precisely the language used by Danton, Robespierre and Saint Just during the French Revolution.'

Alberto had a high voice and the kind of sparse, reddish beard that in Ellie's mind went with that kind of voice. 'Mintoff's methods are those of all the Reigns of Terror that have been unleashed on the world,' Alberto said. 'If the people don't know what's good for them, then those in power will show them, and if they still refuse to understand, then every last one of them deserves to be killed.'

'Once we were all fooled into thinking Russia was going to be the New Utopia. Now we see it for what it is. We cannot allow the Russians to help Mintoff achieve his purpose,' Nonna Rosa concluded.

༼ა༽

According to Nonno Giacomino, back in the 1950s Nonna Rosa had been a Mintoff supporter, something that Ellie could never wholly believe. To all the grandchildren it seemed just another one of Giacomino's wonderful flights of fantasy. It made for an exciting chapter in the Story of Nonna Rosa's Life. So they all pretended to believe their grandfather when he said that during Mintoff's first term of office their grandmother had written a letter to San Anton Palace to congratulate Mintoff for his stance on Saint Jerome and The Beheading of St John the Baptist.

'I should take all of you one day to St John's Cathedral to see those Caravaggio masterpieces, but it would upset your grandmother to have all her grandchildren traipsing about a church,' Nonna Giacomino said.

Ellie cannot remember the quality of his voice, but she has never forgotten his playfulness and wondered how someone with his humour married Rosa, who found nothing funny at all. In clearing the family papers, however, she has come across a photo of her grandparents taken in September 1913. They must have just returned from their two-month honeymoon spent visiting family around the Mediterranean. All her life, Rosa longed to travel but, as things turned out, this was the only time she ever left Malta. In the snapshot, she and Giacomino are leaning over the railing of the first-floor balcony, waving to someone below and laughing. Giacomino's right arm is draped across her shoulders and her head is tilted towards his large hand. Her thick curly hair, which Ellie's so resembles, has been whipped up by the wind. She looks happy, relaxed and surprisingly sexy. Was it the babies born at regular eighteen-month intervals over the next fifteen years of her marriage that changed her, for in addition to the five surviving children there had been three others who had died aged only a few weeks? Perhaps Giacomino was right when he joked that she would have been happier as a politician than as a wife and mother. Rosa's father, whose life's work was an annotated '*Divina Commedia*', never censored her reading material. Among the books in her grandmother's house, Ellie has found a copy of Engel's 'Socialism: Utopian and Scientific'. In the flyleaf, someone has scribbled in pencil in Italian, 'Utopias always end up betrayed', and Ellie wonders if the writing is her grandmother's. On the shelves, there is also an original 1905 edition of Henrietta Elizabeth Marshall's 'Our Island Story', a history not of the island of Malta but of the British Isles. This stands next to Ariosto and Manzoni.

'For centuries those Caravaggios had hung in the cathedral,' Nonno Giacomino said, 'and as time went by they grew darker and darker with grime. The white turned yellow and the black the colour of an oil slick until the Powers-That-Be decreed that the paintings must be removed from the cathedral and given a thorough cleaning. So far, so good, how could anyone object? The trouble came only after the cleaning, because rather than having the paintings returned to the cathedral, Dom Mintoff ordered that they be hung in Valletta's Museum of Art.'

'"These masterpieces belong to the Maltese people," the Dom declared "not to the Catholic Church."'

'This, my dearest grandchildren, is what won him Nonna Rosa's support and even a little affection, which as you know she does not easily bestow. But as much as your grandmother loathed the treachery of the Left, she loathed and feared the priests and their power over the Maltese people more. And so ...' Nonno Giacomino always paused in order to enhance the impact of the dénouement of this instalment of Nonna Rosa's life which he entitled Rosa and the Dom. 'And so in their anti-clericalism, Dominic Mintoff and my wife, though they never actually met, briefly became the closest of allies. A pity that The Dom ruined this good will by abandoning the Grandest of all his Grand Schemes.'

The children all held their breath. Although they already knew that the Grandest of Mintoff's Grand Schemes had been to demand that the British grant Malta the status of an overseas county, none of them ever tired hearing their grandfather re-tell this tale. He was good at creating suspense, pausing to shift his pipe from one corner of his mouth to the other, while the grandchildren sitting at his feet held their breath in expectation. He was a stocky man, with wide shoulders, a thick moustache and a completely bald head, but women seemed to find him attractive, which even the children noticed was a source of tension and frequent outbursts between him and their grandmother.

'Once upon a time, Rosa Coen Toledano had really and truly believed that the British were the sole protectors of the Jews of Malta against the rabid Catholicism of their Maltese subjects. This conviction ran so deep that it led your grandmother to give her support to Mintoff who, being married to an Englishwoman, wanted to keep the British in Malta. Not only was he intent on keeping the British here, he wanted them to grant Malta full English county status. The British, however, wanted nothing to do with this hair-brained scheme. I won't go into their reasons, but their rejection prompted Mintoff's resignation. His supporters were furious. Riots broke out all over the island. In response, our colonial rulers suspended the Maltese Constitution. That was when your grandmother turned against the Dom, and that is why she has remained as unforgiving as a rejected lover, though it is not the British she does not forgive, but Mintoff himself. As far as she was concerned, his failure to convince the Brits that Malta could be like Kent or Essex ought to consign him to political wilderness for the rest of his days.'

Nonno Giacomino had been dead for three years when Mintoff was returned to power in 1971 after thirteen years in opposition.

'*Guarda*! Look at the man!' Nonna Rosa slapped the front page of the newspaper Clementino was holding. When things were bad at home, he often came to his mother's for breakfast, sometimes bringing Ellie and Danny with him, leaving Laura to sleep for hours and hours.

On the front page of The Times of Malta, there was a picture of Mintoff with his thick, dark-framed glasses, which despite his not having a beard Ellie thought made him look like Uncle Alberto's twin. 'What does he do no sooner he's in office again?' Nonna Rosa asked the air around her. '*Scelerato*! The scoundrel! He flies off to China and returns with an I LOVE MAO badge pinned to his lapel.'

'And a seventeen million pound donation to the flagging Maltese economy.' Clementino gave a crooked grin that Ellie once heard a woman say made him irresistible. Ellie had felt briefly protective of her mother. My father belongs to us, she thought, not to people we don't know and who don't know us.

'So who are the greatest enemies of the Chinese?' Nonna Rosa asked. 'The Russians, you'll see. Mintoff is rehearsing for a part as the second Fidel Castro. He's intent on turning Malta into the Cuba of the Mediterranean.'

৵৵

'Do you remember the last great family dinner in this house, just after Dom Mintoff became Prime Minister for the third time, in 1976?' Ellie asks Vanna, trying another tack to ease the tensions between them. 'There was Nonna Rosa jabbing three green beans on her plate and waving them on the end of her fork at all of us. "*Velo dico*. Mark my words."' Ellie picks up a fork and brandishes it in the air in an attempt to coax a smile out of Vanna. She describes their grandmother perched on a stack of cushions, which raised the top half of her torso to the level of the tabletop. '"*Vedrete*. You'll see. The Soviets will soon be goose-stepping down our streets, plundering our money and jewels and imposing uniform drabness on us all. They will make sure that Mintoff succeeds in getting his National Health Scheme through Parliament."'

'I don't remember the details.' Vanna remains poker-faced and goes on chewing.

'Of course, one person's memory is never the same as another's.' Ellie takes a deep breath. 'Surely you haven't forgotten how furious Nonna Rosa was when Mintoff barred all Maltese doctors from issuing medical certificates?' One day she is going to snap and scream at Vanna to stop making those smacking sounds with her tongue as she eats. She should get her adenoids seen to also. Isn't this what Luisa always used to say when they were children? It might improve her breathing.

'Come on, your father was a doctor. If the medical profession weren't willing to accept Labour's plans for a health service, Mintoff would kick the doctors out of the island.'

'Well, yes, of course I remember that.'

'I've never forgotten the day Claire and I were on our way to Paceville and found ourselves in the middle of a huge angry crowd in front of the police station at Spinola.'

Policemen on horseback were trying to hold protesters back, but the jeering made the horses jittery. They snorted and whinnied, and long strings of spittle dangled from their mouths as their riders tugged the cheek straps to stop them from rearing and the bit dug into their jaws. Ellie was reminded of a painting – by whom? Goya? El Greco? – in which a horse's bloodshot eye stares in terror at the viewer. She has been to countless demos since then and still finds that hollow sound of horse hooves on tarmac eerie. She grabbed Claire's hand and they ran as fast they could back to Balluta.

'That evening Nonna Rosa unveiled her Grand Project.'

'Which was?' Vanna seems to be relaxing.

'The Great Soviet Occupation Project. She had an amazing imagination, didn't she? Absolutely loony. We were all going to need a go-between who understood the language of our occupiers, and that *intermediario* had to be a child. Only a child's brain would be malleable enough to enable him or her to learn a new language quickly and speak it like a native. On that count Nonna Rosa sided with the Jesuits. Which of us grandchildren would it be?'

'She kept us waiting for days and days for the answer, I remember that.' As Vanna speaks, she un-hunches her sloping shoulders and stops chomping. 'She didn't like your mother, so that ruled you out. My mother wasn't popular with her either. Apart from that I didn't stand a chance, what with my terrible school results and …'

'…and?'

'…and my big *patata*.' A smile creeps from Vanna's lips to her eyes. 'Madoffi, Nonna Rosa certainly had an obsession with my *patata*.'

'She had an obsession with the big bums of her daughters, her daughters-in-law, and her granddaughters. As far as I recall, those little slaps on our behinds were about the only thing that made her laugh.' For the first time since their reunion, Ellie starts to feel some warmth for Vanna. 'None of us had looks that pleased her.'

'What about Claire?'

'She liked Claire because she was always so neat, just like Uncle Alberto who was so bloody finicky. Plus she was docile. I remember looking across the table and trying to exchange glances with you two, but you both kept your eyes fixed on your laps. I can hear Nonna Rosa even now. *I russi! Maledetti*! In a few days' time they will be throwing grappling hooks over the curtain-walls of Valletta's fortifications and scrambling over like millions of soldier ants. In the dead of night, the Red Army will occupy our capital city and then, village by small village, they will take over the whole of Malta, Gozo and Comino.'

It sounds like hiccups, but Vanna is laughing.

'You do remember, in which case, you must also recall what the nuns used to say. Anyone who voted for Mintoff would go to hell. The nuns got it from the priests, who got it from the Head of the Congregation of the Doctrine of the Faith. The Doctrine of the faith bunch were the ones who started the rumour that three days of total darkness would descend on the island if the Maltese voted in a Labour government. Everyone rushed out to buy candles. I heard my father tell that story so many times. Within twenty-four hours the shops were out of candles. Later on, there were more threats. All Mintoff supporters would end up buried in a *mizbla* when they died. Jesus had their sins recorded in his Great Celestial Ledger.'

❧

'It's horrible,' Claire whined as she and her cousins trudged along the promenade from Sliema to Spinola. Huge waves crashed on the rocks below, spraying the three of them. The late autumn wind blew so hard that they had to lean forward against it. At their feet, rubbish scraped across the pavement like tumbleweed. 'Everyone knows that a *mizbla* is the corner of the field where the farmer throws all the horrible garbage …'

'…and the pig pooh,' Vanna said, 'don't forget the pig pooh, Claire.'

'Surely the two of you aren't so stupid you'd believe what the nuns say?' Ellie quickened her pace, marching ahead with the wind whipping her thick curls across her face. Her cousins were so gullible.

Ellie was angry with them again. They were scared of everything, and they could be so prissy. Like when she took them home and they pretended they had not noticed her mother lying about in her dressing gown. The house was in a mess, the kitchen dirty. Sometimes Laura would rouse herself and offer the children something to eat or drink, but Claire and Vanna would say thank you very much but we're not really hungry or thirsty, as if they were going to catch some terrible disease.

'If Mintoff has become Prime Minister again, it must mean that more than half the island voted for him.' Ellie stopped suddenly and swung round to face Claire and Vanna. 'That's what my father says.'

'So?' Claire squinted against the sunlight piercing the broiling black clouds.

'So?' Vanna echoed.

Ellie skipped backwards. By now they had reached the Coastal watchtower. On the promontory, the gusts of wind were ferocious. 'Work it out for yourselves.' Ellie spread her arms in order not to lose her balance. 'How could tens of thousands of people be buried in the corner of fields? I mean, on this island there isn't even enough topsoil to grow potatoes to feed all the Maltese people let alone in which to bury them.'

'It's not funny, Ellie. It's not funny in the slightest,' Claire said. 'It's not just the Mintoffiani who'll end up in a *mizbla*. The other girls say the *mizbla* is where they bury Jews.'

'They say we will burn in hell when we die. It's horrible,' Vanna said.

'That's so stupid,' Ellie shouted above the wind.

'Oh, it's okay for you,' Vanna retorted. 'Your mother is Catholic.'

'Yes, she's not really Jewish,' Claire said.

'Oh, shut up, the two of you.' Ellie turned round and rushed ahead, but she could not get the *mizbla* out of her thoughts.

৵৵

'My mind is more or less made up,' Nonna Rosa said at that last great family gathering. As she spoke, she screwed up her eyes and nose, as Ellie recalls her doing whenever she was in munificent mode, handing out caramels to the grandchildren. But her generosity was randomly bestowed. It was part of what Clementino called her attachment to a Policy of Divide-and-Rule. Clutching the sweets in her hands, closing her eyes tight, Nonna Rosa would turn her head like a weathervane, then snap her eyes open when she was facing the grandchild who happened to be the Chosen-One-of-the-Day. '*Allora, vediamo*. So, let us see.'

Through the window in the sitting room, which overlooked the street, music floated up from the skating rink below in the gully at Spinola. It took only a scowl from her mother for Marguerita to hop up from her chair and rush to close the windows and shutters. Now there was even less air in the room.

'*Daniele è troppo piccolo*,' Nonna Rosa said. 'Danny's too small. Vanna has not had the best school results lately. Eleonora is of course the smartest of my grandchildren. But Claire has the gift for languages. On Monday she will begin two lessons a week. It has been arranged.'

❧

Soon, the first doctors from behind the Iron Curtain began arriving in Malta. Joseph went on working, arguing with Alberto that they and their colleagues should wait and see if the Prime Minister would allow the island to be flooded by foreign medics. But even when the influx was just a trickle, Alberto began applying for posts in the UK and Canada.

Then the invasion proper began.

Claire and Ellie were standing outside Captain Caruana's Liquor Store on Republic Street in Valletta waiting for Alberto to buy champagne and cognac. There was to be a big meeting of doctors opposed to Mintoff at Claire's house that evening. As Ellie and her cousin stood peering into the window to the left of the front door, two men and a woman planted themselves in front of the shop window to the right of the door, talking animatedly.

'What's the matter?' Ellie asked when Claire fell silent.

'Shush, let me listen. It sounds like Russian, but it isn't. I mean, I don't think it is. I mean, I don't know what it is.'

'Well, say something to them. See if they understand you.'

'What? What shall I say?'

I knew it, Ellie thought, I knew Claire would never have the courage to speak up. For God's sake, she was nearly twelve years old and still scared of the *buttarga*, the fish roe sausages that hung in the *garagor*, the narrow winding staircase that led to the roof. At their grandparents' house, you would never get her to go upstairs at sunset to collect the washing even though she knew that Nonno Giacomino had only made up the story that the sausages were shrunken hanged men.

When Claire's father came out of Captain Caruana's, he did not at first notice the men and the woman staring in his direction and smiling at him. In a country of short people, the Sacerdotes were tall, but Alberto would have stood out even in a crowd of Americans. Behind his back, Nonna Rosa described him as a man with a *puzzo sotto il naso,* a smell under his nose, which is how he looked as he registered the presence of the trio and ordered Claire and Ellie to hurry up and follow him or they would miss the bus back to Spinola. He never once looked back as the girls trotted behind him, and he did not apologise when he nearly knocked over the blind lottery ticket vendor sitting on his box under the arch at Porta Reale.

'No, they're not Russians.' Alberto only answered Ellie's question after they had boarded the No.72 and sat down. 'They're Polish doctors, and they've been given contracts to work at St Luke's. They are the vanguard of the Communist offensive, imported into the island by the Devil Himself.'

The next day, near the Quisisana bus stop, Ellie was waiting for Claire as she came out of Miss Sokolova's.

'What did you learn today?' Ellie marched beside her cousin. 'Go on. Don't be a spoilt-sport. Tell me.'

'If I tell you,' Claire said, 'then Vanna will want to know too, and if I have to teach her that will slow me down terribly.'

'So, don't tell her. She doesn't have to know everything you and I do.'

From that afternoon Ellie walked home with Claire after her Russian lesson and learned the newest Russian words and grammar that Miss Sokolova had taught Claire.

All these years later, Ellie still cannot help feeling a twinge of jealousy that her grandmother had not chosen her. The memory of that is like a bruise in her heart, but she has never forgotten Claire's willingness to share her new knowledge. Vanna says Claire is not interested in returning to Malta, but maybe a phone call from Ellie might change her mind.

Claire

5 Naming of Parts

Today we have naming of sheep
Yesterday we had bikini tops and tomorrow
Tomorrow we shall have climate change
But today
Today we have naming of sheep …

'Does either of you remember the original poem?' I ask my colleagues. Smirking at the laptop screen, I'm pleased with the pastiche and the jumble of fonts.

Through the windows overlooking the Parc Léopold, against the darkening sky, the reflection of the neon-lit conference room appears to be floating in mid-air on the outside of the vast expanse of glass. At midday the sky is as black as night. Rain pelts against the windows. It is hot and humid in the booth today.

Tomorrow we shall bring our Pashminas …

As if I were playing the final bars of a piano concerto, I bang hard on the keys. It is always too hot and humid in interpreters' booths, or else too dry and chilly. But the technician in charge of air quality will have gone off to lunch by now. We must put up with the discomfort. I'm not sure the electronic baton he uses to measure humidity and temperature measures anything at all. He only waves it about to mollify interpreters who are notorious for complaining about stale air, not just bad orators. After the man has passed nothing really changes.

'Hold on to your seat for another dose of knee-jerk negativity.' Simon Pennington raises a flattened palm to signal that he is about to go on mike.

On the third and last day of the Customs Nomenclature Committee/Textiles, the French delegate, who all day long has rejected every proposal any other delegate has made, still fiercely objects to the Committee's classification of bikini tops.

'If they're not sold as part of a set with a bikini bottom – Simon is interpreting – 'they cannot possibly be classified as bikini tops.'

His finger on the mute button, Simon turns to Iris Elizabeth Walton and me and speaking out of the corner of his mouth says, 'It's obvious this guy doesn't have teenage daughters. Mine live in skimpy shorts and mini skirts and buy their bikini tops separately.' He switches on again. Simon has a gift for never sounding as if he is making fun of even the most pompous orator. Yet with the preciousness of a character out of Molière, none of which he spares his audience, he huffs that the definition the Committee has been hammering out for weeks still does not clearly distinguish bikini tops from mere bras.

'On this matter, the French authorities are categorical, and the World Customs Organisation will not accept this definition either.'

'Shit!' Simon sighs having punched the 'off' button hard. 'I'd been hoping this meeting would fold up early.

Now I can see we're going to be here until six thirty.' He crosses his arms and lets his spine sag.

'It's always like this.' Iris Elizabeth puts down her marker pen. 'Just when you think a meeting is going to end early, someone raises ten AOB points. The German delegate still hasn't got his customs classification for the ice hockey shorts.' Iris Elizabeth sifts through the pile of documents in the folder in front of her and pulls out a letter from an importer addressed to German Customs in Hamburg. 'Just think of it,' she says flapping the letter under my nose, 'ten thousand pairs of padded shorts are mouldering in a bonded warehouse in Germany while the importer waits for a decision from Brussels on the duty he is he going to have to pay. Oh, hang on a moment, our Frenchman is about to spout again. Who wants to take him this time?'

I volunteer. On my best days, interpreting gives me the same sense of satisfaction as completing a difficult cryptic crossword. When I'm able to keep up with the speaker, it can feel like gliding in an air stream. But increasingly there are days that seem never ending, like today, when I am driven mad by speakers who turn the most practical things into abstractions without the saving grace of an ironical comment or a complicated grammatical structure that I manage to unravel and transform into something that sounds better than the original. This morning, bikini tops have already taken up hours of rancorous debate. Even more bitter than the discussion on ceramic sheep that took up half of yesterday and carried over to some of today's session. The Committee still has not decided on how to categorise the small statuette that sits to the left of the chairman's nameplate. It has curly tufts of wool glued to its back.

'What do you think will tip the balance?' Simon asks Iris Elizabeth and me. 'Would you say it is "ceramic-ness" that defines that creature's essential characteristics? Or is it the damned thing's woolliness? Millions of euros in customs duty are at stake on the metaphysics of it all. And, hey, weren't these people trying to define the same fucking sheep at the last meeting?'

'And at the meeting before and the one before that,' Iris Elizabeth says. She raises her arms straight up and stretches hard. 'To think that there are people out there in the big wide world who believe the work of an inter-preter is interesting and exciting. They should sit in on a Customs Committee three or four days.'

'It wasn't always like this, was it?' I ask, remembering how once I was genuinely delighted when strangers would say, 'Oh what a glamorous job you have.' I did believe that my work made me interesting and exciting and glamorous. When I first met Yves at that genetic engineering confer-ence, he reminded me that in 'Charade' Audrey Hepburn had been an interpreter. 'Audrey Hepburn,' I sighed. 'We all wanted to be Audrey Hepburn. Even Jackie Kennedy and Maria Callas wanted to be her.' I babbled on, not knowing then that when a man appears to be listening carefully to a woman he is trying to seduce her.

'God, I bet Audrey Hepburn never had to interpret a discussion about ice hockey shorts and ceramic sheep,' I say now.

'Goodness, where did La Hepburn suddenly spring from?' Iris Elizabeth asks.

'Never mind,' I reply. 'Look, the Finnish delegate has raised his hand.' I push the 'on' button with the tip of a pencil, give the floor in English to the Finn, then switch off again.

'The title of the original poem …'

'Sorry?'

'The poem from which you were making the pastiche? It's called Naming of Parts.' Iris Elizabeth speaks without looking up from the page on which she is highlighting key words with her pink marker pen. 'It's full of puerile doubles entendres. The soldier narrator is stuck indoors listening to a lecture on rifle parts: the sling, the breech and the swivel and, wait for it, the cocking piece.' Iris Elizabeth looks over the top of her glasses and swallows a yawn, almost imperceptibly swilling it around in her mouth then quickly gulping it down. Unlike me, she still makes an effort to conceal boredom. I appreciate that letting boredom take hold is fatal even if I can't shake it off myself.

'I'd never thought about the sexiness of the poem,' I say. Iris Elizabeth's sceptical glance makes me stop in mid-sentence. For years she has accused me of sleepwalking through life.

Suddenly, I am no longer so delighted with my spoof. I click on 'Close'. 'Do you want to save the changes that you made to "Naming of Sheep"?' A window pops up in the middle of my laptop screen. 'No,' I say out loud and click again. My mobile phone vibrates. It's the tenth message today from my cousin Vanna. What is the point of opening the in-box? I know what it contains. She wants me to go back to Malta. Even though she knows I can't.

ໆຈ

A couple of nights ago, she stepped up her campaign to get me to return by asking Eleonora to call me. It was strange hearing Eleonora's voice after all these years. There was a slight nasal twang and, even when she wasn't asking a question, she had that Australian rising intonation at the end of each sentence. I was also amused to pick up a touch of Maltese accent, that odd half-bark, half-song. When I commented on it, she retorted, 'Well, to me, you sound so bloody English.' She always did have a quick temper. On the other hand, perhaps she felt offended because she thinks of herself as wholly Australian. If that's the case, I envy her that certainty.

Since leaving Malta as a child I have had no direct contact with her. At first, when my father and I left Malta, we did occasionally receive news of Clementino and his family via Marguerita and Luisa. So we learned that he was applying to migrate to Australia and that he was planning to go out there first to establish himself before sending for his wife and children. Within a year, however, my father and I had practically lost touch with Malta.

When Eleonora and I were small, we used to see each other almost every day. I made languages my career, but I wonder if she pursued her passion for Russian. I should have asked her but the phone call had caught me off guard. Though I felt a wave of warmth for the child I remembered, I must have sounded cold. She was so disappointed when our grandmother chose me, and not her, to send to private Russian lessons. She begged and begged her father to send her too, but Uncle Clementino said he saw no point in it. It was just another of Nonna Rosa's hare-brained schemes. Still, I never knew Eleonora to give up on anything she had set her heart on, and so, on the afternoons of my lessons, she would wait for me outside Miss Sokolova's and when I came out she would pump me for all the new Russian words and phrases. She was so intense. Just like her mother, really. Eleonora never did believe me when I said I had forgotten parts of a lesson. Mostly I pretended I couldn't remember because I hated being pressured by her. But sometimes I actually did not remember. Then, Eleonora would grab hold of my arm and squeeze it hard, insisting that I was not trying all that hard. Her persistence felt like bullying and was impossible to ignore. Aunt Luisa once described Eleonora as an elemental force. She said it in Italian, *una forza della natura*, by which I imagined she was referring to Eleonora's blusteriness, the way she waved her arms about furiously when she spoke and her very loud voice.

After each of my lessons, on our way back to Balluta, she and I would stop by the family pharmacy and I would go over the lessons with her. The pharmacy had been opened in the 1920s by our grandfather Giacomino. After his death in the late 1960s, his three daughters, all pharmacy graduates, had taken it over. I remember the beautiful Art Nouveau façade of the building, the Corinthian columns on either side of the door and the enclosed green wooden balcony on the first floor, directly above the shop window. Inside the shop, it was always dark and as clammy as a cave. The temperature outside had to be in the thirties before the ceiling fan was turned on. I remember too the beautiful fan with its broad wooden paddles decorated with curlicues of brass. The shop had an old oak counter, which had been bought from a bankrupt haberdasher and which still had the inches marked out on the edge for measuring lengths of cloth.

Aunt Luisa usually did the afternoon shift in the pharmacy. Always good with children, she liked us dropping in and would encourage us to study, clearing a space on the table in the cubby-hole above the shop. Sometimes, she would turn a lesson into a game, pretending that she needed our translation services to deal with an angry Russian Commissar. After Nonno Giacomino died, no adult ever dared make fun of Nonna Rosa to her face except for Eleonora's father. So, we recognised that when Luisa joked to us about her mother's obsession with a Russian invasion she was as close to an act of subversion as she was ever able to get. It was Luisa who gave Eleonora and me our first taste of coffee, another act of insurgency, since as children we were never allowed coffee at home. My mother and her two sisters used to pay a man four shillings a week to come by and open and close the cast iron roller shutters that protected the pharmacy window. It was his task to fetch coffee from the café a few doors down the road. When Luisa was on duty alone in the pharmacy, she would dunk sugar cubes in her own cup and let us suck them. Coffee has never tasted so good.

Of Nonna Rosa's five children, I would say Luisa and my mother looked most alike, with the same large mouth, fine, straight and silky auburn hair, and almond-shaped eyes so dark there was no demarcation between retina and pupil. My father always described the two of them as *belle brutte*, which I still believe is much more interesting than being called pretty or beautiful. But I try not to picture what Luisa looks like now as a very old woman for she must be in her mid-eighties at least. Seeing her would give me a clue to what my mother might have looked like had she lived, but I'm not sure I want to think about that. There is something to be said about dying young before your skin sags and your muscles wither. My mother's face would certainly have lost that delicious peachiness of youth, *la beauté du diable*, as the French call it, the quality that makes all young women delicious. Her arms and legs would have become scrawny just as mine are starting to do now. Her mouth would have puckered and unlike me I don't imagine she'd have had the lines smoothed out with laser. She had thick hair and she never reached the age at which she had to start colouring it. Iris Elizabeth once declared that all women over fifty should be shot. Although my immediate reaction was one of shock, there are days now when I look in the mirror and find myself secretly agreeing with her. Elegance is not enough to mask decay. I wonder if Yves' Chinese lover, who is in her early thirties, knows that yet.

Speaking of looks, I have a pretty good idea of what Eleonora looks like now. On a visit to Vanna's in Jerusalem in the mid-1990s, I saw a photograph of her in a colour supplement of one of the Israeli dailies. She was waving her hands in the air in front of crowd at a Peace Now rally. Riots broke out soon after, and she and some European and Australian parliamentarians were expelled from Israel. 'She was asked to leave' is how Vanna put it. The woman in the picture was not a beauty, but she was lean and tanned and she had that mass of curls for which the nuns at school were always persecuting her, forcing her to tie it back and complaining of Eleonora's insolence when strands of hair worked loose.

On the phone last night, I explained that I could not take time off work. Compassionate leave is not usually granted for aunts who are ill and old, and I exhausted my quota when my father was dying and I was going back and forth for months between Brussels and Toronto. It is not as if I have remained close to Luisa and Marguerita.

Within a year of our leaving Malta, my father had begun working for the WHO, which led to his being posted to Geneva and then Brazil. For a few years I went on sending postcards to my grandmother and aunts from wherever we happened to be. But they never wrote back. I don't blame them. After my mother's death, I imagine that Marguerita's and Luisa's lives were frozen in pharmacy routines and chores as their mother's carers. From the perspective of a middle-aged woman without a family, I understand now that they might have had nothing fresh to tell me, nothing hopeful and encouraging. It would have been uncomfortable to keep up a shallow and cheerful patter as they skirted round my mother's murder. But response elicits response, and it is impossible to keep up a one-way conversation. So gradually I stopped writing to my aunts altogether.

❧

'You know, it's dead easy to make a letter-bomb.' I have to shout above the din in the canteen. Two men ahead of me in the queue swing round and scowl. I identify them as Customs experts from the meeting and wonder if they recognise my voice. When I am tense, it has a tendency to crack and sound ugly. Iris Elizabeth is rummaging in her purse for change. Perhaps she is more flustered by the impatient cashier than by me.

'I'm sorry to keep pestering you.' I am close behind her as she looks for a place for us to eat our lunch. Partitions around groups of tables are supposed to muffle the clatter of trays and cutlery, but it is still hard to have a conversation without raising your voice.

Ever since Vanna began assailing me with text messages and phone calls, I have been churning over the story of my mother's murder with Iris Elizabeth, who has heard it many times. Should I go back to Malta or shouldn't I? I want Iris Elizabeth to tell me what to do, though I know her sentiments about family. Like me she is an orphan, but unlike me she has no extended family.

'You don't know how lucky you are to have so many cousins,' she says.

'Large families are over-rated in those cultures that don't suffer under their yoke.'

'Where, for instance?'

'England. People there have this illusion that, if families were more united, their society would be less dysfunctional. To which I give you Sicily and the Mafia, the tight-knit family par excellence. Anyone who's not part of it can go to hell. Anyway, aren't you interested in knowing how to make a letter-bomb? I've been doing all these Internet searches.'

We have set our trays down on a table at the opposite end from the cash tills. From the window there is a view all the way down the rue de la Loi where the debris of yesterday's European farmers' demonstration, which ended in violent scuffles with the police, has not yet been cleared. Barbed wire barriers are piled up in the middle of the roundabout.

'The chemistry is quite simple. The only tricky bit is rigging up the envelope in such a way that it doesn't explode when people merely squeeze the package. You wouldn't want to kill the postal workers handling it. It has to blow up in the intended victim's hands.'

'Claire, you have to stop this.' Iris Elizabeth wriggles out of her jacket. 'I've been watching you at work for the last month. All that crazed click-clicking of your laptop.' She speaks calmly as she reaches for the pepper and, shaking hard, smothers the mushy food with it. 'You're not tuned in to the meetings at all. The delegates notice too.'

'Anyone can do it.' I am speaking loudly again, but I do not know how else to convey my excitement over how easy it is to assemble a home-made bomb. 'All you need is seventy-five per cent aluminium powder, plus a little iron powder. Magnesium is what you use to flash-ignite.'

'I know all that. I learned it in school chemistry. You make a fuse by combining iodine crystals and liquid ammonium hydroxide.' For a moment, I think Iris Elizabeth is making fun of me, but she is perfectly deadpan. There are times when her British coolness drives me to distraction. You ask an Englishman or woman would you like a cup of tea or would you like a month's holiday in the Caribbean and either way the answer is 'Oh, I don't mind.'

'For years I've avoided thinking about the way my mother was killed and what the last seconds of her life must have been like,' I say, banging the tabletop, trying to make Iris Elizabeth react less phlegmatically. If at this moment she were to tell me calmly that I am overwrought, I think I would stand up and scream. 'Lately, I've been having the same nightmare about my mother. Reason tells me that she must have died instantly, but in my nightmare she's been decapitated, and for a few seconds she's fully aware of what has happened to her. I've even looked up decapitation on the Net...'

'Claire, why are you torturing yourself?'

'Listen. There's a website called "damninteresting". Under "Lucid Decapitation", someone has posted an essay by a French doctor, Beaurieux. After attending a guillotining, he wrote that he saw the eyelids of the beheaded person lift slowly. When he called the person's name, the eyes fixed on him. The whole thing lasted about twenty seconds.'

'But this has absolutely nothing to do with your mother's death. You've got to stop this obsessive behaviour.'

I know Iris Elizabeth is right. On the other hand, it is too late to blank out what I have found on the Net, such as a blog by a passenger who'd been on a bus when it was blown up on the Jaffa Road. I was sucked in because the incident happened at a spot I know well, not far from the central market in Jerusalem, and close to where Vanna lived before she and her family moved to one of those settlements on the West Bank. For days after the explosion, which killed dozens of people, body parts were

121

being scraped off the pavement and the façades of nearby buildings. There were legs and arms on trees. Someone found a perfectly intact finger with a diamond and sapphire ring in a pot of geraniums on a fourth-floor balcony. My mother had an engagement ring just like that.

The dismembered bomb victims in Jerusalem pulled me back to the memory of my visit to the church of Nosso Senhor de Bonfim in Brazil. Yves and I had gone on holiday to Bahia together in the late 1990s. All those wax effigies of arms and legs set around the altar or hanging from the ceiling or from hooks on the walls were votive offerings to Christ. We had exchanged complicit glances and smiled condescendingly at the gullibility of people who believe in divine intercession. My mother had not been in my thoughts at all. As soon as we came out of the church into the stabbing sunlight, however, I felt dizzy and my ears began to buzz. Suddenly and unexpectedly I saw my mother before my eyes and threw up.

Yves said nothing. Instead he handed me a clean handkerchief and turned away. He kept several paces ahead of me as he marched all the way back to the hotel. We never mentioned the incident again.

ॐॐ

'Legsarmstoesfingersfeet,' I type then delete. 'Headsrollingintoabasket. Body parts. Naming of Parts.' Delete. 'We are all the sum of our parts.' Delete.

Leaning back in my chair, I stare at Simon. He looks as sad as a beagle. In the last three days he has come in to work with that acrid smell people often have on waking. His thinning hair is greasy and plastered to his skull. Has he broken up with his wife, I wonder? It certainly seems as if there is no one at home to remind him to shower before he leaves for work. What about the teenage daughters? Wouldn't they notice such things?

'The odour of sanctity,' my father would have said. Having been born in the south of Italy and raised in Malta, he knew more about Catholicism than he knew about his own Judaism. 'Saints were hermits. They made it a point not to wash very often. The odour of sanctity is the odour of people who lead isolated lives. It's the smell of loneliness.'

Placing my forearms on the desk, I rest my head on them. I drop a pencil on the floor and as I bend down to pick it up I discretely sniff my sweater and under my arms too. I'm safe. All I can smell is a whiff of the baby shampoo I use to wash cashmere.

Simon is entitled to his family secrets, I tell myself, just as I'm entitled to mine. I have made Iris Elizabeth swear she will tell no one about Yves and his son. She's so adamant about how much she hates gossip, and so I rely on her self-righteousness. The trouble is that when you are stuck all day in a space no more than six feet by four you do tend to talk too much. Close proximity often leads to intimate revelations.

Once on an early morning radio programme, I heard a hostage, who had been imprisoned in a cellar in Beirut for six years, describe the intense emotional closeness that had developed between him and his fellow hostage. 'That experience took us to the edge of ourselves,' the man said and his words have stayed with me ever since. Now that Yves and I are separated, they keep coming back, haunting me with the thought that perhaps I had not loved Yves enough to achieve that kind of closeness. Perhaps I should have insisted that he give up his job in Rome and live with me in Brussels. Why was I so afraid of making him feel trapped? The truth is I do not know what it is like to reach the edge of oneself, and now it is probably too late to experience the sense of liberation, which is what the hostage described.

After the ordeal was over, however, it appears that the two captives never spoke to each other again, which is not unlike what happens to interpreters after a day of being cooped up in a booth. The revelations rarely lead to intimate friendships outside the booth. Although I describe Iris Elizabeth as a friend, what we have rather is a common history that goes back to two terrible years spent at interpreters' school in Paris. The standing joke is that we survived the washing machine-cum-tumble dryer process that passes for French higher education. That humiliation was an acceptable pedagogic technique had shaken Iris Elizabeth and me, forcing us to band together for moral support. This is how we survived the course with no broken parts. More than anything else, I think of us having once been comrades in adversity.

∽∾

Hurry up, Iris Elizabeth, I say to myself as I stand stomping my feet on the corner of avenue des Arts and rue de la Loi. Hurry up or I'll freeze to death.

It was Iris Elizabeth's idea to go to the Belgian Unity Exhibition, a show hastily improvised by a number of her Flemish and Walloon artist friends. As I wait for her to pick me up, I think about the irony of my having ended up living in a country that does not feel it is a nation and whose parts do not make a cohesive whole. If I am unsure about my allegiances, so are most Belgians, and now Belgium is on the verge of beating the Dutch record for the number of days spent without a federal government. Even expatriates like my colleagues and Iris Elizabeth's, on whose awareness the political life of the country rarely impinges, talk continuously about the political situation in Belgium and take sides.

From where I am standing, I see that someone with a sense of humour has put up a giant barometer on the façade of the empty office building to the left of the National Assembly. KAFKA BAROMETER, the sign beneath it reads. Instead of mercury, the gauge is stuffed with fuchsia-coloured worms that reach to within a few inches from the top. Gradually, I discern that the worms are chopped up pieces of red tape. Red tape as in bureaucracy. Red which is really deep pink. I can't help laughing. It's been a long time since I laughed, and it doesn't last when I think again of the monstrous King Léopold II who described the country he ruled over as a small country with small horizons. This is a quotation Yves often cited. But his favourite description came from a former French Ambassador: 'that ratty little country divided amongst itself and incapable of aspiring to the heights'. When Iris Elizabeth called me this afternoon to ask me to the exhibition, I thought I was being clever in repeating the quotation.

'Oh, for God's sake, when are you going to stop sounding like that ex of yours?' she snapped. 'I hate the way the French despise the Belgians. Not just the Belgians, in fact, but anything that isn't French. I mean, if Yves hated it so much, why is he still living in Brussels?'

To make my life miserable, I said to myself only because I knew that if I said it out loud Iris Elizabeth would bite my head off again for wallowing in self-pity.

Standing on the freezing street corner, stomping my feet and clapping my gloved hands, I wonder whether the Belgian vision of the world could simply be the result of the physical surroundings, the way the skies are always closing in on you. Someone must surely have formulated a theory about how low cloud-cover hem a people in mentally.

But I won't run that theory either past Iris Elizabeth.

ॐ

'Sorry I'm late.' Iris Elizabeth waits for me to latch my seat belt before driving on. As they defrost, my fingers tingle. With all the layers I have on, I feel like an Andean *campesina*. 'We need to take the ring road and get off it after the Sheraton. Here's the directory. Look at page 15. Just follow the map and keep an eye out for the bridge over the canal. Up there is the Koekelberg Basilica. We have to turn right just before we get to it.'

I don't want the responsibility of being navigator, no matter how minor that responsibility might be. Rather than traipsing through an exhibition of works by amateurs, in truth I would prefer Iris Elizabeth to change her mind and suggest we go to a café and afterwards take in a film. But I say nothing as we head down the boulevard. It is beginning to snow. Here and there, a light shines in the window of an open-all-hours grocer's. The piles of neatly stacked oranges and granny smiths out front are the only burst of colour in the grey side-streets and empty squares.

'I've really no idea where we're going,' I say as I stare at the map. 'This is not a part of town I've ever been to.'

'Jeezus Christ, Claire, how long have you lived in this city?' Unlike most of our colleagues, Iris Elizabeth likes Brussels and has no plans to ever go back to England. When she left Lancashire, she shed her working-class accent and transformed herself into a cosmopolitan professional with a crisp but classless accent. Now that both her parents are dead, she says she's relieved not to have those pilgrimages to England at Christmas. She's certain that she'll spend the rest of her days in Belgium so much so that eighteen months ago she bought an old farmhouse in the Ardennes and is doing it up by herself. Having become the owner of a small plot of Belgian soil, she has discovered a talent for gardening, which she says 'grounds' her. Iris Elizabeth is the only person I know who is truly content, and this makes her different from most expats with whom we mix.

※

'They cannot help it these expats,' a Belgian friend, who occasionally took me to dinner, once said to me. 'They will always feel superior in some way to us Belgians, even those of them who think England has gone to the dogs.'.'

'You're forgetting I'm an expat too,' I said.

'No, Claire. You are different. You're an exile.'

'But I'm sure the dictionary definitions of the two words are the same.'

'That may be, but as far as I'm concerned there is still a difference. You do not have at the back of your mind a country to which you could eventually return should life here become intolerable. Those people do.'

Thinking of Malta, I saw that Luc Valckenaers was right. If I went back there, I would feel even more of an alien than I do here.

∾

'Perhaps we've made a mistake,' I say as, having parked the car, we stride down the silent street, our heels clacking on the cobbled pavement. 'It doesn't look as if anything's happening at all in this part of town.'

But turning the corner, we hear music. In the yard in front of the hangar in which the exhibition is being held, a brass band is pumping out a Germanic march. Some musicians are wearing court jesters' hats in black, yellow and red, the colours of the Belgian flag. Others wear caps with artificial flowers sprouting out of the top. When they start playing *Hava Naguila,* it begins as a dirge before turning into the recognisable, full-speed Hora and as the players bob up and down, the stems of the flowers on their headgear jig and shiver.

'What an absurd tune for a unification fête.' My breath is coming out in puffs of steam and my throat feels scratchy in the extreme cold. 'I don't get it. Why are they holding this event thing here, in this godforsaken part of the city?'

'It's the names of the streets,' Iris Elizabeth shouts back to me. 'Rue des Wallons and rue des Flamands. Get it? Walloon Street. Fleming Street. We're on the cusp which, to quote the blurb on this flyer, represents the possibility of communal harmony in Belgium.'

What a bizarre way of spending a Sunday afternoon, I say to myself. Iris Elizabeth has always supported young Belgian artists, but it is hard for me to share her enthusiasm.

'*Attention, nom de dieu.* Look out where you're going!' I grab hold of a child weaving in and out of people's legs and who has just bumped hard against mine. He looks shocked and then his face starts to crumple making me realise I'm hurting him.

'Oh for God's sake, Claire,' Iris Elizabeth says as she marches into the hangar.

'These huge splashes of colour on canvas are rather passé,' I say following close behind her. 'These are fun.' I point to the dozen or so buckets on the concrete floor that are collecting the water dripping from the corrugated tin roof.

'They're not installations,' Iris Elizabeth laughs.

'But this must be.' I point to a sign that reads "To be or not to be.be.com." 'Well, at least someone has some humour.'

'Hmm.' Iris Elizabeth bites her bottom lip, unimpressed. 'Still, I'm glad you're starting to cheer up.'

'Let's see what's over there.' I move towards a glass cabinet a few metres away. In it, the artist has placed a minuscule tract next to a miniature model of a printing press. I read out loud. 'People with Flemish surnames are Flemings. People with French surnames are Walloons. And the King of Belgium has no surname because a king is always above the mêlée'.

'I'm sorry,' Iris Elizabeth says.

'For what?'

'For this exhibition being so dreadful. I was hoping for better. What a pity, because it's obvious these people feel deeply that their country is about to shatter into pieces. Poor old Belgium. Poor Belgians.'

Echoes of my grandmother take me by surprise. *Povera Malta. Poveri noi,* Nonna Rosa used to say. Poor old Malta. Poor us.

I stop in my tracks. Ahead of us is a partition with a window cut into it. On the other side, there is a table. My heart starts to race. Leaning over the table, a tall, thin Chinese woman clasps the hands of a baby lying on his back and nuzzles her face in his stomach. The baby kicks his legs in the air and gurgles.

'That's not an exhibit.' Iris Elizabeth nudges me as I stand fixed to the spot. 'It's a real-live woman changing a baby's nappies.'

'Yes, yes, I realise,' I reply, my ears throbbing.

'I was fooled too, just for a moment,' Iris Elizabeth says, patting me on the shoulder. 'At first glance, I thought it was a bit of installation art too or whatever it's called when there are people in it. A teensy bit Breugel-esque, isn't it? You know those scenes? Fat peasants getting drunk. A one-eyed lech with his hand up a woman's skirt. A turnip-nosed boy falling on the ice. A fat man with a bloodied apron slaughtering a pig. And then when you get up closer and take a good hard look you discover in a little corner of the picture a mother playing with a small child. Come on, I see you've had enough of all this Belgitude?'

'Yes, we should go,' I say and follow Iris Elizabeth.

'I guess in the end it's impossible for outsiders to get excited about "domestic" feuds. I can't say this exhibition has made me understand why Walloons and Flemings hate each other so much. It's getting late. Let's get you home.'

At five o'clock the darkness is already starting to close in. I am glad. It makes me feel less guilty about going to bed early. For how else can I blot out the image of the Chinese mother and her baby?

Ellie

6 The Dog that Lies Down Where It Pleases

A fine white powder covers the coarse blanket. As Ellie tilts her head from side to side to relax her neck, white flakes drift down from her hair on the backs of her hands and lap. Overnight, a film of plaster dust from the ceiling has again settled on top of the dressing table, wardrobe, ironing table which, never folded away, stands in a corner, and Luisa's pedal sewing machine. It's as if clouds of talcum blow through the room each night. Through the shutters, shafts of light slice through the haze.

'Bloody hell, Richard, this house is crumbling even as we sleep.' Ellie cradles the phone between her right cheek and shoulder as she peels off the blanket and sheets, throwing up puffs of dust.

'You're not calling me at five in the morning just to tell me that,' he says. It sounds as if he is opening and shutting drawers. 'Yes, I am in the kitchen. I was trying to get dinner started. But, okay, I'm sitting down now, and I promise you have my full attention.'

Sometimes Ellie wishes he were less even-tempered. When emotions are running high, the last thing you want is someone to call you to order. You don't want the strength of your passion or the force of your rage to be underestimated. Richard must surely see that the situation has become urgent. Yesterday, Vanna bought two one-way, non-refundable tickets. Time is running out. In ten days, she will take Luisa with her and leave Ellie in charge of Marguerita.

'You've got to help me find a way of heading her off at the pass,' Ellie says as she opens the shutters and steps out on the balcony. At this hour, there are no fumes from passing traffic, and the cool air feels good on her bare arms. She can smell the iodine from the sea, just as she used to as a child.

'If Luisa is agitated, the airline will not check her in,' Richard says in his café crème voice. 'Even if she gets over that hurdle, she still has to go through passport control, and they're bound to turn away a confused old woman wearing a filthy dressing gown.'

He does not realise, however, that Vanna is a juggernaut. 'No, I'm not using hyperbole. Believe me, she's the size of a World War I tank. You should see the amount of food she cooks every day, enough to feed the entire Israeli Army. It's as if Vanna wants to win the Global Earth Mother Medal and also become Master Chef of the Universe. She claims all her recipes were handed down by Nonna Rosa, and she boasts she's the only grandchild to have kept up family culinary traditions.'

'Ellie, don't forget that, for ordinary mortals, eating is more than just re-fuelling,' Richard jokes.

Ellie controls her urge to snap at him, knowing that he never resorts to jokes to keep others at arm's length or, worse, diminish them. He is right, anyway, about her attitude to food. Whenever they go to restaurants, she gets over the business of choosing from the menu by ordering the first dish she sees, or asks Richard to choose. As a child, she had been a slow eater, something for which she was always teased. Gristle and fat stuck in her throat, but she had liked her grandmother's food, so she suspects Rosa left out one or two ingredients from the recipes she handed down. Nothing Vanna makes ever tastes the way it used to when Nonna Rosa made it. Most of what she produces is greasy stodge.

'I've not achieved anything by coming here.' Ellie leans on the rusty balcony railing. That her feet, white with plaster dust, don't seem to be attached to her is a sign she is tired. 'Not even with the refugees.'

'You didn't visit Ta'Kandja?'

'I didn't, and I didn't see Marguerita either.'

She would have made it if she had not arranged to meet the UNHCR representative. The woman was only on a flying visit to Malta from Pantelleria. Of course, Ellie understood she was busy. If the refugee situation is a mess in Malta, it's a thousand times worse in the detention centres on the Italian islands. Yesterday afternoon was Ellie's only chance to see her, but the bitch made her wait three hours. Afterwards it was too late to visit Marguerita.

'They make the residents go to bed so early. I can see why she whinges so much. I'd do the same myself. Then, when I got back to St Julians last night, there was a crisis. Vanna had called the doctor for Luisa.' She had been managing so well to coax Luisa into drinking fruit juice, and she had even been taking a spoonful or two of custard from her. It had made Ellie feel all maternal. 'It's like feeding a sick kitten. No, please don't laugh at me. She's been eating a little more each day.'

The doctor decided that Luisa needed a shot of vitamins, but when he tried to inject her, she bit his hand, and Vanna had to hold her down. Her strength was astonishing. It disturbed Ellie the way they ignored Luisa's wishes. It seemed so indelicate, as if the doctor and Vanna were talking over her dead body and already deciding where to bury her. Ellie had shouted as she marched out of the room, 'Stop treating her as if there's nothing left of her mind.'

ം∾

Ellie had thought herself immune from the pull of memory. Since her early teens, she had trained herself not to be drawn to the past. Since her arrival in Malta, she had avoided going to most of the places she remembered from her childhood and hadn't been thinking when she'd veered from the seafront and up the hill from Spinola. As soon as she jogged across the road, she caught sight of the pharmacy. Above the shop window, Brian Briffa and Sons, Electrical Goods, had now replaced her grandfather's name which his three daughters, after taking over the pharmacy, had not removed. The Corinthian columns were familiar, as was the old wooden balcony on the first floor, although that was now painted maroon instead of green. Her arms loose and panting heavily, Ellie jogged on the spot as she took everything in. Gradually, she moved closer. To the right of the shop window she found the old brass plaque with the names of her aunts engraved on it: Marguerita W. Toledano (B.Sc.), Luisa R. Toledano (M.Sc.) and Sara M. Toledano (B.Sc. Hons).

Sara. It gave Ellie a jolt. She had forgotten that Sarita had been named Sara at birth, having never heard anyone use anything other than the diminutive, not even when Sarita was in her mid-thirties and had her own child. Then after she died she became frozen in time, as people who die young often do, always sweet, never unkind though that was not always how Ellie remembered her.

Now, looking up above the doorway of the old pharmacy at the white tile with the number 86 written on it, Ellie recalled a scene at her grandmother's. Miriam, Vanna's mother, had called at Nonna Rosa's with a beautifully wrapped package for her sisters-in-law from Morocco where she had been on a visit to her own family. Sarita had been impatient to see what the parcel contained. Had this been the case too with the other parcel, the one that killed her? Ellie shudders as she recalls Sarita ripping off the ribbon and tearing the paper to find the tile with the 86 written in blue in stylised lettering to make it look like Arabic script. The background was white, but the lacy pattern forming the border was turquoise and yellow. 'Now and again, Miriam is capable of showing a bit of good taste. I'll give her this much credit,' Sarita said once Miriam had gone home, and Nonna Rosa and Marguerita laughed in complicity. That was the first time Ellie fully realised that it was not just her mother who was an outsider. Vanna's mother did not belong either, despite her having been born Jewish. Afterwards Ellie felt vaguely depressed by Sarita's unkindness. She could not look Sarita in the eye, afraid her aunt might realise that she had been closely observed and discovered to be cruel. Knowing someone's faults is one thing. Letting them realise that you know their faults can make you feel embarrassed for them.

From that time on, if Ellie knew Sarita was on duty, she would avoid the pharmacy, which meant sometimes missing out on a Russian lesson because this was when she and Claire went over the homework. On the other hand, when Luisa was in charge, Ellie saw the pharmacy as a place of refuge. Whenever her parents fought at home, the pharmacy was her bolt-hole. Not that she would ever have told Luisa that she lived in a constant state of anxiety. It was bad enough when her parents shouted at each other, but silences that might last for days between her mother and father were much worse. At those times, Ellie felt as if she would burst out of her skin. Luisa seemed to know, however, without being told. Why else would she have said that marrying someone you are madly in love with is a huge mistake? The pleasures of conquest soon fade. If a man isn't also your friend, better forget him, Luisa would add.

ౌ

'I went past the pharmacy today,' Ellie says as she sits across the table from Vanna watching her smother the vegetables on her plate with butter.

'Mmm.'

'It made me remember how Luisa used to be. Intelligent, affectionate, funny too. I suppose after seeing

137

what happened when my father married my mother her courage failed her, and then Sarita was killed. How could she cause the family any more anguish? Thinking about her made me feel sad. Who was it who said memory is a dog that lies down where it pleases? It's a great image, isn't it? When we least expect it, the dog gets up wagging its tail and deposits at our feet what we've thrown away. It sounds like the sort of thing Oscar Wilde might have said, doesn't it? But I don't think it was Wilde. I don't think it was Proust either.'

'Why is it that whenever people talk about memory someone always cites Proust?' Vanna retracts her short neck into her shoulders and goes on chewing. 'Personally, I never read him.'

The degree of absorption she brings to the task of stuffing food into her mouth makes Ellie's nerves feel raw. All around the dining and sitting rooms as well as her bedroom her cousin has set little dishes of jelly babies, milk chocolates, toffees, nuts and raisins, sweet and salted liquorice. Within arm's reach in any part of the house, Vanna always has something to nibble on. No wonder cockroaches come crawling out at night.

Ellie looks away at the glass-fronted cabinet which Vanna has moved to the centre of the wall in an attempt to hide some of the peeling plaster. Despite Luisa's obvious distress with this new set-up, Vanna has re-arranged all the furniture in the house. And now Ellie sees she has also re-shuffled the dinner services and the glassware on the cabinet shelves. 'She just bloody well has to leave her mark on everything. Perhaps she thinks of it as some sort of victory over this decaying pile, and over the rest of us.

138

Perhaps it gives her a sense of exclusive ownership,' Ellie said to Richard. 'She likes to think that she alone cares about the aunts.'

On the top shelf of the cabinet, the Bakelite tray, which had been a wedding present from one of Rosa's brothers, Samuele, is propped upright. Great Uncle Samuele had gone to Manaus as a young man. The search for husbands and wives in Nonna Rosa's generation had taken her brothers and sisters away from Malta, but none had gone as far as her eldest brother. They settled instead all around the Mediterranean, in Bologna, Marseilles, Alexandria and Tripoli.

Richard's father and mother were often confused when Ellie talked about the comings and goings from the island of one generation after the other.

'I don't understand,' George Radcliff once said. 'What were all those people doing milling round the Mediterranean?' It sounded contemptuous to Ellie. Was Richard's father accusing her of being a liar? Immediately Ellie was on the defensive. 'They weren't milling around the Mediterranean. They were living their normal lives. The Mediterranean was their home. Not any individual nation-state. They were true cosmopolitans.'

'Ah, yes, cosmopolitans.' As he turned away, George Radcliff drew on his pipe. If he had been anyone else, Ellie would have gone after him, tugged at his shirt and forced him to explain what he had meant by the tone of his voice.

'Don't be angry,' Richard said to her later. 'My mother and father just need simple answers. It's enough for them to know you're Maltese. You don't have to go into all the complicated history.'

But Ellie has never been able reduce it to something simple. Her mother might be Catholic, but her father was Jewish. Richard's mother and both sets of his grandparents were English. Whenever Ellie meets Maltese people, they always point out that Toledano isn't a Maltese name. Well, it's not part of that small pool of typical Maltese surnames like Grech, Agius, Mifsud, Zammit, or whatever. But if she says she is a citizen of the world, people think she is being facetious, or, worse, a smart-arse.

Looking at the tray, Ellie remembers that visitors to the house often used to say how beautiful were the exotic butterflies embedded in the glass base, with their satiny turquoise, emerald and orange wings. But how were the butterflies caught and killed? As a child, it had upset Ellie to see the pin piercing their fat bodies and holding them in place. How could anyone be so cruel, impaling them under glass on a serving tray? 'I hate it,' Ellie had said one day, astonishing yet another woman guest who had been admiring the tray's beauty. 'It's cruel,' she had said, turning to her father in the hope he would back her on this, 'and so unfair.'

'Well, Eleonora, that's a good lesson to learn.' He smiled at the woman with whom he seemed to share a secret which someone Ellie's age could not possibly understand. Ellie remembers hot disappointment flowing from her stomach to her legs as he added that the world was full of injustices and pain. 'Sooner or later, she'll come to see that for herself,' he said to the visitor over her head. Then finally looking at her, he added, 'Cheer up, *hanini*. You'll get used to it.' But Ellie never has.

She pushes her plate away wondering why, in the evening, the smell of the chemicals from next door always seems more pungent. With the tips of her fingers, she rubs her temples in a circular motion. Ever since her arrival, the seepage has given her a scratchy throat. At this moment, her head feels as if a barrel hoop has been pulled tight around it. No one would ever describe her as fastidious, but it is hard not to feel queasy at the sight of the blistering plaster on all the walls.

'Scrofula, the King's Malady,' she says out loud.

'Sorry?'

'Scrofula, a word from our school history books. These walls look as if they've caught a good dose of some horrible skin disease.'

'History, mishtory, the problem is the Russians haven't been here for more than a year. Their house needs airing.' Vanna leans over her plate, as protective of her food as a lioness with a freshly torn-off shank of wildebeest. 'Mind you,' she says, shovelling mashed potato into her mouth, 'I'm not one hundred per cent sure that if someone lived there all year round the stench of those damp-proofing chemicals would go away completely.' She pushes the mashed potato into her left cheek where it forms a bulge. 'Apparently they've fired the housekeeper. Not that she came by all that often. But when she did, at least she opened up the place for a bit.' Vanna dabs the corner of her mouth with the back of her wrist. 'Anyway, let's get things clear. You still think you're going to be able to stop me taking the aunts to Israel. Should I deduct ...'

'Deduce...'

'Deduce, whatever! Should I deduce that you've found a decent place for them here on the island?' Vanna reaches across the table and stabs a meatball on Ellie's plate then pops it whole into her mouth. 'Or have you and our dear cousin Claire hatched some brilliant plan in your telephone têtes-à-têtes? Have you, for instance, convinced her to come to Malta, because that'd be a good start, I'd say.'

'You know as well as I do why Claire won't return. She and I have talked about that, and about what she thinks we should do…'

'How pally, but then you always were thick as thieves. Oh, I know it's corny, but it fits perfectly.'

'Listen, Vanna, Marguerita is eighty-nine-years-old.' A voice inside Ellie's head tells her to stay cool. 'And Luisa is eighty-five. In eight, almost nine decades, the sisters have never lived apart. That's longer than any married couple. You can't take one aunt back to Israel with you and leave the other.'

'They won't be separated for long,' Vanna says, and with her plump fingers, tears strips of flesh off a chicken thigh.

'Long or short, the bottom line is they are very old and very frail and you can't ship them to a place where they don't speak the language and where they know absolutely no one.'

'They know me, and Ephraim. Unlike the rest of the family, we've never forgotten them. My father and I came back every year. The children have been here with me on holiday. Marguerita and Luisa know them.'

Ellie takes a deep breath. 'Listen, Claire and I have looked at the situation from every angle. She and I both have some savings. We can keep the aunts in Malta if we pool our funds.'

'I knew it. I just knew it. You and Claire have been deciding things behind my back. I'm not surprised. You think that money is the only solution. I suppose Claire was the one who suggested that we pool our money. But if she's not interested enough to come to Malta, then she has no say in these matters.' Vanna rips a thick chunk from the loaf of Maltese bread and dunks it into the gravy. It is impossible for Ellie to get Vanna to look her in the eye. A trapdoor has slammed shut in her brain. Someone has to prise it open.

'Oh, Vanna, if it was traumatic for you and me to be uprooted as children, imagine how much worse it must have been for Claire being transplanted to the Swiss Alps …'

'Scotland.' Vanna chomps as she speaks.

'What?'

'After Sarita's death, Uncle Alberto took up a post in Scotland, and then he got that job with the WHO in Geneva.'

'I defer to your superior knowledge,' Ellie says, making Vanna scowl at her sarcasm. 'But have you considered that the reason Luisa is upset is that some of your plans for her have penetrated the mists in her head. Perhaps she realises that you want to take her away from the only place she has ever known. Perhaps she doesn't want to go.'

'How do you know that?'

'I wasn't saying I knew. No one can know what's going on in someone else's mind. But up to yesterday she had been managing to get a bit of food down, and drinking.'

'In case you haven't noticed, when our backs are turned, she spits out everything.'

'Ah, here we go.' Ellie presses her temples harder. 'You're jealous. No, don't look at me like that. You're jealous because I was managing to get her to drink and eat. You couldn't bear it so you called in Dr Bonnici.'

'Jealous. Who's talking jealous? I'm talking practical. So far I haven't exactly seen you do all that much. I mean, I don't consider lecturing a confused old woman on illegal immigrants, tuna farms and the situation in Palestine as much. Yes, I've heard you when you're alone with her, pottering about in her room. It's completely ridiculous. As if in the state Luisa is in she should understand a word of what you're saying, as if she should have sympathy for your political views.'

'Well, I just so happen to recall that Luisa was bloody furious when your father started talking about moving to Israel during all the trouble between Mintoff and the doctors. Luisa was never a Zionist.'

'To quote your own words, you know nothing.' Vanna speaks through a slit between her plump lips. 'You know nothing about the choices my father was forced to make. Your father gave up Medicine. How surprising was that? He gave up whatever he started. Then he cleared off to Australia, and Uncle Alberto also turned his back on Malta. My father stuck it out far longer than most of the island's doctors. You have absolutely no idea how difficult it was for him. The doctors' strike destroyed his life. It destroyed our family. My mother was so miserable that when she went back to Morocco she threatened not to return to Malta, and then the parcel bomb …'

Vanna stops, realising that she is in danger of going down the path she has been trying to avoid ever since Ellie's arrival. No one found out who the bomb was intended for. The family thought it was Miriam who should have been killed, not Sarita. Her mother could not go on living in Malta knowing that this is what her in-laws all felt.

'At any rate,' Vanna lowers her voice, 'how can you possibly know Luisa was an anti-Zionist? You were twelve when you left Malta. How many times have you come back in the last forty years? I haven't exactly seen you rushing back whenever there's been a crisis.'

Ellie has no answer. It is true that over the years, in emergencies, Vanna has always been the one to hurry back to Malta.

'Do tell me, Ellie,' Vanna ploughs on, 'who brought Luisa back from the brink of death three years ago? I know you live on the other side of the planet, but you were in Rome at the time. What conference was that for? Climate change? No, let me guess. The rights of Palestinian refugees. What else could it possibly be? A topic too important that you should interrupt your visit to Italy and make an emergency detour to Malta.'

'I'm not going to be drawn into arguing about that.'

'So okay, let's say we should follow your advice. Let's say we should stick the aunties in a retirement home in Malta. You know what will happen? You don't? Well, consider this. All the old people's homes on the island are run by the Church. It's obvious the priests will take charge and try to convert the aunties. Believe me. I know my Maltese. This is what will happen.'

'Marguerita would never allow anyone to convert her.'

It's hard for Ellie not to burst out laughing, but she keeps her voice steady. Here were the old religious divisions again carried down from the old generation to the next.

'Marguerita might not allow it. She still has the good luck to have her wits about her. What about poor Luisa? Her mind has gone …'

'As I've said before, God, if the bastard exists, will know it's not a true conversion and ignore it,' Ellie says. 'It's crazy to think you can take the aunts with you to live in the Occupied Territories. Aunt Marguerita will certainly not be able to get on a plane for a while. It's going to take months before she's able to walk again. And there are all sorts of other serious medical complications. She has diabetes. That's what the doctor told me at the Home. It's what made her pass out and fall down the stairs and break her shoulder and leg. Marguerita and Luisa hadn't seen a doctor for over twenty years.'

'I suggest you should go and inspect a few retirement homes for yourself.' Vanna looks up from her plate. 'Instead of trying to make visits to illegal boat people in detention centres perhaps you should take a look at some horrors closer to home. How many times have you been to see Marguerita?'

Ellie has been expecting this question. 'It's not my fault if I've been prevented from seeing her again.'

'Been prevented.' Vanna gives a dry laugh. 'So it's circumstances that control you rather than the other way round? Very convenient.'

৵৵

This morning Ellie is determined not to be diverted. She's not going to let Vanna accuse her again of not caring. So, after her morning jog, she takes the spine-jolting bus to Valletta, only realising she has made a wrong connection when she reaches Buggibba. In backtracking, she wastes over an hour, and it is close to midday when she reaches Mosta.

Ellie knocks softly on the door of her aunt's room. No reply. She opens the door. Marguerita is asleep, propped up on so many pillows that she is almost sitting upright. Her head has rolled back, her mouth, from which the dentures have been removed, is wide open. Of the five siblings, Marguerita and Clementino looked least alike, but Ellie is struck by how much at this moment her aunt resembles her father on his deathbed. He was thin and shrunken and, with his toothless mouth wide open, he looked like a drowning man gasping for air. Ellie and Danny had searched for his false teeth all over the hospital ward, channelling their energies into the hunt and thus avoiding having to speak to each other. They only gave up when the duty nurse pointed out that the dentures would be removed anyway at the crematorium. The next day, Danny went straight from the funeral to the airport to catch his flight back to New York.

Sliding a bentwood chair across the room, Ellie places it next to her aunt's bed. Marguerita's skin looks like burnt wax paper. Her forearms are blue, her finger-tips purple. Poor circulation. No wonder she had passed out. As Ellie squeezes her aunt's clammy hand, Marguerita wakes up with a start.

'So at last you've come again.' She blinks hard. Her eyes like all the eyes of Nonna Rosa's children had once been dark brown, without any graduation between iris and pupil. Now, they have turned a slimy grey, the *arcus senilis*. The term pops up in Ellie's memory. Way back in the days when Luisa had coached her in Latin, she had explained that this is what happens to old people like Nonna Rosa. Now both Luisa and Marguerita's eyes have that watery grey outline around the pupil.

'You've been on the island for two whole weeks,' Marguerita grumbles, 'and this is only the second time you've found time to come to see me. We hear nothing from you for decades and now you expect me to be grateful. When was it you turned up looking like a hippie and ex-pected us to put you up with your long-haired boyfriend?' Marguerita struggles to heave herself completely upright. '1987,' she puffs. 'And now you and Vanna have come to Malta to steal my money and Luisa's and take possession of our home.' She leans her concave chest forward. Though keeping up the stream of recriminations, she allows Ellie to plump up the pillows that are propping her up and put an-other one behind her. 'How is Vanna, by the way? What's she up to? She promised she would get me out of here, but I've seen no evidence of anything of the sort.'

'She wants to take you away from Malta – to Israel.'

'Yes, she did mention Israel. She's mad. You can tell her for me that I'm not going anywhere except back to my own home. It's typical though, typical of all of you. Your people abandoned the island and now you want Luisa and me to do the same. But old doesn't mean we can be shunted about against our will. No one has the right to brainwash us.'

'Brainwash?'

'Yes, that's what your mother did to your father. She made him abandon Judaism, and then he abandoned Malta and went to Australia. Men are so weak.' Marguerita pulls her hand out of Ellie's grasp. She has always been irascible. Who was it who said that as people grow older they become more like their true selves? 'Look at Joseph. Miriam talked him into settling in Israel, of all places.'

'But isn't it the ambition of all Jews to settle in Israel?' Ellie grins as she thinks of Vanna.

'It's the ambition only of Jews who don't have a homeland,' Marguerita barks, 'refugees, exiles, drifters. My brother Joseph had a perfectly good homeland. I blame that Moroccan wife. Her family were poor and ignorant. They all ended up in Israel, and they made sure Miriam and her family would end up there too.'

'But they had nothing to do with it. Uncle Joseph was forced to leave. He couldn't keep on defying the Medical Association of Malta. When he decided to break the doctors' strike, he became a social pariah.'

There are times in Ellie's life when she is suddenly pulled right back to being a child again, banging on her mother's door, begging to be let in. It is a recurring nightmare. Her mother is in her bedroom, but she does not answer. Or her mother is being carried off to hospital by ambulance and she is banging on the neighbours' door for help. There are times when she is outside in the dark and pouring rain, tapping on the window of a brightly lit room where a family is seated around the table. They do not hear the tapping. In another variation, a social worker, accompanied by a policeman, has come to take her and Danny away. She has phoned her father in Queensland, but he has told her there is nothing he can do. Danny clings to Ellie's arm as the social worker tries to tear him away. It is the policeman who manages to pull the brother and sister apart.

'Sorry. I can't hear what you're saying. What were you saying about Joseph and the doctors' strike?' Marguerita cups her right hand to her ear and screws up her face.

'Never mind,' Ellie says and is relieved when a nurse's aid comes into the room with a bedpan and jostles her out.

❧

'You know something, Vanna,' Ellie says when she gets back to the house in the late afternoon. 'Why should Claire get out of dealing with this situation? Marguerita and Luisa are just as much her aunts as they are ours. I'm going to call her again tonight.'

Claire

7 Island of Dreams

'I'm sorry, *hanini*. There's no room for exiles in this house.' Vanna steers me outside into the sunken courtyard at the back of our grandmother's house. 'You'll have to sleep out here.' She gestures towards two wrought-iron garden tables standing by the kitchen door.

The tables are painted bright orange just like my Japanese dining table, but they have slatted tops and some of the slats are missing. I could easily fall through the gaps.

'You'll need to push them together and lie on top as best you can.' Vanna puffs as she pushes the tables together. 'I'm sorry that this one should be a little wobbly.' She pulls out half a sheet of newspaper from her apron pocket, folds it several times and bends over.

She has a huge *patata*. Nonna Rosa used to say we all had enormous *patatas,* but Vanna's was the biggest. This is what I remember as I watch my cousin put a wedge under one of the legs of the smaller table. She was always greedy, and she still habitually flicks her tongue out like a lizard. A feeling of disgust bubbles up inside me. There are crumbs stuck in the corners of her mouth, but as soon as she licks them off more appear. Vanna thinks she can hide her fatness by wearing a brightly coloured shift patterned

151

with palm leaves and giant flowers. It reminds me of the tents that nineteenth century missionaries decreed native women must wear once they had converted. Perhaps Vanna is hiding evidence that she's pregnant again. She must be pushing fifty. It would be disgusting if she were expecting another baby, I tell myself. As repellent as having her head shaved because she's a married woman. We were never an Orthodox family. Her wig is a rich chestnut colour, thick and shiny, but it sits askew, giving her a slightly crazed look. Vanna has a double crown, her mother used to brag. When I first heard the words, I took them literally and was bewildered. 'It's just Miriam's way of boosting poor Vanna's morale,' my mother said. 'What else does that child have to commend her?'

'Look, Vanna, I haven't come all the way to Malta to sleep outside on wobbly tables, or down among the strays.'

I look up at the garden ten steep steps above the courtyard. On top of the crumbling perimeter wall, a *claque* of indolent felines lolls in the dying sunlight and from behind the fat-bellied terracotta pots, in which Nonna Rosa grew jasmines when we were children, three mangy cats blink at me through gluey eyelids. From the corner of my eye, I glimpse a cat slithering off the wall and settling on her back on the rim of the empty garden pond. I see her teats are swollen.

The Neptune in the middle of the pond was listed among a ship's cargo of gloves, hats, shoes, furniture, crockery, linen, blankets and curtains that my Florentine great grandmother brought to the island as part of her trousseau. For as long as I could remember Neptune had been handless, but once he had a mane of waist-length sinuous weeds, and now I see they are badly chipped. Rusty streaks run down the damaged locks and stain his muscular thighs, which two nymphs grasp, their mouths open, half in ecstasy, half in desperation.

'Well, if you won't sleep out here, I shall have to ring the Hôtel de la Gare,' Vanna says. That doesn't sound right. There are no trains in Malta, so how could there be such a place? Vanna digs into her pocket again and pulls out a headset with mouthpiece which she plugs into a wall socket above the garden tap. 'Sorry, the line is dead,' she says and does not offer to try again.

I have already picked up my suitcase, which feels much heavier than it had on arrival. I walk through the kitchen and, as I cross the dining room, the eyes in Beatrice's portrait follow me. I feel them searing my back as I step out and fall down, down into an abyss of darkness.

෨෬

I had known what I was letting myself into by starting analysis. But I thought I would be able to keep the intimacy that a patient/analyst dialogue requires under tight control by doling out my nightmares in small doses. Nonetheless, in the last few weeks, I have felt less in charge. Already on the bus to Laurent's, I start to feel queasy. Next door to his apartment block, there's a small supermarket and a few days ago, before my session, I went inside and threw up in their loo. It is hard to look Laurent straight in the eye, a childish reaction, I know – if I can't see you, then you can't see me. Or rather, you cannot see into the deepest recesses of my mind. On the other hand, if I don't offer some of my dreams for dissection, there's a risk Laurent will become exasperated and call off the therapy. So I'm glad that tomorrow I will have this gift of a richly symbolic dream. No doubt, there's a huge subconscious seam to be mined from sex-starved nymphs, an impotent sea-god and a female cat rolling over to expose her obscene pink belly and enlarged teats.

'I only hope he won't start linking up Vanna's pregnancy in the dream with the nausea I felt as the cat rolled over,' I say to Iris Elizabeth. 'I expect him to be more original than that, smarter.'

'In other words, you want the poor sod to jump through hoops,' she jokes. 'Just like the other analysts.'

Lately, we have been meeting outside work two or three times a week. I can see I have a depressing effect on her and that depresses me too. My unhappiness is a concrete block weighing us both down, but to my surprise she hasn't wholly given up on me.

'You know, a break-up is never the fault of one party only. When you were with Yves, I sometimes felt he struggled to keep you – how can I put it –entertained? No, more than that – dazzled.'

It's like being punched in the solar plexus.

'That's unfair,' I say as I fight back the rising nausea.

'So why don't you give Laurent a fighting chance?'

Gulping down the remaining half glass of white wine, I start gathering my coat, scarf and handbag.

'I've read Freud,' I say as I knot my scarf. 'I know all about Jung's archetypes of the subconscious.' If only I could wipe out that curl at the corners of Iris Elizabeth's lips. You don't have to be that clever to pick out all the symbols of alienation in my dream.

'So why the hell are you paying an analyst seventy-five euros an hour?' She picks up her coat and handbag. 'Come on.' She hooks her arm round mine. 'Let's walk back home via the Mont des Arts. It's bloody freezing, but when it's like this there are no clouds. It'll be lovely to see the stars.'

'The dream didn't end with my walking out into the night, you know?' I am calm again as I tell Iris Elizabeth how the scene switched from my grandmother's house to a room at the Hôtel de la Gare. Trains or no trains, there was a station hotel on the island after all.

'By definition, station hotels are places where people pass briefly. They don't unpack their bags, and they lie awake anxious about missing their early morning train. Fifty euros, please, or a glass of Armagnac when we get to your place.' Iris Elizabeth squeezes my arm. 'I can't stay long, mind you.'

This is her way of signalling that she is only prepared to go so far as a sounding board for my misery and, of course, it would be wrong to drag her down with me. The rest of the dream will keep until I see Laurent. I am keen to hear what he has to say about the symbolism of my not being able to open the hotel's windows, which overlooked Balluta Bay. The handles on the frames were only there for show. As I watched people swimming and heard the laughter of children, the panorama before me seemed both very far away and within arm's reach. In the room it was as hot and stuffy as an interpreters' booth. I would have liked to dive into the sea from the balcony and join the swimmers, but I could not get out. Filled with longing for human company, all I could do was press my nose to the pane and watch as the sea grew choppier.

A line of brown scum lapping against the rocks reminded me of being sent out as a child in the early morning to test the wind direction. If it blew from the north, sewage and rubbish would wash up on the shore, and I was not allowed to go swimming. Now, I wished that before checking into the hotel I had taken note of the wind direction. I might have been able to warn the swimmers that they were in danger.

I could hear the mosquito hum of a sea scooter before I saw it rounding the headland, bouncing hard on the water and heading straight for the group of swimmers in the middle of the bay.

'Watch out!' I screamed. 'Watch out!' I banged my palms on the windowpane until they stung, shouting to the bathers to get out of the water. They all had their heads turned away from me, then one of them, a woman, turned around. When she waved back at me, it was in the slowest of slow motion. My dread turned to terror. I screamed again, but my vocal chords felt as if they were being ripped out of my throat. I had to close my eyes tight to hold back the tears.

When I looked again, the sea scooter was out of view, and the silence was so profound that the air above the water shimmered like the air that hovers above a mirage. The sea had turned blood red and bobbing on the water were the severed heads of dozens of swimmers.

I woke up with a jolt, feeling a searing pain across my chest. In the few seconds of wooziness between sleep and full consciousness it seemed to me that the world was a broken place, and that the deep ache of longing for a time when it once was whole would never leave me.

※

The answer to Iris Elizabeth's question only comes to me in the middle of my next session. I pay Laurent seventy-five euros for fifty minutes because he does not use the clichés of my previous therapists who accused me of 'being out of touch with my feelings'. He is always mindful that language is as much my business as it is his and seems to know words have a shape and weight.

'It's probably because my cousin Vanna keeps phoning me that I've started dreaming so much,' I tell him, determined to shed the diffidence that has up to now marred our twice-weekly encounters. 'Though I can't remember everything, I know I've been dreaming all night. Every morning I wake up feeling hollowed out, just as I had for twelve whole months after my mother died. She appeared to me in my dreams, and I'd wake up exhausted and crying. In the end I had to ask her to desist, it was too upsetting, which is when I stopped dreaming altogether, though it seems to me that in my waking hours I'm always in a dream, living with a sense of unreality that has only got worse in more than twenty years in Brussels.'

'A sense of unreality?'

'The sense that the landscape we move in is not real. Is it because few of us feel our lives have turned out as we imagined and that we should be living a different life? I can't tell. Lately, I've been unable to shake off that feeling. Everything seems to have a dream-like quality. Each morning on my way to work, I walk across the Square

157

Ambiorix. You know the one. I loathe the way the trees around the perimeter are espaliered, a brutal imposition of French culture on the Belgians. Salvador Dali would have loved that square, the way the branches of one tree intertwine with the branches of trees on either side of it, dancing in some kind of macabre Greek dance. Each tree has been forced to grow in a two-dimensional plane and so is both a cross and the thing that's crucified.'

Laurent Bertrand's eyes open wide in surprise.

I hesitate. 'Well, I was born in one of the most fanatically Catholic countries in the world,' I say. 'In my first years at school, my teachers were all nuns.' I re-arrange myself on the couch. 'When I leave the square, I carry on up the rue Michel Ange. It's weird. Someone has embedded a pair of sunglasses in a small square of cement among the cobblestones. The glasses first caught my eye on a sunny day in spring. There were the lenses shining like the wings of a fly. Over time, however, they've cracked, and now all that's left are the empty metal frames. Doesn't that sound as if the world is a sort of dream? Or, more like it, a nightmare?'

Laurent's particular quality of stillness can make me nervous. It comes to me now that the image in my dream of Vanna as a lizard is drawn from him. I have always thought that his heavy eyelids are like a reptile's and that at any moment he might shoot out his tongue and lasso an unsuspecting insect – or me. But at this moment, as he leans forward, I find myself responding to his intense concentration. So I tell him how the sense of dread – a melodramatic word I have avoided using up to now – carries over from my sleep.

One way of shaking it off is to switch on the radio to a calming BBC voice, a human presence. But the voice ebbs and wanes, and static threatens to drown it. When the bark of the France Inter announcer bursts through the airwaves, I jump out of bed and turn the radio off. I shower and dress in a hurry, but at six-thirty it's still dark outside. My corner café will not open for another hour and a half, so I sit at my desk and watch and wait for daylight. I'm all dressed up with nowhere to go.

'Lately, I've been thinking a great deal about an old friend, Luc Valckenaers. He used to say I was fortunate to be a woman without a country. "I envy you," he'd say. "It must make you feel liberated to know no place can lay claim to you."'

'What happened to him?'

'He got married and inevitably our friendship took second place, but I did argue that one could take the opposite view, that having no place to lay claim to might be a burden and a source of isolation. Though I have lived in Belgium longer than in any other country, I have few Belgian friends, and I've carried over no friendships from my school days in Malta, Scotland, England and Switzerland. My father and I lost touch with my uncle and cousins in Australia, and Vanna is the only family member I have seen in the last thirty years.'

Throughout previous sessions, I have hardly taken my eyes off the carriage clock on Laurent's mantle-piece and not just simply because I was trying to avoid his gaze. This time, I have glanced at it only a couple of times and am therefore surprised when he says our fifty minutes are up.

❧

The feeling of calm and lightness does not last. I wake up on yet another Sunday in which time stretches endlessly ahead. But on opening the living room window, I unexpectedly feel and smell a touch of spring in the air. It is only the end of February. Winter isn't over yet, but on roadsides and in parks, daffodils and crocuses will burst into bloom only to be decimated by the next spell of frost. Nature is not always fair. I have never forgotten the English-born teacher who, at the International School in Montevideo, which I briefly attended during one of my father's UN postings, taught us Chaucer. She was adamant that children like us, who had been born and who lived in countries where there was no clear demarcation of seasons, would never be able to appreciate the opening line of The Canterbury Tales and understand the full force of April's sweet showers. She spoke to us as if we were benighted heathens, and it is true we did not understand. I wonder what she would have to say these days about someone, like me, who finds the thought of all that seasonal renewal utterly depressing.

Across the courtyard, slices of light break through the half-closed Venetian blinds. Mme Dierieckx, who owns one of the ground-floor flats on the other side of the courtyard, separates the slats to look out, but when I wave to her she does not see me. In this building, she is the exception, a woman who lives in the same *quartier* in which she was born. At eight-five, she has never been abroad, not even to France or Holland, both only a short train-ride away. Despite her Flemish surname, she is a French-speaker, which is not unusual in Brussels. Because of the country's political divisions, the city is actually a Walloon island in the middle of a Flemish ocean. How ironic that I started my days on one island and look set to end them on another.

Although it is not yet seven o'clock, in the first-floor apartment directly opposite mine, the Costa Ribeiros are also awake. Mme Dierieckx waging war against them because they do not sort out their rubbish, and she ends up having to do it. She complains to me that it is all one can expect from *étrangers*, a word that translates not just into 'foreigners' but also 'strangers'. When she asked me to tell them they must put different kinds of refuse in different bags, she said I should speak in Portuguese 'so they can't pretend they haven't got the message'. I suspect I came across as a sad and lonely middle-aged woman. Now, when they see me trying to strike up a conversation with their daughter, whose name I've learned is Eva, the mother calls out from the first-floor landing not to pester the senhora. Eva reminds me of myself as a child. After years of hard work and skimping in order to make a home for them, her father collected her mother and her from Madeira last November and brought them to Belgium. But Eva does not yet seem to have got over being uprooted.

I am reminded of my own first months in Scotland after we left Malta. My father would get up before dawn, wake me and get me ready for the school bus, which in winter would pick me up when it was still dark outside. In my memory, Scotland remains a place of never-ending night. We had landed on a November day to a city of low skies and winds which, as my father explained, blew all the way to Glasgow from Siberia. Brussels must appear equally hostile to Eva, who came to Northern Europe also at the beginning of winter, and I wonder if she too dreams of her island. I shivered in my light winter coat as my father and I queued for a taxi to take us to our temporary lodgings. Around us, everyone was grey-skinned, with thin, bloodless lips, but they did not seem to notice the cold. My father ended up taking off his jacket and wrapping it round my shoulders.

He was distracted, and I could tell that his mind was on matters more important than weather. Where would we settle? Could we really put the past behind us? How was he going to bring up a child alone? In Scotland, we knew no one, whereas in Malta we had known almost everyone, and everyone knew our family. A native Italian-speaker and unused to the Scottish accent, my father often had to ask people to repeat what they had just said. This could create problems with his patients. Sometimes, in public places, he would turn to me to translate for him and I am sorry to say that when I was trying hard to blend in I became embarrassed by his failure to understand. Once, anticipating he would ask for my help, I slunk off. It's a cliché to say children can be cruel, but it does not make it any less true. After he had caught up with me, he was not angry. But when the UN job came up soon after, he did not hesitate to uproot me once more.

The only time I ever saw him show strong emotion was six months after our arrival in Glasgow. One morning, he was trying to plait my hair, but not knowing how it was done, he was clumsy. The three strands were uneven and hair kept working loose. He joked that he would never have made a transplant surgeon, but there was no mirth in his laughter. Only now do I suspect that 'transplant' was a play on words and I do not believe I'm reading too much into it. Having failed to raise even a smile, he looked suddenly wiped out. Sitting down on the edge of the bed, he let the hairbrush drop onto the floor, unable to control the trembling in his hands. Ever since we had left Malta, I had been waiting for him to give me the lead to cry, but even then he did not break down completely, and so I do not remember having ever properly mourned my mother's death. The pity of it was that even when my father himself was dying we managed to skirt around the subject of how my mother had died and the effect her death had had on us. I do not hold my father responsible for my thinking of life as nothing but shadows, though I have often felt that he gave me a head start in seeing things this way by never speaking of my mother. He did not re-marry, and I do not remember him ever having a girlfriend or getting close to anyone, male or female, ever again. When I married Yves and settled in Brussels, I know he felt very lonely, though he never complained to me when I made my weekly telephone calls to him in Canada where he spent the last ten years of his life.

On the second floor across the courtyard, yet another light switches on. I can see the Latvian moving about in his kitchen, preparing breakfast. Last summer, his wife and two daughters came to stay in Brussels. Within twenty-four hours of their arrival, they had set about washing the windows, scrubbing the terrace, watering the desiccated pot plants and lugging IKEA flat-packs up the narrow stairs of the main building. On sunny days, the teenage girls would sit on the windowsill tanning their long legs. How at ease with their bodies they were. As a teenager, I was never like that. In the evenings, the whole family sat down to feasts, music and laughter.

After his family left, the Latvian's sad old expression returned. He reminds me of that friend of Charlie Brown. What was the little boy's name, the one who had hula-hoops of flies whirling around him? I can imagine Dr Kalnins with whorls of black dots buzzing around his head as he stands in the middle of the Square Ambiorix in his shabby raincoat feeding the fat pigeons. Whenever we meet on our way out in the morning, he makes childish jokes about the weather and the dog shit on Brussels' pavements. He says his wife will not come back here because of the shit, he reiterates, uttering the word loudly without embarrassment because he is unaware there is a more polite way of putting it in English. 'And I still have two years left in this terrible city.'

༄

My Sunday has not turned out as expected, with the hours dragging on until sunset when I might respectably return to bed and to oblivion. Yves has dropped by this afternoon to ask for a divorce. When he phoned he did not warn me what the visit would be about, but I was not surprised by his request. Deep down I know he will never return to me, but for as long as I am able to call him my husband, a sliver of hope remains lodged like a shard of broken glass in a tiny chamber of my heart. It hurts terribly, but just as shrapnel, penetrating deep into a soldier's body, worms its way out decades after he has been shot, so, I tell myself, I must be resigned to the hope of a reconciliation with Yves taking years and years to work itself out of my heart.

My stomach lurches with longing as, with his back turned to me, he stands by the window commenting on the messiness of the Latvian's terrace: the ugly satellite dish, the motley array of flowerpots and the blue tarpaulin that covers the rabbit hutch where the previous tenant kept two Géants des Flandres. Those grotesquely huge rabbits had once been a source of shared merriment. I cannot remember when I last laughed long and loud with Yves, or with anyone else. Yearning for that sense of closeness we once shared and for his touch, I imagine reaching out and running my hand across his shoulders and down his back. I have always been aroused by his tremendous physical beauty. Now, I picture us sinking to the floor and making furious love once more.

'*Eh bien*, I see that Dagmar and Lydia are still living here.' Yves keeps his gaze firmly on the neighbours on the ground floor across the yard. They are sitting down to their supper.

Yves and I often made fun of the subtle power shifts between Dagmar and Lydia, concluding that sometimes it was Dagmar who was the lion tamer and Lydia the poor shabby big cat, and sometimes Lydia the master and Dagmar the slave. Only in retrospect do I recognise how cruel we were. When we guessed right, we would discreetly exchange knowing glances. I had imagined that this complicity would bind us together forever.

'The truth is I'm bored with their teasing of my being a vegetarian,' I say, hoping I shall be able to hold to Yves a little longer. 'When they invite me to dinner, they heap vegetables on my plate but dish up huge steaks for themselves always cooked *bleu*. One night they even had a whole pig's head.'

I prattle on while he takes the divorce papers from his brief case and, without comment, lines them up in piles on the kitchen table. 'I guess I didn't hide my disgust all that well,' I add, 'so they don't invite me to eat with them very often now.'

'I'll leave these papers with you,' Yves says, his voice displaying no emotion. 'I'm not demanding anything, but I would not be unhappy if you were willing to give me one of those Norwegian watercolours on the staircase.'

'They're a pair,' I say, hearing the whine in my voice and wishing I could undo the damage, 'a wedding gift from my father.'

With or without the painting, Yves will soon walk out of the door and, probably, I will never see him again. After which I will be consigned to the divorced women's corner, making fun of her ex's faults and flaws, exaggerating them in the company of all the other abandoned wives and lovers who bury their pain and failure by joking about the man who had walked out on them.

'I hope this whole matter will all be settled quickly and *à l'amiable*.' Yves touches my forearm as I see him out. Despite myself, I feel the burning flow of desire move from my womb to my thighs.

ৡৄৢ

'Escort services. Based on Article 38/3 of the Penal Code, the advertisements of this magazine may only publicise meetings of a non-sexual nature. If there is evidence that this is not the case, please notify the Publisher and the ad will be suspended.'

Leafing through the film and exhibition listings, my eye is caught by a disclaimer at the top of the classifieds section.

'Vanessa. Prestigious, elegant lady. 24/24 hours, 7/7 days. Discretion guaranteed.'

'Seventh Heaven. High-class men, women and/or she-males. Your place or ours. All major credit cards accepted.'

'Millennium. Massage combined with cosy atmosphere. Available from 12 noon to 3 a.m. French, Dutch, German, English and Spanish spoken.'

'Guaranteed', 'accepted' and 'spoken'. How clinical and detached. Not 'we guarantee', 'we accept', 'we speak'. On the other hand, 'cosy' conjures up an image of scones, jam and clotted cream, which is what you might expect from a magazine that targets English expatriates. At what stage, I wonder, would the tea ceremony take place? I suppose if it were before sex, customers would feel more comfortable about exposing their bodies. After sex, a client might not want to sit across a table, sipping tea and nibbling biscuits with a stranger. I also wonder about payment. Do the high-class men, women and/or she-males turn up at the client's place with a large leather bag from which they extract their electronic reader? Does the client have to slot in a credit card and key in a security code? Is a tip expected?

As I pick up the phone, my body feels heavy. I am aware of its defects: the dry, puckering skin on my thighs and the tops of my arms; the stringy neck; the blue-veined hands; the breasts that are beginning to sag.

'Our fee is two hundred and fifty euros an hour.' The woman on line sounds as if she is standing next to me. Although she speaks with a thick Flemish accent, her English is correct. 'Not including VAT, of course. We can send a gentleman around straight away if you like. Whatever time is most convenient to you. Your escort can call you on his GSM when he's five minutes from your place. Will you be paying in cash or by credit card?'

'Cash,' I say. In less than a quarter of an hour I can rush out to an ATM, draw out five hundred euros and be back at home.

Before she hangs up, the controller, or whatever one calls a woman in charge of an escort service – the procurer, the secretary – tells me that the young man she is sending to me is much in demand. Does that mean he has a list he ticks off as he works through his schedule for the day? As soon as I have let him in, I will go into the bathroom and get into a bathrobe, leaving him in the bedroom to undress and climb into bed. I want none of the social niceties suggested in the advertisements. I'll be firm. The escort will do exactly what I tell him to do and then he will leave.

Having eaten only one slice of toast today, I feel light-headed. But at this moment I'm too anxious to eat. If I can hold on to the feeling of detachment that comes with hunger, when the man arrives it will be easier to go through with the performance.

The doorbell buzzes. I can see him on the intercom screen, shuffling in the cold at the entrance and running his fingers through his hair. He must be in his late twenties, and he reminds me of the very young Robert Wagner whom I once had a crush on as a teenager. As soon as he steps into my apartment, he takes my hand. But I pull it away when he says, 'Cold hands, warm heart.' It's not only the corniness that makes my stomach lurch but also the flatness of his smile.

'Look,' I say, 'I hope they've briefed you. I'm going to the bathroom. The bedroom is on that platform, up those stairs.'

'Well, okay. How long have you booked me for?' He looks over his shoulder at his reflection in the entrance mirror. Although I have addressed him in French, he chooses to speak English.

'My French is considerably better than your English,' I say. This is bitchy, but I must make it clear that I am in charge. If I speak French, then he must follow. As French is not my first language I can say things I would be reluctant to say in English. I can be insincere and tell lies more easily.

A spark of anger flashes in his eyes but, in less than a second, the smile is pasted on his lips again. He has uneven teeth that are very white and a slightly effeminate mouth, small and red and fleshy.

'Lips is a penny,' I say, quoting from Under Milk Wood.

The man looks bewildered but turns away and climbs the winding staircase to the bedroom. From the half-open door of the bathroom downstairs I see him getting undressed. He looks over the edge of the platform railing and then walks around the bed a couple of times before testing out the mattress. The way he bounces up and down makes him seem so young, and I feel a tenderness for him I do not want to own. This visit is a business transaction, after all. Once into bed he lies still, waiting for me. I climb in next to him before removing the bath towel wrapped around me like a toga.

In the end, I do not manage to come. I should have known that I was not going to smother the simmering anguish I have turned against myself. Instead of giving him the money in one neat batch, I spitefully count out what I owe him, fifty Euro note by fifty Euro note.

When he leaves, I go back to bed trying to blank out what I have done. To know another man's body intimately now seems too much of a challenge. I cannot imagine repeating my story to one man after another or getting used to the rough skin of a stranger's feet, his slack belly, smells and snoring.

Waking up at around nine in the evening, I am ravenous. But the only thing I have in my fridge is a jar of raspberry coulis. In the cupboard I find a mix of almonds, sunflower seeds and rock-hard sultanas. I put a handful in my mouth, but the almonds and seeds are rancid, and I spit them out into the sink. There is half a baguette left over from Saturday morning on the counter. I dunk it in the coulis.

Mangia come la gente – eat like a human being – I hear my grandmother's voice in my head. *Non sei un cavallo* – you are neither horse nor savage. Sit down and eat.

When I look at my reflection in the window, I am a savage, stuffing bread into my mouth while coulis runs down my chin, and as pale as a Hammer Horror Heroine. Raspberry sauce drips on my pyjama bottoms.

The floor is sticky under my bare feet. It makes my toes curl as I hobble across the room, pick up the phone and dial my aunts' number in Malta. Vanna is the one who answers.

Ellie

8 Boat People

Claire had been a prim child, always perfectly turned out in her Little Monaco Princess dresses. Ellie had hated all the outfits handed down to her, but she especially loathed the blouses with the hand-embroidered bunnies and chicks on the collars. Had Claire rebelled against the prim way her mother used to dress her, Ellie wondered? As the doors of the arrivals' hall slid open, there was her answer. Among the casually dressed holiday crowd, Claire stood out in her severe charcoal grey suit, unadorned by jewellery, and with a pale blue suede jacket draped over her shoulders. On the strap of her handbag, she had knotted an Hermès silk scarf. As a schoolgirl, Claire had always managed to keep her school-bag looking brand new from one year to the next. Not a single scuff. No messy ink and food stains on the inside like Ellie's bag. Now, Ellie couldn't help noting that the expensive luggage had no scratches or dents on it either.

'I won't be staying at the house with you and Vanna.' Claire stiffened as Ellie spontaneously hugged her, jerking her head back to avoid being kissed on the cheek. 'I've booked myself into the Phoenicia. It's more convenient. Don't worry, I'm not shirking my duties. I'll be at the house by eleven thirty every day, without fail.'

So where the hell is she now? Ellie paces up and down the parapet. They had all agreed Vanna should have lunch ready early today so that Ellie could arrange a visit to one of the refugee camps. Surely Claire hasn't forgotten? Ever since her arrival, she has been wandering around in a zombie state. Okay, Ellie understands that it is hard for her to be back in Malta. She also understands the reason for Claire not wanting to stay at their grandmother's or in a hotel in St Julians. Everywhere you go, a memory jumps out at you and it feels like a punch in the solar plexus. God knows Ellie has experienced that herself. But spending every morning at the National Library scouring old newspapers for stuff about her mother's murder will paralyse Claire. Ellie has always said that the trouble with the world is that people get so easily stuck in their own little lives and their own little miseries and fail to glimpse the bigger picture.

At least Claire is alive to Vanna's plans to bundle Luisa off to the airport and onto a plane to Tel Aviv. She's being bloody cagey about her date and time of departure, but it isn't hard to work out. She won't be on a flight via Frankfurt or Munich. The connection time is too long. Even via Rome, you're talking more than ten hours on planes and in airports and an arrival time in Israel at two or three next morning, which would be very difficult with a confused and frail old lady in tow. No, Vanna is bound to be booked on the Larnaca flight, which leaves at two fifty in the afternoon.

From the threshold between the kitchen and the courtyard, Ellie watches Vanna shuffling pots and pans on the shelves under the sink. Ellie rarely dreams, but now and again she has one recurring nightmare. In it she is looking down from the ceiling at her own naked body laid out on a forensic pathologist's slab, an image her subconscious has absorbed from countless television crime series. As the pathologist cuts into her chest, the sound of skin being torn catapults Ellie into consciousness. The sound of tearing lingers in her head and makes her edgy and irritable for the rest of the day.

Although she cannot recall having dreamt at all last night, her nerves feel raw again. Only Richard knows how tired she gets of the rage she carries inside her, that burning tightness in her chest, which makes her feel as if she'll explode. She has rung Claire's mobile phone half a dozen times since eleven thirty-five, but all she gets is her infuriating voicemail, and at the Phoenicia they insist that Mrs Perez is not in her room. If Claire doesn't show up in the next fifteen minutes, Ellie will have to risk leaving Vanna alone with Luisa. She has to be down at Spinola to meet Joe Agius, the diver who's taking her to look at the tuna pens, and then to a meeting with Rosemary Vassallo who, she hopes, will have finally allowed her to go officially into a camp.

'For God's sake, Vanna, stop messing about with pots and pans for a moment. I want you to know I've mailed the Russians.' Ellie tries to appear calm despite Vanna's continual rummaging. 'Yesterday afternoon, when I was picking up Luisa's prescription at Grenfell Pharmacy, I met their old housekeeper, Censa. The pharmacist introduced us.'

'I could have told you her name, and the name of her village, for that matter.' Vanna pulls out two dented pots nestled inside a battered, rusty colander and bangs them on the floor. She is out of breath, and there is that familiar high-pitched whistle from her nose.

'Okay, big deal, so you knew her name and the name of her village, but I bet you didn't know she still hears from the Russians. They've settled in London and have no plans to come back to Malta. Not even on holiday. Censa says they don't intend to sell the house, either. She gave me the name of the guy's company, and I found his email address on the Net.'

'Why should you need his email address?' From deep in the cupboard Vanna's voice sounds muffled.

'So that I can write to him.'

'You know, the bottom of this pot is almost worn right through. This has got to be one of the things Nonna Rosa's mother brought from Italy with her as a bride.'

'Listen to me, would you? If the Russians aren't coming back, that helps solve our problem. Well, at least part of it.'

'How's that?' Vanna slowly pulls her head and shoulders out of the cupboard and, leaning on the sink, hoists herself up.

'Promise not to dismiss the idea out of hand. We can rent the Russians' house for a few months and move Luisa and Marguerita into it. I've spoken to Claire, and she thinks it's an excellent idea. Once they're out of this dump, it'll be so much easier to find a carer to live in. And while the aunts are installed comfortably next door, we can hire some builders to make the place habitable again.'

In slow motion, Vanna bends down to pick up one of the battered pots off the floor. 'Who, may I ask, will be paying for such renovations? You and Claire might have money to throw away, but I do not.' Even after she has set the pot on the counter, Vanna does not turn around. Ellie is tempted to walk over and pinch the rolls of fat on her cousin's back. It'd only be a small act of violence, just to make Vanna pay attention.

A little roughness used to work when Ellie was lumbered with babysitting her cousin. 'No dolls,' Ellie would say. 'No teddy bears. Let's pretend I'm Robespierre. No, hang on, I'm Ivan the Terrible. Why don't you hide in the garden and see if I can flush you out of your hidey-hole?'

At first Vanna would go along with everything Ellie ordered her to do. But after a couple of hours she would start getting listless. Soon she'd be whining that she was starving and wanted to go home to her mother. No use telling her that she could not go home until her mother came to collect her. At that point Vanna would start to howl and scream enough to burst Ellie's eardrums. Ellie wonders if Vanna remembers the day she found a way of making her stop.

'You asked for it,' she said, scooping the convulsed child off the floor. Though at the age of six Vanna already weighed a ton, Ellie dragged her upstairs and, in the bathroom, dumped her fully clothed in the tub.

'Even if I should have the money'– Vanna twists round at last – 'and even if we should be able to carry out all the works this place needs' – she crosses her arms – 'the aunties would never agree to an outsider living in. How many times do we have to go over that again?'

'I really don't know why you bothered to ask Claire and me to come to Malta, Vanna. All those phone calls, what were they about when you'd already made up your mind about everything? What are you trying to prove, that you care about Luisa and Marguerita more than we do?' Ellie turns on her heels.

On top of the sideboard in the dining room, by the carriage clock, there's a yellowing photograph in a silver frame. In it, Luisa stands behind Vanna, aged ten or eleven, with her hands gripping her youngest niece's shoulders. Vanna came across this snapshot a week ago, put it in the frame and set it in full view on the sideboard. She seems to have forgotten that the hands resting on the shoulder were a prelude to Luisa frog-marching her out of a room. 'An Immovable Force', Luisa used to call her. 'How come, wherever I turn, Joseph, that child of yours manages to be right there under my feet?' Without waiting for her brother's reply, Luisa would steer Vanna out of everyone's way. 'One more thing. Joseph, for Heaven's sake, please prescribe something to clear up your daughter's nasal passages.'

'Vanna is rolling down a hill so fast that she'll end up crushing us all,' Ellie said to Richard.

'Come on, Ellie,' Richard said, 'it's not like you to let a Road Train run you over.' If he managed to make fun of her faults without provoking a defensive outburst, it was because Ellie recognised there wasn't a single spiteful bone in his body. 'Just go ahead with your own arrangements for Luisa and Marguerita and present Vanna with a fait accompli.'

As Ellie brushes past the sideboard on her way out, she picks up the framed photo of her cousin and Aunt Luisa, turns it facedown and shoves it behind the bowl of fruit.

❧

The air pressure had been building up all day. Now, after a torrential downpour, every object stands out as clearly as if an artist had used black ink to draw the outlines. North of the Equator the light seems less bright than in the Southern Hemisphere, or is it only homesickness that makes it seem that way? Looking out of Rosemary Vassallo's office window, Ellie sees a sunbeam break through the low, black skies like something out of an Annunciation painting. She gets up and opens the window wide. Breathing in deeply, she feels as if she's been underwater for hours and has suddenly shot to the surface.

Claire is keeping an eye on Vanna today, giving Ellie time to write up her Greenpeace report on the state of the tuna pens around Malta and the pollution they're causing. Animals are dying from disease by the thousands, and renegade tuna are spreading infections among wild fish. Since she has the use of Rosemary's office, she might as well get on with other tasks too. On Monday the Russians sent a standard lease form attached to an email. Ellie filled it in straight away and sent it off. The problem remains how to find that little jewel: a woman the aunts will not reject, Luisa out of confusion and fear, Marguerita out of rage and suspicion. Vanna might have been right when she said it was unrealistic of Ellie to think she would find a carer from among the refugees at present flooding the island. It was Vanna's mixed metaphors, however, that made Ellie's teeth ache: 'You can't play God and kill two birds with one stone.'

So far Ellie's Internet searches have taken her as far afield as nursing agencies in northern Italy whose registers are full of Filipinas and Peruvians, but they haven't produced results. Bugger Vanna! As for Claire, it's obvious she's waiting to see whoever comes out the winner, Vanna or Ellie. Well, Ellie has no intention of losing. If she's said it once, she's said it a million times, you can't take two old women, who are sick and frail and disoriented, and transplant them to a place they do not know.

'Boat People Malta in the Mediterranean,' she types and hits 'Enter'.

Results 1-10 of about 326,000 entries.

'Okay, let's see what this bastard has to say.' She clicks on the You-Tube entry at the top of the page.

'How many illegals can you cram into a lifeboat?' The young man on the screen has a grating laugh, and a five o'clock shadow. 'Well, just take a look at this bunch of blacks trying to scramble on to a boat. Looks to me as if they're trying to get into the Guinness Book of Records.' He shoves his face forward, exposing foxy, stained teeth. 'Joking aside, *hbieb*, how many more of these scroungers is the Maltese government going to let in before the Maltese people wake up to the truth that Malta is being invaded?'

'Wow!' P. Cremona kicks off the comments in the comments section. 'Two years later and Malta still hasn't sorted out those wogs.'

'Viva Berlusconi!' C. Agius cheers. 'The Italians have got the right idea. They've voted for a Prime Minister who knows how to get tough on economic refugees stealing our jobs from us.'

'Could the Social Policy Minister please clarify what exactly illegal immigrants are entitled to?' asks E. Sciberras. 'Do they receive help that hard-working native Maltese tax-payers are not entitled to such as free dental care, medicines, phone cards and electricity?'

'Illegal immigrants rape and rob us and are never punished. Go to Birzebbuga or Marsa on any given day and you'll see fights breaking out between drunken Africans and the local population who are only trying to go about their business in a normal way. The Afros piss in public including in front of little children. They peddle drugs at the gates of our schools.' J-P Caruana.

On the back of Rosemary's office chair, Ellie has flung the cardigan Claire lent her a few nights ago when, angry with Vanna, she had stormed out of the house. After Claire had caught up with her near the coastal watchtower, Ellie joked that cashmere was too delicate for her and that beige really didn't suit her sallow skin. Despite her joviality, however, she was touched by her cousin's gesture, wanting to prolong the unexpected moment of closeness between them. Hadn't they been friends when they were children? Okay, it was unfair that they'd excluded Vanna, but this time Vanna is working bloody hard to exclude herself.

As Claire and Ellie strolled back to Balluta, crossing the well-lit Peace Garden, Claire fell silent. 'You must remember' – Ellie tried a different tack – 'how we used dive off the rocks at this same spot when we were kids.' Claire just shrugged her shoulders. She didn't seem to catch on that Ellie had asked the question not in order to test her memory but in an attempt to keep the communication open between them. The trouble with Claire, Ellie thought, is that when you throw a ball to her, instead of her bouncing it back, she hugs it to her chest. For someone whose business is words, she's bloody untalkative. Perhaps it's only through the words of others she's able to speak at all.

'Enough of You-Tube.' Ellie clicks to The Independent of Malta. The house of one of the paper's star columnists has been attacked because the journalist had spoken out against growing racism on the island.

'In the middle of the night, arsonists, whom the police have not been able to identify, leaned five tyres doused with petrol against her back door. Before setting fire to the tyres, they poured more petrol on the road in front of the house and scattered smashed glass on the tarmac to stop the journalist and her family from escaping. Luckily no one was killed, and this was not the first such arsonist attack. Seven vehicles belonging to the Jesuits have also been set on fire.'

'Eight actually,' Ellie says out loud. Since Rosemary Vassallo works alongside the Jesuits, in Ellie's view she should be counted as one of them, which makes it a total of eight.

Ellie had been in Sliema at Rosemary's office when Rosemary's teenage son phoned to say that their car was going up in flames on the road in front of their house, before his eyes. 'Shit, Mum, and all these stupid people are just standing around in the street watching.'

'Why the hell are you calling me?' Rosemary shouted. '*Madoffi*, phone the fire brigade and the police, now!'

As she rushed out of her office, Ellie was close behind.

'Sometimes, I think we're on the brink of civil war,' Rosemary said as the two of them climbed into a cab. 'Just like the seventies.'

৩৵৵

A Jewish woman from Greenpeace in Melbourne had given Ellie Rosemary Vassallo's address. Nora Rosenfeld always peppered her conversations with Yiddish words like *schlepp* and *mensch*, assuming that because Ellie was part Jewish they shared a common language. How typical of an Ashkenaz not to have any idea about Mediterranean Jews. Anyway, it annoyed Ellie to have a label stuck on her forehead. There is never an escape from it and, if anything, it is worse in Malta. Every day since getting here, she has bumped into people who can't resist reminding her of her missionary uncles. They claim her as one of them, whereas Vanna claims her as a Jew. Her father's family always did. If only they knew how close Danny and she had got to becoming Russian Orthodox.

The attempted conversion took place about a year after Clementino had brought Max the Black Labrador as a present for Danny. Their mother whirled into the house at ten thirty at night and ordered Ellie and Danny to put on their best clothes. While hustling the children to get ready, Laura prattled on in that frenetic way Ellie always dreaded. 'But, Mum, I can't. I've got stacks of homework to do.' Even if an assignment had been set weeks ago, Ellie only ever completed her homework the night before it was due.

'Hurry up, we're going to midnight mass.'

'What?'

'Yes, we're going to midnight mass at the Orthodox Church,' Laura said, 'with Irina. She's invited us. No, not those jeans, Ellie! Let me braid your hair. Oh, okay, leave it a mess like that, if that's what you want. But you have to wear a skirt. What about one of those pretty dresses Claire gave you? It'd be more respectful. Quickly, we have to catch the train to Strathfield.'

To begin with, Ellie had liked the idea of her mother having a close friend. It took the pressure off Danny and her. Ellie also liked Irina Demetreeva's being Russian, although she had been born in Harbin in China, which had once had this huge community of White Russian refugees. During one of her good periods, Laura had struck up a conversation with Irina on a bench at Town Hall station. For weeks afterwards it was 'Irina said this', 'Irina thinks that', 'Irina, the Russian Oracle'. Ellie eventually mumbled to Danny, 'God, you'd think Mum was in love with that woman.'

'Irina knows loads of people and she's so kind.' Laura wittered on as she sat knitting a cardigan for her newly found friend. She never knitted for her children or for herself, but Irina had asked her to and, well, she felt inspired to knit again. Irina will help us if we need help. Irina is only a phone call away.

Laura remained on a high for so long that Ellie even began to hope that it would last forever, that she would never fall into depression again. Too bad if she didn't seem to notice that there was something creepy about Irina keeping a portrait of the murdered Romanovs above a chest of drawers in her hallway. On each of the Name Days of each member of the Russian imperiall family, Irina would light a candle below the picture. She lit a whole row of candles the evening she invited Laura, Ellie and Danny to dinner at her place to celebrate their forthcoming conversion.

'But I don't want to be Russian Orthodox,' Ellie had protested, having had the ends of a loose strand of hair burned by the candle she'd been holding during the Orthodox Easter midnight mass. Now, as Irina led Laura, Ellie and Danny into her dining room, with her heels click-clicking on the parquet floor, Ellie noticed she was wearing pink slippers exactly like the pink slippers Laura still had dozens of in those boxes stacked in the hallway at home. Throughout the meal, Irina kept her pug dog on her lap, feeding him bits of gristle and fat from the same hand she was using to dish up the food. At the end of the meal she passed round the largest tin of Quality Street chocolates Ellie had ever seen.

'No thanks,' Ellie said, trying not to show her disgust at the string of spittle dangling from the dog's mouth and the way it crunched the caramel Irina had popped into its mouth with its little pointy teeth. 'No thanks, I don't like sweet things very much.'

After the meal, Irina led them into a dark and chilly front room where the Oldest Woman on the Planet, Irina's mother, sat in an armchair wrapped in a floral peasant shawl.

'Come on, Ellie, try out some of your Russian.' Laura poked her daughter in the back.

'I don't remember any.'

'Yes, you do. Don't be shy.'

But after Irina and her mother had corrected Ellie five times in the course of a single sentence, she lost interest in trying to be nice to her mother's new pals. Laura would have a huge fight on her hands if she insisted on the conversion. No priest with a bushy beard was going to tell Ellie what to believe in and do. Thank heavens that never came about.

Within a few days of that lunch at Irina's, Laura slid into depression again, and Ellie does not remember her dear friend Irina even phoning to ask if she could be of any help.

৵৵

'Have I already mentioned that your father and my father were at school together?' Rosemary looks up from her file. 'My family knew your family well.'

'Jeezus, I've lost count of the number of people who, since I got here, have stopped me in the street and told me what good family friends they were,' Ellie says. 'Oh, shit, I'm sorry. I didn't mean to sound so bloody aggressive.'

She had come here to push Rosemary to exert more pressure on the authorities and now she was blowing it. If she doesn't control her temper, she's never going to get into any migrant camp. Ellie cannot lay all the blame for her pugnacious mood on Claire and Vanna.

Rosemary, however, remains calm, gracefully gesturing for Ellie to sit down on the chair on the other side of her desk. On it, the jumble of papers is piled so high that Ellie can only see the lawyer's head. That her own chair is lower than Rosemary's makes her feel uncomfortable, as if she were a naughty child being spoken to by a headmistress, so she gets up and prowls the room instead while Rosemary starts to clear a space on the desk, throwing documents on the floor beside her chair. They hit the ground with a thwack, which sounds to Ellie like a reproach for her rudeness.

'You know, my grandparents and parents always went to your grandfather's pharmacy,' Rosemary says. 'After he passed away and your aunts took over, we continued going there. I remember Luisa, Marguerita and Sarita very well. Oh, now it's my turn to say sorry,' she adds without a hint of sarcasm. 'It's probably very upsetting to talk about your Aunt Sarita.'

'Actually I'm glad to hear her name spoken out loud for a change.' Ellie walks back to her chair.

At last, here is someone who knew Sarita and who might understand how terrible it is to sit down each evening to dinner not only with two lugubrious cousins but also with the gloomy ghost of her murdered aunt.

'What happened to her affected us all.' Rosemary's words are surprising. Where has Ellie seen that ad exhorting people to drive more carefully, on television or at the cinema? Everything takes place in slow motion. A young man is knocked over by a car. Like a pack of cards, a long line of people standing behind him fall backwards too: his mother, father, grandfather, girlfriend, colleagues and friends. On impact, their bodies distort and turn into splashes. 'The police locking the doctors out of St Luke's, that was shocking to those of us with doctors in the family. But letter-bombs! Perhaps you know this already, so stop me if you do. After your aunt was killed, the police rounded up dozens of striking doctors and arrested them – including my father.'

Ellie remembers nothing about the round-ups, but she does recall three detectives coming to the pharmacy to carry out a search. They were bomb experts from England. The whole family had been outraged that anyone should think the chemicals that went into the letter-bomb might have come from the pharmacy. Ellie, however, has always attributed the unexpected investigation to the general atmosphere of suspicion and distrust that gripped the island at the time. After all, how could the police possibly know anything about the bitter internal divisions within the Toledano family?

'They searched our house from top to bottom too,' Rosemary continues, 'turned everything inside out and took away boxes of papers. There was this rumour, you see, that the Medical Association of Malta had targeted your Uncle Joseph, and that the bomb had been intended for him. It was no secret that all the other doctors hated him for going on working against the medical association's injunctions.'

Still, it is hard for Ellie to imagine doctors getting mixed up in sending letter-bombs.

'In our family' – she leans forward, clasping both hands tightly – 'we were never completely certain who the bomb had been intended for.' Pushing the bracelets and bangles up her arm, she rests her elbows on the desk. It feels good to air the story with someone who had also lived through those turbulent times.

'Miriam, Uncle Joseph's wife, always maintained that on the afternoon of Sarita's death, when she called in at their house, she had just come from the post office and had brought the parcel with her. The confusion about who the bomb had been intended for was caused by Sarita having also picked up the mail from my Uncle Joseph's window-sill. It looked as if that mail and the parcel-bomb had been delivered together and the bomb had been intended for Joseph, whereas Joseph was certain that one of the patients Alberto had refused to treat must have been responsible. It was part of the class war being waged against the poor. Well, that's what my father always said. Not that I ever rated his opinions, but in this case I tend to think he was right.'

'You know'– Rosemary too leans forward – 'for months after your aunt was murdered, most of the doctors who refused to work received dozens of threatening phone calls and anonymous letters.'

It is news to Ellie that the post office intercepted other letter and parcel bombs. It must have happened after her family had moved to Australia. On the other hand, she does know that most doctors held firm for more than a year. Tolstoy was wrong when he said that all families were unhappy in their own way. At the time, all the families of Maltese doctors were miserable in the same way. How many hundreds finally emigrated?

Ellie listens intently as Rosemary speaks about her father not being able to work. He was so stressed that he developed diabetes. After a year, he finally gave in and took up a job in a Saudi hospital.

'Has anyone ever told you that now and again your Aunt Sarita's case still pops up in the local papers? Hard to believe that after all these years, the letters to the editor are still so vitriolic from both the Mintoffiani and the anti-Mintoffiani.'

'At least, there was no You-Tube those days. But joking aside, they were terrible times for everyone. Our family was split apart.'

And so was Rosemary's. Her father felt that if things had got to the point where people were blowing each other up, it was time to make his escape. He left his family behind because he didn't want to interrupt the children's schooling. But he always planned to come back, sooner rather than later. How could anyone have known that the strike would go on for ten years and that he would return only when he retired?

'He never adjusted to living abroad.' Rosemary said. 'Instead of being a big fish in a little pond, he became a little fish. It's a cliché, I know. *Madoff*! We have got gloomy, haven't we? Let me tell you something more cheerful. You and I are practically related.'

'At this moment, I must admit I'd be happy to have a relation who's on my side. Even a pseudo-relation would do.'

'Well, your Aunt Luisa and my father were in the same year at university and at one time it seems they planned to marry. But your grandmother banged her shoe on the table …'

'So it wasn't just a family myth that Luisa had been disappointed in love? You know, I've come across some old photo albums in my aunts' house. I used to remember Luisa as being such a lot of fun. She was good with kids, and we loved her much more than we loved Marguerita, who was always so sour. In the albums the look of dis-appointment with life, no, more than that, the look of despair, became more and more deeply etched in Luisa's face with every year that passed. With every page I turned, that's the story the photos in the albums told me.'

'Let me tell you something I've never told anyone before.' Rosemary lowered her voice. 'Your aunt called me here at the office after she'd read the announcement of my father's death in The Times. That was in 2000. She wanted to send flowers, she said. Later that evening, when I went over to my parents' house, I saw her sitting in the back of a Wembley cab which was parked outside. But my mother opened the door before I had a chance to cross the road and speak to Luisa. When I looked out of the front window an hour or so later, the car was still there. I should have gone out then and asked her to come in, but I didn't know how much my mother had known of the old love affair. Anyway, I thought, if Luisa had wanted to come in and pay her respects surely she would have done so. As a pharmacist, she was, so to speak, in the same line of business as my father. That was reason enough for her to call. I looked out the window several times and she was still there. Around nine o'clock I no-ticed the cab had at last gone.'

'Poor Luisa! I believe it was lack of courage that wrecked her life. She had seen what had happened when my father married my mother, who was Catholic, and decided that she couldn't face the same hostility from her mother.'

'My father also lacked courage. He could have mar-ried your aunt and the two of them could have gone to live somewhere else, but he was always afraid of leaving the island. Until all that business with Mintoff, he had loved his life here. This is where he belonged. It was the aggression of former patients who had in the past worshipped him that drove him out. Still, who can blame them? If you've got a very sick baby it's hard to have sympathy for a doctor who refuses to make house calls, let alone open his surgery door. I'll never forget my father turning away a woman whose teenage daughter needed help. The girl had been complaining of severe abdominal pains. But why I remember the mother more than anyone else my father turned away is that a few days later the girl died, and shortly afterwards my father made up his mind to leave Malta.'

∽∾

Still, waiting for official permission to visit a detention centre, Ellie has hired a car and driven out to Hal Far, in the south of the island, where hundreds of boat people are trapped behind barbed wire. According to the UN report, some of them live in a disused hangar while others shelter in containers or tents.

The landscape all along the route depresses Ellie. Concrete boxes now blight the view on the seafront where, when she was a child, beautiful villas with Rococo-style façades had once lined the promenade. And who the hell bribed the local council to allow that monstrous blue skyscraper to go up near the casino? On windy days, brown scum washes up on the rocks. The diver who took Ellie out to see the tuna pens told her that these days the sea is too polluted for sea urchins.

The diver had used the Maltese word, *rizzi*, reminding Ellie that when she and her cousins were children *rizzi* was the word everyone used even when speaking English. When they were small, it was always Luisa who pulled out the spines from the soles of their feet if they stepped on one of those spiky carapaces. Feet stained with Mercurochrome had once been part of the rituals of summer holidays.

Despite the bright sunshine, it is desolate at Hal Far. Like everywhere else on this rocky island, there is little vegetation. Few cars pass by here, although Ellie notices there is a bus stop across the road from the camp, which at least means the refugees can get to Valletta or to other towns and villages and have a chance to look for work, with or without a permit. All over Malta, you can see boat people labouring on building sites.

As Ellie climbs out of the hire car, she has to hold on to the door to stop it from slamming against her. The wind, which whips fine gravel against her bare shins, is icy. The Gregale blows from the north-east, Luisa had taught her nieces and nephew, and brings showers and hail in winter. The word comes from *grecale* meaning Greek and it blows from the island of Zakynthos. Their aunt had gone on to list all the winds of the planet.

Taking a large orange from the fruit bowl on the sideboard, she used it to represent the earth. 'This is how winds are formed as well as hurricanes, monsoons, gales and sea breezes. Leveche, Levantades, Marin, Libeccio.'

Luisa went through all the names, and reciting them is still one of Ellie's party pieces when she is feeling relaxed.

Ellie crosses the road. On the other side of the barbed wire, she sees clusters of tents pitched in the middle of a small field of dry yellow grass. Close to the tents, shipping containers stand in a row next to a stack of cement pipes, about six feet high. A car speeding past toots the first few notes of 'Colonel Bogey' at her. Fuck you, too! Ellie rubs her eyes hard to clear the grit.

When she opens them again, she sees a tall black man standing close to the barbed wire. He is wearing a T-shirt with the iconic print of Che on it. Behind him stands a solitary tree, leaning in the direction of the wind. With its blackened trunk and leafless branches, it looks as if it has been stuck by lightning. Next to the tree, a group of men sit on the ground. Heavy eyelids half open, they are chewing blades of grass, suspended in time, waiting. 'Our lives have become nothing but waiting.' This is what a refugee in a detention centre in South Australia had once told Ellie. The words had felt like a punch in the stomach.

'Hi, I'm Ellie Radcliff.' She hopes she sounds friendly but not over-familiar as she walks towards the wire. Even if the man cannot escape her curiosity, he must have time to work out for himself that she means him no ill. She cannot assume that he will be grateful for a stranger's interest. On the contrary, he might not want anyone to be a witness to his humiliation. 'How many of you are there in this place?' Feet crunching gravel, she moves forward slowly. If it weren't for the dead look in the African's eyes, he would be a handsome man, tall and lean with a beautifully shaped shaven head. It's not often you come across such truly black skin. Ellie is tempted to reach through the wire and touch the man's bare arm. It is an instinctive urge as is the wish is to assail him with questions, but a voice in her head says, for once in your life, don't be so impetuous, take things slowly. Before you stands a wounded being.

'Eight hundred, maybe it is more. I do not know.' He shifts his weight from one leg to the other. 'You are with the delegation?'

'Sorry? What delegation?' One question at a time, the inner voice reminds her.

'The delegation that comes to see for themselves. One of the Eritreans who live here, he hanged himself last week. We are told there is to be official visit. Today the Dutch Ambassador comes to see for himself. There will be many policemen.'

'I came to see this place. I didn't know anything about a man who hanged himself. It wasn't in the press. I'm really, really sorry. Look, I don't have official permission to be here.' Ellie sticks her hands into the pockets of her thin cardigan. She can't leave without giving the man something. Not that a cherry-flavoured life-saver will assuage the guilt she feels about his being on one side of the fence and her being on the other, but she always has a packet of life-savers on her. This time, however, all she's able to fish out of her pocket is a single stick of chewing gum, gluey and covered in lint.

'Hamed Hendane.' The man puts his long arm through the wire and shakes Ellie's hand. The skin of his palm is cracked and greyish and rasps the skin of her hand.

'I'm not with any delegation, but take my word for it, I will come back.' She sticks the gum back in her pocket before walking away.

193

❧

Ellie does not return to Hal Far. Rosemary is only able to get her permission to take a look round the Ta' Kandja detention centre. I've seen better jails in South America, Ellie says to herself as she follows the lawyer down a long, dark corridor. They stop when they come to a room, no bigger than a police cell, where two women and a teenage boy sit on a mattress on the floor, their heads lolling like dead sunflowers, their eyes staring into nothingness.

'Madonna,' Rosemary says, 'they told me that the toilet cistern had leaked onto the floor. But I wasn't expecting this.'

The cell is ankle-deep in filthy water, and no one's made the slightest attempt to clean up properly. Even if they had, it would be impossible to rid the place of the stench of piss, Ellie thinks. The women should never have been put here in the first place. What's the point of NGOs writing up all those human rights' reports when no one in authority takes a blind bit of notice?

Ellie follows Rosemary into another cell. As they enter, the five occupants stop speaking. In the silence, Ellie can hear the wheezing from their lungs.

'You know' – Rosemary waves her arms as if she is making a speech to a vast audience – 'at this time of the year and even up to early spring most people held in here end up with really serious respiratory infections.'

She speaks of how all year round there are countless cases of scabies and other skin infections because of the poor hygiene. The inmates don't even have something as basic as soap unless Rosemary brings some. It's hard to get proper medical treatment once they fall ill. There is no infirmary, nowhere to go when people have an infectious condition and have to be kept in isolation. Rosemary's NGO has been campaigning for an infirmary for more than a year. Some of the detainees have been at Ta' Kandja for as long as three years waiting for their residency applications to be processed.

In a cell even smaller than the last, they find the Somali woman Ellie has asked especially to see. She is sitting on a low stool nursing a baby, a dirty cream-coloured shawl wrapped around the two of them, with only the top of the baby's head exposed.

'So this is Aïsha el Fazaa.' Ellie crouches to bring her face to the level of the mother's face. 'The whole world knows Aïsha.' Against the light streaming in from the broken window behind Rosemary, Ellie cannot see the lawyer's expression. 'Who hasn't seen that newsreel of her being winched off that Spanish trawler as she went into labour?' Ellie unfolds the edge of the shawl. 'Shit, shit, shit!' She jumps up.

'What?' Rosemary moves forward.

'The kid's crawling with lice.'

'Madonna, come on. Let's get someone to see to this.' Rosemary picks the baby up gently without, as far as Ellie can see, stiffening in disgust.

'She can't stay here,' Ellie says as she trots behind Rosemary down the long draughty corridor, with Aïsha shuffling behind. 'We've got to get the mother out of here,' she shouts. 'Her and the baby. Can't you do something about getting her a work permit?'

ೞⲟⲁⳁ

It was an old *soixante-huitard*, settled in Australia since the early 1980s, who taught Ellie how to stop someone shivering from cold. She had met him on a rainy winter's day in Melbourne, outside the French Consulate where a crowd was gathered to protest against French nuclear testing in the Pacific. Pascal Aymonnier was bragging about how he had climbed the barricades during the student riots in Paris back in 1968 and braved tear gas and dodged CRS truncheons. It was not just his height and thinness that reminded Ellie of an El Greco painting. It was the greenish grey tone of his skin. The hippie clothes were a little out of date, even by then, but what bugged Ellie most of all was the touch of French elegance Pascal still had, despite the casual appearance he affected, the well-chosen combination of tones and the noticeably expensive leather shoes. Still, after they were arrested and crammed into a police cell with half a dozen other protesters, it was Pascal who came to the rescue when Ellie began shivering uncontrollably.

'I must be coming down with something,' she said as she fought a wave of nausea. 'Maybe it's flu. I never feel the cold, but right now I just can't seem to get warm.'

'Back in '68 …' Pascal got up off the cell floor.

'Give it a rest, Pascal, willya,' one of the other protesters, a genuine hippie, grumbled.

Seated on the edge of a bunk, Ellie was hugging herself, shaking with cold. Ignoring the teasing, Pascal ordered her to remove her top. 'No false prudery,' he said. He was being serious. Her clothes were soaked right through. If she preferred it, he would make everyone in the cell promise to close their eyes and keep them closed while she undressed. She didn't have to remove her bra.

Slowly, feeling weaker than a child with an earache, Ellie pulled off her sweater. All her strength had drained away and her limp limbs, her back and her shoulders throbbed painfully. She didn't have enough energy to grumble when Pascal ordered her to lie down flat on her stomach. Having pushed up her hair, he put his lips to the base of her neck then moved them very slowly down her spine, exhaling warm breaths with every kiss, all the way down to the hollow in her lower back. Within moments, the shuddering had stopped and the whole of Ellie's body was tingling with warmth.

'I learned this in a Paris police cell during the *Evènements* of '68.' Pascal stood looking down on her, beaming with pleasure at his achievement just now. 'A student doctor taught me.'

Ellie hasn't thought of Pascal in years, but in the wake of the last heavy downpour, as she stands shivering in the midst of a straggle of demonstrators before the Maltese Parliament, Pascal comes back to mind. Should she ask Rosemary to blow down her back? It's an intimate thing to do. She would have to explain the technique, which she has used many times since the great anti-nuclear demonstrations. The last time was in the desert in South Australia. No one who hasn't experienced it can know how cold it gets in a desert at night. Ellie and fellow demonstrators had camped out close to a detention centre where the inmates had set fire to buildings and a number of them had gone on hunger strike. Not only did the police surround the centre, but Australian soldiers were hauled in as back-up.

Plus ça change, Ellie thinks, as she stomps her feet trying to get warm. It has been raining heavily on and off all night, and a chilly wind slices the Square. A week ago, at Hal Far, some detainees set fire to their huts, and now six of them, including two women, have gone on hunger strike, demanding better housing and faster processing of their asylum applications. In response, on Monday morning, the right-wing Alleanza Nazzjonali Repubblikana descended en masse on Valletta, rallying in front of the Auberge de Castille, then jack-booting down Republic Street. Shoppers milling on the city's main street were forced to retreat to the pavements as Alleanza thugs marched towards Palace Square chanting racist slogans and menacing boat people and refugees and their supporters.

Reacting to that, Friends of the Earth, the Peace Lab and the Third World Group have organised their own rally, drawing up a roster of demonstrators to camp on Palace Square in front of Parliament. We'll show the bastards! By which Ellie means not only the Alleanza mob but also politicians.

'You'll have to hotfoot it over to the aunts' house, I'm afraid, and spend the night there.' Ellie called Claire at the Phoenicia. 'I don't know when I'll be back. But this demonstration is very, very important.'

On the first afternoon of the vigil on Palace Square, despite the jeering of the Alleanza mob and the terrible weather, the pro-refugee demonstrators remained upbeat. Mounted police brought in to protect the MPs as they went in and out of Parliament prevented a scuffle by pushing the Alleanza hecklers back to the perimeter.

Shouting at the Greenpeace supporters to also get back, they tugged hard on the reins of their skittish horses. Ellie had heard that eerie sound of hooves clomping on cobblestones many times before.

'How Many More Torchings Before Someone Dies?' Wearily she sets down her placard. After a second night of wind and driving rain, it lies soaked on the cobbles with its lettering bleeding into the sky blue background.

'In 1943 Malta Stood Up To Fascism! Don't Let The Fascists Take Over Now!' Rosemary Vassallo is still holding up the placard her son made for her. Her wet hair is matted on her forehead and there are dark crescents under her eyes. Her pale skin has turned grey from lack of sleep.

Though Father Francis, Rosemary's Franciscan friend, seems to be dozing, he's still sitting upright on a collapsible fisherman's stool with his home-made sign: 'Do Not Turn Away The Stranger From Your Door!'

Yesterday, around six in the evening, driven off by the heavy showers and razor wind, the Alleanza mob had finally drifted away, leaving behind them pavements littered with rubbish. 'Hardly surprising,' Ellie remarked, having gone round picking up crisp bags, hamburger cartons and dumped polystyrene cups. 'Believe me,' she said to Rosemary, 'I'm not doing this out of civic-mindedness. I need to move to get some sensation back into my hands and feet.'

By nine o'clock the police guard in front of the Parliament was thinned out to three unhappy constables, each with a droopy moustache and eyelids as heavy as a bloodhound's. This morning at two o'clock the House was still in session. The massive wooden doors of the building that had once housed the headquarters of the Grand Master of the Knights of Malta were still wide open. Through the pillars on either side of the doors the light in the courtyard appeared to Ellie like a beacon in a hurricane. Black limousines, tyres swooshing through puddles, glided past the huddle of protesters stamping their feet and clapping their gloved hands in front of the palace.

At night, Valletta turns into a ghost city, emptied of tourists and shoppers. Ellie remembers how special it had once been to be brought to town by her father. Sometimes they used to visit a Jewish tailor who had his shop on Palace Square. The old man would let Ellie and Danny scramble up the narrow stairs and sit on the wooden horse which he used to measure legs for riding breeches. On these excursions, Clementino would meet up with musicians at Cordina's on the corner of the Square. In retrospect, Ellie wonders if the violinist Caterina Fortuna had also been her father's lover. She was always present at those gatherings at Cordina's and attentive to Danny and Ellie in a way that, in retrospect, seems to Ellie stagy and exaggerated. Clementino would often return home late saying he had been rehearsing a new song with her.

In Malta it is hard to keep secrets, and Laura would have inevitably found out about such an affair. Who is there left to tell Ellie what really happened? Her mother was the last person to ask. Marguerita would purse her lips just like Nonna Rosa used to do and deny all knowledge. A pity Luisa's memory has gone. She would have been able to tell Ellie.

Exhausted and with her eyes gritty from lack of sleep, Ellie managed very early this morning to slip away from the Square, taking a wide detour down narrow back streets and alleys and up again to a pharmacy on Republic Street where she bought a toothbrush and toothpaste. There were no Alleanza supporters out yet. The road was still clear round Cordina's where, in the basement, Ellie stripped down to her underwear and, dampening a paper towel, rubbed her arms, legs and feet as best she could. Laura used to say that when Ellie was in the womb, when the '1812' was played, Ellie would kick hard as soon as the Russian Imperial Anthem and the Marseillaise began battling with each other. It's this battle of anthems piped into the loo that drives Ellie out of the café without ordering coffee or a pastry.

Back at the square, she takes position again, watching as Father Francis strolls up to the three constables, hands clasped like a royal consort's behind his back. He says something that makes the policemen laugh. Funny how not knowing why people are laughing can make you feel so excluded and alone. Ellie shudders. Throughout the whole of the previous night's vigil before the Parliament, she and the priest had kept each other awake arguing about the existence of God. Father Francis thought he'd won the case in favour of a higher being at the point when Ellie seemed unable to explain the genius of Mozart. The truth was, however, that because Father Francis is such a likeable man, Ellie only let him think he had won the debate. With anyone else, she would have snapped that Mozart is always what scoundrels and religious fanatics pull out of their sleeve. And anyway, if there is some higher force directing our lives, Mozart is perfect proof of the cruel randomness of the way that force acts, bestowing some people with too many gifts and others with too few.

Last night, Rosemary's son brought heavy-duty yellow raincoats for both his mother and Ellie. But the beach umbrellas the boy had thought would also be useful are hopelessly not waterproof. By mid-morning Ellie feels chilled to the core. Not even Father Francis's strong, sweet coffee produced from a giant flask can ward off her queasiness as her blood sugar plummets. Rosemary moves in a daze from one protester to another speaking softly and encouraging them to hang on. Now and again her whole body gives one violent shudder.

'Come on!' Ellie suddenly unfolds her legs and arms. 'Come on, sit down here on this orange crate!' She takes her friend by the elbow. 'I'll show you how to get warm. Take your raincoat off. Your sweater, too.' Placing her mouth on Rosemary's thin blouse, Ellie blows up and down her spine. Soon Rosemary is purring.

'Now, it's my turn.' Ellie gives her a quick hug.

'The two of you should take a look at this.' Father Francis hurries over to them waving a bright orange flyer in his right hand. 'Our Alleanza friends have been very busy during the night.' The photograph on the flyer must have been taken using a mobile phone. In it, Rosemary Vassallo's face is contorted with anger as she holds up a fist at the Alleanza supporters. The flank of a police horse cuts across the left-hand corner of the frame. Below Rosemary's picture the caption on the leaflet reads, 'Rosemary Vassallo, Greenpeace Ringleader'. It identifies the woman standing next to her as 'C. Toledano, Australian Provocateur'. Well, they've got the initial wrong. It's E not C Toledano. And shouldn't provocateur be provocatrice? Ellie crushes the flyer and shoves it into her pocket. She bends down to pick up her placard again.

Something is happening at the top of the square. Shit, don't tell me the cops are going to let the Alleanza thugs through? Ellie moves forward as two constables lower their outspread arms to let a woman in past the barriers. What the hell? It's Claire.

'I've brought you a few things,' Clare says. She holds up a shopping bag with some sort of designer logo on it.

Ellie notices a fleck of plaster on the shoulder of her jacket. It must have been torture for her to spend a night in Marguerite's room. She imagines her lying awake with plaster dust from the ceiling descending on her like fine mist.

'Don't look so worried,' Claire smiles. 'I'm not staying, but I had to get back to the Phoenicia to take a shower and while I was there I thought you could do with a change of clothes – and a toothbrush. There's a taxi waiting for me and I'm going straight back to St Julians.'

'Oh, shit!' Ellie looks over Claire's shoulder.

'What?' Claire swerves around.

'I don't bloody believe it. They're letting someone else through.' Ellie straightens up, placing her weight evenly on both feet spread wide apart and holding her placard up high.

A woman is rushing towards them brandishing a furled umbrella. As she runs her full breasts jig up and down. She is shouting, but neither Ellie nor Claire can make out what she is saying. A constable lunges forward to block the woman's way. As she dodges his grasp, he slips to the ground. From the other side of the barriers, Alleanza supporters give a triumphant cry. When another constable blows his whistle, the crowd howls him down. Father Francis trots forward to meet the woman, but she pushes past him. Raising her umbrella higher, she advances until she is only a couple of feet away from Ellie and Claire. Thinking the woman is about to strike a blow, Ellie steps in front of Claire to protect her. Instead, the woman lowers her umbrella. Ellie expels a deep breath. Her muscles relax.

The woman takes one more step forward. Who is she, and where does that look of hatred come from?

'A murderer, your father is a murderer,' the woman shouts, raising the umbrella again. But instead of striking, she screws up her lips, and then she spits. Ellie remains nailed to the spot – bewildered, dismayed. 'That's for your father.' The woman spits again.

Claire

9 Certainties

The first gob hit me, not Ellie, the spit landing on my shoulder. My mind locked. The second hit my cheek. I felt the sour taste of vomit well up at the back of my throat. My vision blurred.

'Bitch! Alleanza bitch!' Ellie lunged forward.

'No.' A priest in a cassock caught her arm. 'Please don't.'

Two policemen grabbed hold of the attacker. Pulling her jacket down, they pinned her arms to her sides. Stocky and broad-shouldered, she looked strong, but she was easily subdued. When she stumbled, they pulled her hard back onto her feet. As they chivvied her along, she twisted around, and for a second our eyes met. Like a fish, she opened and closed her mouth, but no sound came out. If the policemen had not been propping her up, she might have sunk to her knees. They had to half-carry, half-drag her over the cobblestones that were slippery from the previous night's storm.

'Oh, shit!' Ellie slapped her thighs. She clutched her head and took deep breaths then, swerving around, said, 'For fuck's sake. You were supposed to be keeping an eye on Vanna. I wasn't asking much, was I?' She pushed back a clump of hair that had fallen across her face.

I could not speak. In dreams I have often found myself standing naked and humiliated in front of a crowd, and that is how I felt at that moment.

'Here, *Sinjura*, use this.' The priest gently placed one hand on my forearm. Five other people shuffled to form a protective circle around me as I took his handkerchief.

'Give that to me,' Ellie said. 'Shit, Claire. It was nice of you to bring me things, but you shouldn't be here!' She twisted a corner of the handkerchief and dabbed the shoulder of my jacket. It was pointless. None of the clothes I was wearing would ever feel clean again. I would have to leave them at the hotel. Anyway, I no longer liked them; beige and white were the colours Yves would have chosen for me.

'This spit was meant for me,' Ellie said.

'Who was she?' I asked.

Ellie's daubs were becoming more like little punches.

'God knows. One of those anti-immigrant fascists spewing their hatred at me and my friends,' she said as she stepped back. 'Still, no real damage done.'

'Why would she call your father a murderer?' I plucked at the cloth on the shoulder of my jacket anxious that the spit might have seeped through to my skin.

'She's a nut case,' Ellie said. 'She can't possibly know who my father was, unless she's the daughter of one of his former mistresses. Now, there's a thought. Maybe she meant murderer metaphorically. I mean, who knows what she meant? She was hysterical.'

As Ellie took hold of my arm, there was a strong whiff of dank wool from the cardigan I'd leant her. I could also smell that slightly vinegary odour I sometimes get on my skin when I'm worked up. There must be a genetic component to skin odour. It would show me up as a liar if I were to deny that Ellie and I are related. When we were children, I often said she wasn't my cousin. She was so intense, so messy and so loud, and I admit to prissiness. I didn't want people to associate me with her.

'Let's go and have a quick coffee at Cordina's,' Ellie said. 'Then you'd better hurry back to St Julians, and hope to God Vanna hasn't done a disappearing act with Luisa.'

'When I left the house, Luisa was snoring, and Vanna was getting ready to tackle the roaches with her broom.'

'Ah, yes, the daily battle, the one she always wins,' Ellie said.

'Didn't you say she's sure to have booked the afternoon flight via Cyprus? It isn't even eight yet. She won't have had time to pack. Getting Luisa dressed is not easy, and then she has to get the two of them to the airport.'

'Still, you never know,' Ellie said.

When we were young, I was afraid of Ellie's sudden rages and her equally sudden enthusiasms. After I'd started going to private Russian lessons, she decided that she had to learn Russian too. She didn't let up until I agreed to teach her everything I was taught. 'Come on, you must remember what Miss Sokolova said this afternoon,' she would say and later, when I was tired and not at all in the mood to speak, she would bully me for more lessons.

Ellie splashed through a puddle as she jostled me across the square. 'Vanna is crazy enough to have booked a flight via Frankfurt, even if it means shunting Luisa around a transit lounge for hours.' Alleanza supporters were out and about so, just in case, we went into Cordina's through the side entrance on Palace Square.

'I still don't get it. How did that woman know who your father was,' I asked while we queued for our docket at the cashier's desk. On an empty stomach, the smell of buttery pastries made me feel nauseated, as did the gardenia-scented bleach used to wash the tiled floor. 'I really don't understand.'

Above the hissing of the coffee-machine, it was hard to make myself heard, and in any case my voice sounded tinny to my ears. Throughout my life I have constantly struggled to pitch it low so as to make it more seductive to my listeners. Yves used to say that he had fallen in love with my voice. Under stress I usually lose control and sound like a witch in Macbeth. When I am in charge, on the other hand, I can sound cold even if I don't mean to.

'My face has been in most of the papers since this Greenpeace vigil started,' Ellie said, as she hooked her arm into mine again. 'The Alleanza has distributed thousands of flyers with the photos and names of pro-immigrant activists.'

'But she wasn't accusing you of supporting boat people. She was accusing your father of murder. It doesn't make sense. Listen, couldn't she have been after me? Couldn't she have meant my father? Maybe this has nothing to do with refugees. Maybe it's something that goes back to the doctors' strike. My father made enemies then. All the doctors who refused to work made enemies.'

'Okay, let's say she was really after you. Could you tell me how she knew that you're your father's daughter? You were a child when you left Malta. It was so long ago. Come on, let's go outside. It's too dark and stuffy in here. I think we're safe sitting outside for a few minutes.'

On the small square in front of Cordina's, a sullen teenager was unfolding chairs, banging each down before the tables. In the watery sunlight, the air was chilly as I followed Ellie outside. We sat silently as a waiter brought us our tray and laid everything out.

'Here, drink some of this water first.' Ellie poured it for me. 'You look dreadful.'

There was a burning hollow in my stomach, and my skin felt tight and dry as paper. Ellie scrunched up a handful of paper napkins, which she had taken off the top of the cakes counter. After moistening them with mineral water from her bottle, she offered them to me. 'Here, have another go at your shoulder.'

'It's fine, the jacket's fine, honestly.' I took a sip of coffee, but it was strong and bitter, and it brought on a coughing fit.

'Hey, calm down! Drink some more water, and try a piece of this.' Ellie pushed an unbuttered toast triangle towards me on a small plate. Overlooking us, impervious to the turmoil of the living people below, Queen Victoria stood on her high, stone plinth. There was a ring of pigeons squatting on her crown, oblivious in their turn to the droppings deposited all over the queen's face and shoulders.

'Piss off,' Ellie hissed, clapping her hands and stamping her feet, as two pigeons swooped down and landed close to us. 'You know, I'm still thinking about that crazy woman.' She pulled her feet up on her chair, forming a tent with her long peasant skirt. 'Maybe you're right.' She drummed her fingers on the table so hard the bracelets on her arms rattled. 'Maybe she has nothing to do with the Alleanza mob. Maybe she did know your father.' She looked up at me. 'Perhaps she was a former patient,' she said, 'but she still got things wrong.'

'Sorry?'

'Take a look at this.' Ellie pulled out a piece of orange-coloured paper from her pocket and, smoothing it flat, pushed it towards my side of the table.' Can you see? They've put C. Toledano under my name, C. for Claire, not E. for Eleonora. The woman was trying to attack me because she thought I was you. Without knowing it, she hit her real target.'

'I've never set eyes on her before …'

'Don't look so bloody worried.' Ellie reached out to stroke my hand. 'Come on, if you're not going to drink that coffee you'd better get your skates on or Vanna will have whisked Luisa off to Israel before you get back to Lapsi Street. I'll walk with you up to the Porta Reale so you can catch a taxi.'

❧

At Floriana, I ordered the taxi driver to stop. I couldn't go back to my aunts' house, not straight away, not the way I was feeling: exhausted from the previous night's sleeplessness in that creaky, sagging bed that was once my grandmother's, and soiled from my encounter with that midget madwoman. There's no hot water in the house, and I had to take a shower, wash my hair and change into fresh clothes. I got out of the cab and walked the short distance back to the Phoenicia. The steaming shower and a complete change of outfit, however, did not stop me from feeling unclean.

How was I going to face another day in that ruin? I'm no good with old people. Since coming back to Malta, I've learned that about myself. The loathing of my body's encroaching decay began a few years ago. Other people's decay frightens me too, and I seem to be of little use to my family. Marguerita views me with increasing suspicion, which I don't know how to appease, and even the faintest whiff of stale urine from Luisa makes me feel sick. It's obvious my presence disturbs her though she doesn't know who I am.

I couldn't stay holed up all day churning over who was right or wrong, or why that unknown woman had called my father a murderer. Have I blanked out so much that I've lost that memory too? I went over and over the questions in my head as I got on a bus at Porta Reale.

Wedged in the right-hand corner of the perspex partition between the driver and the passengers, the jo-vial bearded face of Padre Pio on a prayer card smiled benignly at me. The Italians have an expression, *buono come il pane*, good as bread, if you translate it word for word. I think a translation that captures the real meaning of the Italian phrase should be 'warm as freshly baked bread'. There's nothing as comforting as chewing bread still warm, fresh from the oven. It's not for nothing that breaking bread is at the heart of much religious ritual. In contrast to Padre Pio, Dun Ġorġ, with his wax-effigy pallor, stared blankly at me from the left-hand corner of the partition. I must admit that looking at him I am reminded of my father: the tilt of the square chin, the *puzzo sotto il naso*, as Nonna Rosa used to say. A man with a bad smell under his nose, Dun Ġorġ certainly did not look like someone who, alive or dead, would have had his image posted at the feet of AC Milan. The team members' individual portraits had been arrayed in horse-shoe formation and, in the middle, the Madonna, draped in a blue gown and a red cape, floated above cotton wool clouds, beams of sunlight radiating from her head. In the past, men and women would have crossed themselves before the Madonna as they got on and off the bus, but nowadays no one seems to care.

I reflect that in my life I have been drawn to people who are assured, even when reason and experience tell me that in this world nothing is sure. One of Yves's attractions had been how certain he had been of his *bon goût,* for instance, or of the breadth of his *culture générale* – now there's another term which, translated literally, does not convey the self-confidence of the French term. General knowledge isn't quite the same, and to admit to being cultured is not something Anglo-Saxons comfortably do. Most of all Yves had never doubted that he was truly French, a certainty I envied most in him. As a Jew and not a Catholic, I am acutely aware of not being wholly Maltese.

It is so easy to be swayed by people who appear to be sure of themselves. I can read a book that brilliantly presents a new reading of historical events, for example, and be equally dazzled by a historian presenting the opposite view. Because neither Ellie nor Vanna appears to have doubts, each is equally capable of winning me over. I swing from one view to the other daily, even several times a day. I've been waiting since my arrival to be given a task that will have made this trip worthwhile.

Two stops after Floriana, an old man got on the bus. As it pulled away from the kerb, he crossed himself. At last, that familiar gesture, and the memory of the day I tried out what it felt like to flutter my hands across my chest in genuflection. I must have been nine or ten. Sitting on the top step of the parapet at the front of my grandparents' house I had, out of boredom, been counting the women dressed in black scudding to evening mass in Indian file along the pavement-less street. I recognised a couple of older girls from my school and waved to them, but they did not wave back. Out of the classroom context, they didn't seem to recognise me. What was it like to go to mass, I wondered, and did it make you feel different? It was something I would never know because churchgoing was something that THEY, the Maltese, did and we, the Toledanos, did not.

Although my father's family name, Sacerdote, is an Italian translation of Cohen, the Cohens were a different kind of priestly class. It has nothing to do with going to church. 'Superior in their shunning of idolatry,' is how my grandmother put it.

In the late afternoon, the stone walls on the other side of the street gave off their radiant heat. From one of the wrought iron gates that led to the back of the houses facing the seafront, Tonino Zammit's mother was calling for him to come indoors and get ready for church. Tonino would sit all day long on a kitchen chair planted on the roadside. He had a wizened child's face but a balloon man's body. We were supposed not to stare at his dirty white vest, which was full of holes, and his fly, which was always unbuttoned. We had to show our superiority – there was that word again – over other people's children by not making fun of Tonino or calling out names. Continuously plaiting and unplaiting a rosary through his fat fingers, he would mumble under his breath, but I could never make out the words. Sometimes, for apparently no reason, he would work himself into a frenzy and prowl up and down the road. Only the parish priest could soothe his anguish. Leading him back to the chair, Father Vincent would place his hand on Tonino's pinball head and murmur a prayer. This scene always ended with the ritual fluttering of hands across the two men's chests, something Ellie confirmed to me only a couple of days ago.

Since the doctors began their strike, I had grown anxious and jittery and was often on the verge of tears. Now that my father was unable to work, the smallest things would make him explode: a dirty cup in the sink, the scraping of cutlery on a dinner plate, a window not properly shut at night. He never did have the inner tranquillity that might have allowed him to spend whole days reading, for instance, or listening to music. Nor could he release his pent-up energy through physical exercise, which he despised. Sometimes his anger was aimed not at Mintoff but at my mother who did not share his eagerness to leave Malta. She thought that we should stick things out, which was what killed her in the end of course. But loving her work as a pharmacist, she was not prepared to sacrifice her career and move to Italy where my father was born, or to England, although her qualifications would have automatically been recognised there. Late into the night my parents would argue. Through the two foot thick stone wall that separated my bedroom from theirs, I could hear them. I remember Luisa coming to our house two or three times to mediate a truce. 'Mintoff is not just destroying the medical profession,' my father would say to my mother's elder sister, 'he is destroying my family.'

Watching the women going to mass, I raised my right hand and moved it down from my forehead and across my chest as I had seen people on buses and the girls at my school do. I imagined it would have had a calming effect, but there was no sense of peacefulness. One lunchtime my mother had dropped me off at my grandmother's after another fierce argument with my father. She had walked out of the house, slamming the front door, with me running behind her. 'Make a wish,' I said to myself, screwing up my eyes. 'Cross my heart and hope to die,' is what girls at school used to say. 'Cross my heart and hope to die.' The words whistled through the wide gap between my two front teeth as I crossed myself again.

In an instant, my grandmother was on the parapet, tugging my arm so hard that I was forced to my feet, yelping with pain. It felt as if she might pull my shoulder out of its socket, but the pain was not as sharp as the insult of her fury. It was more usual for me to stand by and watch Nonna Rosa turn other members of the family into her victims, not only Laura, who wasn't Jewish, but also Miriam, who was a simple woman with little education.

Having pulled me indoors, my grandmother shoved me into an armchair and shouted in a mixture of Italian and Maltese that she would really give me something to bawl about if she ever caught me doing what she had just seen me doing. She could not even bear, she said melodramatically, to let the name of my crime pass her lips. But she uttered it all the same: *Sacrilegio.*

༤

The minaret was straight ahead. Above the mound in the centre of the roundabout, I saw that the gates of the Moslem cemetery were wide open. I'd got on the wrong bus.

'Stop! Stop here!' I reached for the bell cord. The woman sitting next to me huffed with exasperation.

'*Sinjura*, this is not a bus stop.' In the rear-view mirror, the driver's eyes narrowed to slits, but he slowed down enough for me to hop off safely.

The Jewish cemetery is located next to the Moslem cemetery, but its gate was locked. Had some subconscious force directed me here? Vanna is all self-righteousness when she boasts to Ellie and me that she alone has tended the family graves. A few days ago, she tried to get the two of us to pay a visit to the cemetery with her. 'No point in disturbing ancient ghosts.' Ellie's words were trite, but I felt the same.

From Vanna, I knew the caretaker of the Moslem cemetery also keeps the keys to the Jewish cemetery. So

I stood my ground when a man wearing a knee-length rubber apron and green gum-boots advanced towards me shouting, 'This is private property.' I put my right hand out to him, keeping it held out while he removed his garden gloves. Instead of shaking hands with me, however, he scratched the tip of his nose. Undeterred by his rebuff, I asked him if he would kindly open the next door gate and offered him my French passport.

I used to travel on my British passport, but I've let that expire. A French passport at least spares me the kind of interrogation which took place at UK passport control whenever an alert officer peered more closely at my place of birth. Since there is no St Julians anywhere in Britain, I would sometimes be asked where I was really from. Once, I tried being flippant by answering with a question: do you want the long or the short version of my story? The officer was not amused.

As it turned out, the caretaker of the Moslem cemetery was unimpressed by any kind of passport.

'A passport does not prove that you are entitled to enter the Jewish cemetery,' he said. He spoke English not with a Maltese accent, but with the guttural bark of an Arabic-speaker. 'I cannot let just any strange lady in there,' he said and began moving off. 'People have been known to desecrate graves.'

I have read somewhere that a thought is formed in our brain several seconds before we are aware of it. 'Here, why don't you take this,' I said and hurried after the caretaker pulling off the wedding ring I still wore. Certainly, its removal was a gesture that I had not planned. But once the thought had burst into my consciousness, I did not hesitate. The ring was tight on my finger, and I had to twist hard to get it over my knuckle. At our very first reunion, Ellie had asked me in her typically blunt way why, given I was no longer married, I still wore it. I had no answer and in front of the caretaker I realised there was no answer that would not make me appear pathetic.

'Keep it as a security,' I urged the man. 'I swear to you' – I tried to disarm him with a smile – 'I have no intention of vandalising the cemetery and absconding with the keys.'

In the end, he decided to phone the head of the Maltese Jewish Community to obtain permission to let me in. He was on the phone for some time. When at last I turned the key to the gate, it felt reassuring to think that though I have never met the head of the Community he nonetheless knew who I was. Being a member of the Toledano clan was identification enough.

Unlike the Moslem cemetery, which is a well-watered oasis with a warm smell of rich soil and succulent vegetation, the Jewish cemetery stands on stony ground. Tombstones tilt in all directions in the tall dry grass that grows around them. I had no memory of having ever visited this place before, but I must have come here at least once, when my grandfather died. As for my mother, I had not been allowed to attend her funeral. No doubt the grown-ups thought it would be too upsetting. At any rate, I cannot recall that day. Nor where I spent it. By the first anniversary of my mother's death, my father and I were living abroad. From Vanna I also knew that it was my mother's sisters and Joseph, their brother, back on a visit from Israel, who erected her tombstone after the ritual twelve months had passed. On that first anniversary, I don't remember my father and I speaking about my mother let alone commemorating her passing. Both of us remained locked in our own sadness and grief.

I had to search for my mother's grave. The first tombstone I came to with a name I recognised was that of my grandfather's younger brother, Abramo, who had enlisted in the British Army during the First World War and been killed in France. It took me several seconds to decipher the Hebrew inscription on his tomb and to work out from the dates of the Jewish calendar etched on it that he had died in 1917, at the age of nineteen.

I could no longer hear the sound of traffic on the other side of the cemetery wall, but my ears were buzzing as finally I stood looking down on my mother's grave, nestled between her mother's and father's graves. Whereas her parents' tombs are huge, with tall obelisks, hers is as small as a child's. I quickly pushed aside the thought that the size of grave was a reflection of the very little that had been left of my mother's body after the letter-bomb had exploded in her hands. You-Tube images of body parts scattered in the rubble on a street in Baghdad came into my mind.

Bending down, I picked up a smooth, white stone. It was a reflex action, dredged up from somewhere deep in my memory. For only at that moment did I remember that when Jews visit a grave they do not place flowers on it but rather set down a stone. Some people say that stones not only mark a visit to a graveside, but are also the means by which the living keep the dead from haunting them. Other people see stones as a symbol of the permanence of memory, compared to the transience of fresh flowers. Both explanations seemed valid to me as I placed my stone on my mother's grave and, speaking out loud, asked her to forgive my father and me for abandoning her here, for this is what we had done by failing to pause occasionally to remember her together. From around her grave I tore out a few tenacious weeds, but I was glad of this small struggle with nature which diverted my attention from the pain in my chest and helped me hold back the tears.

As I left, the shadow of the minaret glided over the corner where my mother lies. In my light winter coat, I shivered. As I trudged back to the bus stop, cars spewing fumes whizzed past me, drivers tooting their horns when I drifted on to the roadway. Only after hailing a passing taxi and asking the driver to take me to St Julians did I realise I'd forgotten to collect my wedding ring.

I called Ellie and left a message. 'This is Claire. Sorry to get your voicemail, but I thought I'd let you know that Vanna hasn't done a disappearing act yet.'

৽৵

Over the last few years, I've often heard friends talk about the decline of a mother or a father, or both parents, and considered myself fortunate to have been spared that worry. My mother was thirty-seven when she was killed. My father died relatively young too, aged fifty-seven.

I know I was only a child at the time, but why did no one ask if I wanted to go to my mother's funeral? Since the visit to her grave last Friday, I've felt surprisingly energised. When Vanna first asked me to go through our aunts' papers, I thought it would be straightforward. What I feel now is that I'm being initiated into something that at last brings me inside the fold of ordinary human experience: settling the affairs of the dead. As I sift through old letters, photographs, receipts and certificates, I build a picture of my grandparents' and aunts' lives. It feels as if I'm breaking through the misery and inertia, which have paralysed me over the last eighteen months. There are dozens of postcards that date back to my grandparents' days, and to the days before I was born, when my father and mother had travelled all over Europe. It's painful to read my mother's short but always jokey messages on the cards and to see how happy she had been. But it's a pain I should never have been spared.

I am not sure whose solution is the right one, Vanna's or Ellie's, but now I feel less squeezed between their certainties, less paralysed. All three of us have been behaving badly. I've tried to appear impartial, which is, I know, an excuse for not acting. My cousins have been fighting a tug-of-war, ignoring the wishes of our aunts, and ignoring that each has a will of her own. Luisa's dressing gown is filthy and reeks, but she's determined not to part with it. You have to hand it to her. Despite her confusion, she stubbornly refuses to be told what she should wear. When she zips her mouth shut and refuses to eat or drink, I'm no longer sure we should force her. As for Marguerita, why should we treat her as if she doesn't know what she's doing when she banishes us from her sight? The three of us have forgotten that our aunts were once professional women. We've stuck the label 'old' on them and erased their personalities.

221

Going through the half dozen savings-account books and the pile of statements from banks in Scotland, Switzerland and the Channel Islands, I have totted up the equivalent of almost four hundred thousand pounds. Back at the Phoenicia, I go on line and print out withdrawal forms. These will have to be filled in and signed by our aunts. With twenty minutes still left of my session on the Internet, I turn to the Times of Malta website. On the front page, there's an article about a sea rescue of African refugees. The poor sods had set out from the Libyan coast in a small boat and, though their traffickers had apparently given them a compass, none of them had known what the instrument was for. Clicking to another page, my eyes are drawn to a short article about an altercation on Palace Square. A photograph of a more youthful woman than my attacker appears at the bottom of the column, but I nonetheless recognise the face. 'Bingo,' I say out loud, making the businessman at the computer next to mine look up for a moment.

'Barbara Galea, aged fifty-four, was held for four hours in police custody but has now been released on bail. Her case is due to go before the court in early April.'

So now I know the woman's name, though I still do not know why she called my father a murderer, for I'm assuming Ellie was right and I was the intended target. It's in the Monday edition of the Times that I come across an insert with a black border.

'Thirty years ago today, detectives from Scotland Yard arrived in Malta to continue the investigation into the death of Sarita Sacerdote, M.Sc., née Toledano. Since the Maltese Police have given up all hope of finding the people responsible for the letter-bomb which killed the pharmacist and young mother, it is hoped the English police will be able to solve the case.'

I read and re-read, hoping to extract more information from these four and a half lines. But that's all there is. The backdated issues of the newspaper do not stretch back to the 1970s. I'll have to look at the microfilms in the library.

❦

The duty librarian is officious, correcting my mistakes without smiling when I try to speak to him in the shreds of my Maltese, a language I have rarely spoken since leaving the island. I have, however, made up my mind to ignore his scowls and grunts each time I ask him for another batch of microfilms. I'm on a mission and am not going to be embarrassed by my mistakes. My eyes sting and my back aches. I've been in the library four hours today and my search has taken me to newspapers dating back to 1956, during Mintoff's first term of office. This was the year he made his initial proposal to nationalise the island's medical service. Confronted with fierce opposition from Malta's medical profession, he had already threatened to recruit doctors from abroad.

Over the weeks and months, the papers give a blow-by-blow account of the conflict between the doctors and Dom Mintoff. I skim through the headlines: Maltese Students Demonstrate In London, Medical Students Chained To Railings, Pay Cuts For Doctors, Health Minister Grants Licences to Libyan Doctors, Licences Granted To Polish Doctors, Maltese Doctors Suspended,

Blue Sisters Expelled From Island, Doctor Refuses To Treat Sick Dockyard Worker, Lock-out At Saint Luke's.

In an issue dated 4 June 1977, I come across my father's name. I'm surprised to see just how prominent he had been in the campaign against those reforms. I read on. When the Medical Association of Malta set up campaign headquarters at the Astra Hotel in Sliema, journalists sought my father's views. In an article dated 14 June, my father is quoted as saying, 'We are living under a dictatorship.' He had a thin voice but could sound authoritative. 'Only a dictatorship would ban doctors from taking their orders from their own professional body. Under this new arrangement, we're supposed to defer to civil servants, which is an outrage and an infringement of our human rights and liberties.'

The photograph accompanying the article shows my father wearing one of his elegant, made-to-measure suits, but his neck looks scrawny and his face is haggard. 'We will win this battle.' He was adamant. 'You'll see. The whole world will see.'

Soon after my father's call to defiance, however, the government tabled another Parliamentary Bill aimed at bypassing the Medical Association of Malta completely. Mintoff, I read on the microfilm, had been working up to this piece of legislation since the 1950s. All through his years in the political wilderness, his obsession had not weakened. He would bring to heel the middle classes as represented by the island's medical profession. Now under a new law it would be the Ministry of Health, not the medical association, that would issue licences to foreign doctors, and all local doctors who wished to continue

224

working in private hospitals would also have to be authorised by the Ministry.

For the next few days my father's photograph appeared in every edition of the paper, either alone or alongside leading members of the medical association. Malta is a small island. Everybody knows everybody else's business. The government continued to vilify the profession, depicting the doctors as arch enemies of the poor.

The atmosphere at home became more tense and volatile. My parents quarrelled more fiercely. At my grandmother's, the adults were constantly at each other's throats. My father and Nonna Rosa, both great opponents of Mintoff, stopped talking to Uncle Joseph, who had continued to work. My Russian lessons were stepped up. Instead of once a week, I now went to Miss Sokolova's three times. People think it's funny when I tell them I started learning Russian because one day my grandmother had a brainwave during a family dinner. They're surprised when I explain that many Maltese, not just my grandmother, felt that the island was about to be invaded.

By the end of 1977, my mother finally gave in to my father and agreed to leave Malta. Immediately, my father relaxed. He reassured her she hadn't made a mistake; she would be able to continue as a pharmacist if we settled in England or Canada or Australia. We would leave very soon. But it was not soon enough. If we had left within the next couple of weeks, my mother might still be alive today.

It is hard to imagine her old. Would she have resembled her sisters? Would she, like them, have ended up suspicious and angry? When I began going through my aunts' papers, I came across a snapshot of my mother I had not seen before. She is standing in the back court-yard of her parents' house, holding me up high like a sports trophy to face the photographer, probably my father. I must have been about eighteen months, and it was wintertime, for I am bundled up in a thick jacket and knitted cagoule. On the back, in fading ink, I read: 'Dr Shackleton, I presume!'

I recognised my mother's handwriting from the scribbled notes I had seen in her Maltese Grammar. My mother had a sense of humour. This was a new dimen-sion. She had not always been the martyr to the doctors' cause after all. It had been what her early and violent death had done to her.

The library is about to close, but I scroll quickly through the next few pages of The Times. In 1977, a Martian landing on the island might have thought that Malta was on the brink of civil war.

'Doctor's strike claims its first victim.' I stop scroll-ing. The caption below the photograph of the victim reads, 'Carmela Galea, aged 20', and the story begins, 'Yesterday, the bitter struggle between the government and the MAM ratcheted up several notches with the death of Carmela Galea, aged 20. Miss Galea, who lived with her parents and brothers and sisters in San Ġwann, bled to death in her own home because her family was unable to summon a doctor to her bedside.'

It takes me just seconds to place the name and face. Carmela Galea used to clean my aunts' pharmacy twice a week. Shooing us all out early on Wednesday and Friday evenings, she would wash the floors and polish the brass fittings on the counter and shelves. On her knees, she scrubbed the front doorstep and sloshed the dirty water across the pavement. I vividly recall the smell of bleach as the water evaporated in the lingering heat of a Maltese summer evening. Carmela was a big-boned girl, not unlike those heroines one sees in 1930s Soviet posters extolling the New Woman. Uncle Clementino, Ellie's father, used to describe her as sexy, which always brought a howl of protests from the women in the family. Nonetheless, it was true. Men seemed to be attracted to Carmela. Sometimes, I would see her on the seafront, leaning on a railing, one foot resting on the lower rung, her skirt sliding up her leg to reveal a strong, well-sculpted thigh. There were always men buzzing around her. Another time, on board a bus, I caught sight of her standing on the kerb. Before the bus pulled out, I saw her bending down slowly to pick up a paper bag that she had dropped on the pavement. As she straightened herself, her thick glossy hair, which had been caught up in a giant clip on top of her head, came tumbling down over her shoulders. Out of nowhere, half a dozen young men appeared as she raised her arm to push her hair back up on top of her head. At that moment I understood what Uncle Clementino had comprehended as 'sexy'.

The librarian, who has cleared the tables, is slamming drawers shut. Fifteen minutes left before closing time and I'm now on the fourth page of a Saturday edition of The Times. And there it is, a short article about a certain Tony Galea of San Ġwann. He had been arrested for causing an affray at my aunts' pharmacy.

'Miss Marguerita Toledano, Miss Luisa Toledano and Mrs Sara Sacerdote née Toledano called the police after Mr Galea had appeared at their pharmacy threatening them and refusing to leave when instructed. He demanded to see Dr Alberto Sacerdote, the husband of Mrs Sara Sacerdote, but the doctor was unavailable. Before the terrified pharmacists, Mr Galea smashed the glass front of a cabinet in which prescription medicines were stored, sustaining cuts to his hand. The pharmacists have, however, declined to press charges.'

In the silence of the library, I am aware of the cold penetrating the soles of my fleece-lined boots.

Vanna

10 Flight

Claire's skin was always pale, but now it looks to Vanna as if someone has dipped a brush in ash and painted her all over. She hasn't removed her jacket and is wearing boots. Nonetheless she is hunched up from the cold, and the veins in her hands are mauve–blue. In winter, sunlight does not reach this part of the house until after midday and then it is too brief to warm up the room. The smell of chemicals is at its most pungent here, but Claire is so absorbed in her newspaper cuttings that for once she seems able to block out her surroundings. Still, what is the point of her wasting time sifting through the ashes of her dead mother? The whole thing happened such a long time ago. Though she keeps pressing her, there's nothing more Vanna can tell her.

'You know' – Vanna comes up quietly behind her and leans the broom against the wall – 'I find the only way to get warm is to relax your muscles.' She would like to place her hands, red and rubbery from washing clothes in cold water, on Claire's shoulder, but she is afraid her touch will not be welcome.

Suddenly, she feels tired, with a fatigue that penetrates right to her bone marrow. Surprising, she thinks, how low-level rage eats up more energy than happiness. The warfare with her cousins has not only drained her but reduced them all to childish recriminations. One fragmented set of memories is pitched against another. Old rivalries seep to the surface. Who suffered most? Who was loved most? Not to mention who once loved and still loves the most? They can't agree about past events let alone about the future. Vanna still believes she feels the fragmentation of the family more deeply than her cousins, but perhaps it is time to make peace with Claire even if she can't do so with Ellie.

'The blood doesn't circulate properly when you tense up,' she says, trying to sound as warm and gentle as she can. 'That's what my mother told me. We were living in a tiny, damp flat in Rehovot just after we arrived in Israel. I was so miserable.'

Ellie said pity was a passive, hateful emotion, but though it might sound odd to others Vanna feels great pity for the unhappy girl she once was. When she thinks of Claire as a motherless orphan, she pities her too.

'I don't know how you can bear to crush cockroaches even when they're dead.' Claire doesn't turn to face Vanna and speaks *au bout de lèvres* – prissily – just as Vanna's mother used to say. It's not that Vanna doesn't understand perfectly that irony can be a strategy for keeping others at arm's length, but in her experience people get caught in a whirlpool when they respond to sarcasm with more sarcasm. All Claire has to do right now is turn round and smile and Vanna will forgive her glib remark. But Claire keeps her gaze steadily on her papers and so the moment is lost.

Ellie was right about pity after all. From now on, Vanna's resolve will not weaken. She will not allow herself to forget for a single moment that Claire is here to keep a close eye on her while Ellie charges around Malta. Claire's pretext is so transparent: she is here to help sort out the family papers, but she brings along photocopies and printouts of ancient newspaper articles and spends most of her time sifting through them. She does nothing else that could be described as real help.

Vanna has seen her delicate nostrils quiver as she sponges down Luisa. No question of her getting her hands dirty. 'Once you've changed thousands of nappies, nothing puts you off,' Vanna said to Claire and, no, she doesn't care if it made her wince. She won't take it back. When Luisa reaches out and grabs her hand, does Claire imagine that she doesn't notice her prising her hand free, as if Luisa had leprosy? You should have seen her when she was cutting Luisa's toenails. Doesn't she imagine she will grow old eventually and need someone to clip her hardened toenails too?

As for Ellie, she can believe as much as she likes that she'll manage to get a work permit for that Somali woman who is her little protégée in one of the detention centres. Her other newly discovered 'best' friend, Rosemary Vassallo, collects her each morning, and they trundle from one government office to another trying to get the necessary residency papers, after which Rosemary delivers her back in the evening. By the time that permit comes through, Vanna will be gone with Luisa, and she will come back and collect Marguerita soon afterwards. You may be able to pay poor asylum-seekers and refugees to clip toenails, dress suppurating bedsores, rub lotion into flaking skin and wipe an invalid's bottom, but strangers do not perform these acts for love.

'You're not still at it, *hanini*?' Ellie appears in the archway between the sitting and dining rooms. She has been out jogging, and her face is shiny with sweat. 'Isn't it a bit late to be sweeping up roaches?' For a moment, Claire looks up and exchanges one of those knowing smiles with Ellie. To Vanna, the two of them look much older than their true ages, but that's what happens when there's no flesh on a body. 'Has Claire spoken to you about the drama on Palace Square?' Ellie bends down to untie the laces of her trainers, which Vanna has many times offered to scrub for her. So what the hell, let her insist she likes those shoes the way they are – stained with red Aussie dust and looking as if a dog had chewed them for breakfast. 'She was really shaken by that woman, you know.' As she removes her socks, Ellie speaks in a near whisper so that Claire can't hear, but she needn't worry because Claire's nose is firmly stuck in the newspaper articles she has spread out all over the desk, coffee table and armchairs.

In the kitchen, Ellie picks at the vegetables Vanna has left on the chopping board in readiness for the evening meal.

'I am sorry she is so upset,' Vanna says and deftly moves the board out of reach. 'You don't have to be as fastidious as her to feel disgust when a stranger spits on you.' She picks up a dusting cloth and returns to the dining room. 'The thing I don't understand is how she got mixed up in that demonstration.' She steps in front of Ellie and starts re-arranging the ornaments on the sideboard.

'She'd come with a change of clothes for me.'

'Oh, how thoughtful, is this a sign of change?' Vanna raises her voice and ignores Ellie's flapping hands. 'To think that I was imagining she came back to Malta to pamper herself in a five-star hotel.'

'Moo.' Ellie bites into the skin of an orange she has taken out of the fruit bowl on the sideboard and starts peeling it. Vanna clenches her jaws. If she opened her mouth, she would let fly at Ellie about the way she thinks it's okay to deposit orange peel on the dining table. One day when Vanna had been on a London bus with Ephraim, she'd overheard a standing passenger say in Hebrew, 'When this fat cow gets up, there will be room for two of us,' which just goes to show that you should never take it for granted that no one within earshot will understand. The world has become too small for that. At Oxford Circus, she and Ephraim had to fight their way out of the crowded bus. 'Moo,' Vanna said, stepping deliberately on the feet of the woman who'd insulted her. She remembers how good revenge felt, but now she shrugs her shoulders and disappears into the pantry where she rummages for a rubbish bag. Ellie can moo as much as she likes. Sticks and stones!

'Anyway, why is Claire pestering me more than she's pestering you?' Vanna re-emerges. 'I won't stand for her accusing my father of being a strike-breaker. The other doctors didn't give a damn.'

'You can't blame her for wanting to know what really happened. I'm curious too.'

It makes Vanna smile how quickly Ellie and Claire have become fist in glove, just as they were as children. Vanna always felt like the spare rubber tyre. One of her worst memories of her cousins' complicity has to do with Henry VIII and the dissolution of the monasteries. She had been absent from school for two weeks with flu. There was homework to do, but it had slipped Claire's mind and now she only had one day left to finish the assignment. Ellie stepped in to help and ended up getting Vanna into hot water.

'Well, of course you'd expect them to say Henry VIII was a monster, not the Pope,' Ellie said, throwing her arms in the air. 'Actually, the one was as bad as the other. In history, you'll find very few people with purity of purpose, which doesn't mean that we should give up on mankind.' Can you imagine? Already as a twelve-year-old she spoke like that. God knows where she got that kind of stuff, but she was always memorising famous lines. Clementino dubbed them her 'party pieces' and Ellie glowed in the warmth of his praise. 'My genius little monkey,' he used to call her. What surprises Vanna is that, despite all the bad things that have happened to her, Ellie retains a belief in the enduring goodness of human nature. In principle, of course, such faith is attractive, but Vanna finds it exhausting being around idealists. On the other hand, she no longer holds it against Ellie for sabotaging her homework. People can become so bogged down in childish resentments that they turn their hurt into an excuse for bad behaviour. Vanna has no intention of falling into that trap.

Soon, anyway, she will be gone far away. She has worked it all out carefully, step by step. It helps that

Ellie is convinced she's booked on a flight via Larnaca – whereas she is returning to Israel via Frankfurt – and that their aunties' passports have expired. Ellie has dropped her guard and thinks it's safe to stay out all day running around like a headless chicken. It's helpful, too, that Claire keeps disappearing for two or three hours to go to the library in Valletta. What Vanna's clever cousins don't know is that before they got to Malta she had arranged for new passports for Luisa and Marguerita, and she will be going in the next couple of days to collect them.

Mind you, Vanna hasn't said anything to Marguerita about this because she's in a constant rage whenever she visits her. Claire and Ellie don't see that side of her.

'She isn't abusive with you because she doesn't know you so well,' Vanna tells them. 'She's only on her best behaviour because you are strangers to her.' They don't hear her declaring that she will never leave Malta and the next day that she is over-the-moon to be leaving. Who can say what mood she will be in tomorrow, let alone next week or next month? One thing is for sure, she will not stay here once Luisa is safe in Jerusalem among the people who truly love her.

'Actually, I take some of the blame.' Vanna scoops up the orange peel from the table.

'Blame, for what?' Ellie pulls out a chair. 'Come on, sit down a moment. Stop fussing and give me the peel.'

'Claire wouldn't be raking over those old newspapers if I hadn't convinced her to come back to Malta. But if the detectives from Scotland Yard were not able to solve the crime, it's ridiculous to believe she should be able to solve it herself more than thirty-five years later.'

Since Ellie's arrival, these are the first calm words Vanna has spoken to her. Perhaps it's time to call a truce. After all, she thinks, they are two happily married women with children. Claire is the odd one out.

'Oh shit!' Ellie thrashes the air. A flying cockroach has skimmed past her face.

For a moment it disappears and then Vanna spots it high on the wall above the sideboard. 'Leave it to me.' Removing her apron, she advances towards the giant roach as it scurries towards the brass chanoukia. 'Take that!' She slaps the apron so hard against the wall that the chanoukia crashes to the floor.

Claire springs up from her chair. 'What happened?' She appears on the threshold of the dining room.

Ellie rolls her eyes and says nothing, but if she thinks Vanna hasn't noticed her exchanging conspiratorial glances with Claire, she is mistaken.

'Here, give it to me.' Vanna grabs the fallen chanoukia out of Ellie's hand. 'It'll take more than a wipe with your tee-shirt to make it shiny again. I've been meaning to take it down and give it a good polish.'

∽◦∾

All along it has been Vanna's intention to take the chanoukia with her when she leaves for Israel. No one will notice, least of all her cousins who do not care about the family's history on the island. There is very little in this house that she can remove, after all. The furniture was made for villas with huge rooms and very high ceilings – impossible to find in Israel. The crockery is mostly chipped, the silverware too cumbersome and old-fashioned. There is some fine linen with hand-embroidered monograms, but who has the time to iron bed-sheets, pillowcases and hand-towels?

Sometimes Vanna plays a game in her head, imagining a knock on the door at two o'clock in the morning. If she should be thrown out of her home with only one small suitcase, what would she take? When Vanna and her parents left Malta, they had only two bags between three people for their new life. It is a good lesson in finding out what matters to you, she thinks. When Uncle Alberto left with Claire, you should have seen the amount of luggage, though Claire denies it. Her story is that they left with hardly any possessions and that's probably because she imagines she has a monopoly on heartbreak. People have to outdo you in everything, even in suffering. By rights, in any case, the chanoukia belongs to her since it was a present from her mother's mother on her only visit to Malta when everyone was so cruel to her.

Mémé Claudette. Vanna is not ashamed to admit that her mother's mother was illiterate. She had many good qualities to make up for her lack of formal education and, anyway, as the eldest of thirteen children, how could she have had a chance to finish school? Nonna Rosa thought herself so clever, so above everyone else, especially Vanna's mother and her Moroccan family. She was always going on about helping her father annotate Dante's *Divina Commedia* when she was young. She'd left school at fourteen, hadn't she? Uncle Clementino used to joke her father only put her in charge of the index cards to make her feel she was the centre of the world.

The problem was Nonna Rosa went on thinking she was the centre of the world for the rest of her life.

It was through Nonna Rosa's first cousin Livia Bensoussan née Coen, originally from Rome, that the Toledanos learned of Vanna's mother's family, the Haddids of Tangiers. Livia had married a certain Henri Bensoussan who was an old friend of the Haddids … Since there were no eligible Jewish girls on the island, it was not surprising that Nonna Rosa was petrified that some Catholic girl would get her fangs into her other son. Miriam had one great asset, she was Jewish, which is why Rosa overlooked her paltry dowry.

Vanna remembers Cousin Livia very well – the piece of flesh that wobbled under her chin, the watery eyes that slanted at the outer edges and the rings on every short, fat finger. Cousin Livia was always telling salty jokes and laughing at them herself while slapping you on the back, even if you didn't get them which, being a child, Vanna hardly ever did. Livia used to come to Malta every two years and lord it over everyone because her husband was so rich. Money meant that no one laughed behind her back when she called magazines books, or looked down their noses because she only read scandal stories in Gente. Each week, she bought the Settimana Enigmistica, but she couldn't do even the easiest crosswords.

She brought her only daughter, the apple of her red-rimmed eyes, to Malta, just once. Edith Bensoussan was studying at the Conservatoire in Paris to be an opera singer and she went around the house in St Julians singing arias all the time. It was embarrassing the way she would stand at the top of the stairs and make the stairwell echo. Too much vibrato, Nonna Rosa sniped whenever Edith did her Tosca act. Just like Callas, she would add, but Vanna thinks that was only to get up Uncle Clementino's nose because he was such a fan of Callas and her vibrato.

There is something else Vanna remembers about Cousin Livia. It's a story that doesn't put Sarita in such a glowing light. Vanna was sitting in the niche under the spiral staircase one afternoon when she overheard her auntie and Livia whispering on the landing upstairs.

'Can you imagine this?' Livia said. 'Miriam's grandparents don't speak a word of French, only Arabic. Worse, it was rumoured that they were once so poor they couldn't afford underpants for their children. You know something? I once saw one of Miriam's aunts lift her skirt and squat in a lane in the souks to pee.'

Vanna never discovered which of her grandmother's seven sisters Livia was referring to and she admits this will sound cold and callous, but for a while she couldn't get out of her head the image of that squatting great auntie, and it made her unkind to her grandmother Claudette too, dodging her kisses and hugs whenever she could.

'You should have seen Miriam's mother coming off the boat,' Sarita went on. 'She looked just like a *caffone*, a Sicilian peasant, what with all those big wicker baskets filled with food.'

'Just what Vanna needs, sweets to make her even fatter,' Nonna Rosa scoffed as she emptied the enormous plastic bag of home-made makrouds and dates stuffed with marzipan into the rubbish bin the moment the Moroccan grandmother had left the house.

No wonder Vanna's mother vowed never to return to Malta, not even to fulfil her husband's dearest wish to be buried on the island. Vanna had had to travel alone to bring back his body so that he could be laid to rest beside his mother and father and Auntie Sarita. When Vanna's father was alive, it was a source of great bitterness between her parents that he repeatedly said he didn't want to be buried in the Land of Israel just as her mother had said she didn't want to be buried in Malta. Vanna had countless times heard her parents arguing about it. And de *fil en aiguille* – inevitably –their arguments would lead back to her mother's belief that the Toledanos couldn't stand her to be alive when their favourite daughter and sister Sarita had died.

It is true that Vanna's father did sometimes toy with the thought that Sarita had not been the intended target of the letter-bomb. Vanna could tell he was turning that idea over in his head each time he had three or four glasses of wine and then fell silent. He and her mother would then start speaking to each other between gritted teeth thinking she could not hear them. Could the bomb have been meant for him? There was the matter of that operation in which that girl had died. Could her family have been out to take revenge? Vanna's mother was right about one thing. Malta was not a place for them especially after what had happened to Sarita.

༄

Vanna's stomach has been in knots from the moment she woke up before dawn and couldn't get back to sleep again. Her tongue feels fur-lined and her eyes are as red as if she's got conjunctivitis, but she's made it to the airport. Hard to believe how easy it was and that within forty-five minutes she'll be boarding the plane with Luisa. As she told Ephraim last night, for the last few days Ellie has been totally caught up with the story of immigrants setting fire to their detention centre. She just can't help sticking her nose in the business of strangers. Perhaps she thinks Vanna has given up listening to her telephone conversations with her husband in Australia who is begging for her to come home in case she should be thrown off Malta again, which apparently happened on her last visit. Ellie is living in Cloud Cuckoo Land, however, if she imagines she can set up an unknown woman and a child in their aunties' house.

Luisa is calm, thank goodness for that. The anti-histamines that she gave her last night and again this morning have not worn off and probably won't wear off for another few hours. Vanna keeps her fingers crossed she will not panic once they are mid-air. Thank goodness the airline people are well prepared. When she phoned them to explain that she was travelling with an elderly auntie, they reassured her that the airport security staff would be ready. Check-in, amazingly, only took ten minutes.

A couple of days ago, when Vanna went to Valletta to collect Luisa and Marguerita's passports, she also bought Luisa a brand new dressing gown. She says blithely that she bought a 'new' dressing gown, but at the end of the season she had to search high and low for something that was cheap and attractive. The new gown is a pretty dusty pink, which can almost pass as a light overcoat. Just the other day, when Vanna was secretly packing, she found a couple of berets at the bottom of Luisa's wardrobe and a beret now covers her aunt's hair which badly needs washing and cutting. Vanna will see to it once they are in Israel. When Vanna and her cousins were children, other women wore hats, but Luisa always preferred berets, which she wore tilted on her head as if she were Juliette Greco. It was the tilt that irritated Nonna Rosa, and, though Luisa was a grown woman and a professional, whenever she went to work wearing a beret, her mother would re-adjust it so that it sat like a tea cosy rather than as something an apache dancer might wear. Nonna Rosa would also tug at her skirt, telling her that it was too short, but then she was always tugging at everyone's skirts.

Vanna had a little scare a couple of nights ago when Claire went into the *garagor* after she had been to the toilet. The flush often gets jammed, and Vanna is usually the one who has to adjust the flushing mechanism. Of all evenings, Claire decided that she would have a go at adjusting the cistern herself. Vanna couldn't help wondering whether that was another sign she was emerging from the torpor which had prevented her from coming sooner to Malta. But if Claire saw the suitcases in the alcove under the staircase she obviously didn't realise they were packed and so her suspicions were not aroused.

Vanna did get slightly nervous, however, when in the middle of supper Claire started talking about Carmela Galea.

'The two of you must remember her,' she said. 'She used to clean the pharmacy twice a week. I've worked out that she was the younger sister of the woman who spat on me on Palace Square.'

The air around them hummed. Ellie set down her fork and leaned back in her chair. As Vanna slowed down her chewing, her gaze alighted on Claire's hands. How square the fingernails were, how like her own, and how like Ellie's. With their palms flat on the table, it was noticeable how far their thumbs curved backwards in exactly the same way.

'I only vaguely remember Carmela,' she said, breaking the silence. 'Funny how each of us recalls such different things. Here's something, for instance, that I remember very well. When their mother was ill, Ellie and her brother used to stay at my house. No, Ellie, don't look at me like that. It's absolutely true.'

'And you're never going to forget my mother's bouts of depression.' Suddenly, Ellie seemed deflated. It was not what Vanna expected. She had only brought up the matter because Claire's words had triggered the memory of how she shared her room with Ellie and Danny and her bed with Ellie, which was always so uncomfortable. Even in her sleep Ellie would throw off the blankets because she felt so hot. What's more, she tossed and turned all night long and never gave Vanna any peace. Danny was the lucky one because he always got the truckle bed that was normally kept under Vanna's bed and he, needless to say, slept like a top.

'Well, at least we agree about one thing,' Ellie said as she got up from the table and began to pace around the room.

'Things get so mixed up in my head,' Vanna said, looking to Claire for support. 'All this business with Carmela Galea's sister spitting on you reminds me how patients often came knocking on my father's door in the middle of the night. When he refused to make a house call, they insulted him. I can't be one hundred per cent sure that I haven't rolled a number of separate incidents into one, but I think I'm right in saying that during the week leading up to Auntie Sarita's death Ellie and Danny were staying overnight at our place. We were all woken up by a knocking on the front door. Another patient looking for a doctor, that was my first thought. With every day the strike lasted, emergencies became more common, too much for my father to handle on his own. Sometimes he had to turn people away.'

ಲಿ

Sitting up in bed, the two girls strained to hear what was being said out on the front parapet. The moonlight was streaming in through the slatted shutters on the French windows, Vanna remembered. She and Ellie had had to step over the truckle bed where Danny was still asleep and pad barefoot out of the bedroom and onto the landing.

'Shush, stop breathing so loud,' Ellie hissed at Vanna.

From the landing there was an unobstructed view to the front door. The lights in the entrance hall, the sitting room and the kitchen were on full. Luisa was downstairs, which was surprising, and she was talking excitedly so that Vanna's father had to keep asking her to keep her voice down or she would wake up the whole house. They could hear another man's voice.

'I think that's my father,' Ellie said. 'What's he doing here in the middle of the night? Oh God, it must be my mother.'

Vanna doesn't remember how she managed to stop Ellie from running downstairs. But she does recall hearing her mother clattering about in the kitchen and then appearing in the downstairs hallway. She has a very clear picture in her mind of looking down on the top of her mother's head as she passed the bottom of the staircase unscrewing one of those Italian *cafetiere*. There was a small, pink bald patch already at the top of her scalp even then. It wasn't for religious reasons that she started wearing a wig in Rehovot, but because by then she had lost all her hair.

'Vanna, Ellie, please go back to bed,' she said without glancing up.

Back in Vanna's room, the two girls watched from the front balcony as Vanna's father and Luisa hurried down the street with Clementino. Vanna had seen her father racing out so many other times in the middle of the night on emergency calls to patients. He always dressed in a hurry and his shirt was never tucked properly into his trousers, but he was untidy, and it wasn't unusual for him not to have tucked his shirt in completely. He always had his beautiful battered leather medicine bag with him, which had been a gift her mother had brought him back from Morocco on one of her trips home. When Miriam died, Vanna found it at the back of a cupboard.

'That's all I remember about the lead-up to your mother's death, Claire,' Vanna said as she heaved herself up from the table. 'I couldn't squeeze out a single more memory, not even to save my life.'

❧

'Come on Luisa,' Vanna pushes the wheelchair to the other side of the check-in hall. The airline representative has told her to sit by the car rental counters for a moment. They are going to come and collect her and Luisa once the call has been made to board the plane to Frankfurt and then they will take Luisa straight through in the wheelchair as soon as everyone else has boarded. All those security checks, Vanna thinks. She remembers the days when friends and family could accompany you to the steps of the aircraft. The thing is not to risk Luisa getting in a panic by boarding her too early, which would disturb other passengers. She seems to be perking up, which might be good or bad. When little children pass by, she reaches out to touch them. She'll love my children, Vanna thinks, I know she will, and they will love her. Thank God she brought along the last of the home-made macaroons. She checks and re-checks that the passports and the boarding passes are in her handbag. That's the trouble when you have a black lining in a deep bag. It's hard to find the things you need. Claire gave her this stupid expensive bag as a present when she arrived in Malta, but the pocket for documents is impossibly shallow. Already Vanna has managed to lose an expensive biro, which must have fallen out when she and Luisa were in the taxi and she was rummaging for money to pay the driver.

'Please could you keep an eye on my auntie?' she asks the nice young man at the car rental counter next to which she has parked Luisa's wheelchair. 'The airline official said she would come and collect us in twenty minutes' time. I won't be gone more than a couple of minutes. I'm just going to the ladies.' She turns back to Luisa and pats her forearm.

'Who are you?' Luisa asks her for the umpteenth time this morning. There is a coin of spittle in the corner of her lips, which Vanna wipes with her clean handkerchief. 'Do I know you?' Luisa looks dazed as Vanna carefully adjusts the beret on her head, trying to tilt it in the way she used to like so much. How tiny she is, how shrunken, she thinks. Even a light touch can bruise her skin. Vanna is now one hundred per cent sure that had she agreed to leave Luisa in the hands of strangers she would shrivel to nothing in no time.

'Auntie, I'm Vanna. You know me, of course you do. I'm just going to the ladies'. This kind gentleman will look after you.'

'Who is he? Do I know him? And do I know you?' Luisa rubs her eyes then clutches the sides of her head. '*Madoffi*, I used to be so clever once, and now I have become so stupid.' She has said this many times before, but it remains unbearable to Vanna. Where the hell is the woman from the airline? She's got to take them to the gate before Luisa starts fussing and getting well and truly stressed. 'Why am I wearing this coat?' Luisa plucks the front of the new dressing gown and then starts unbuttoning the top button.

'No, don't, you'll be cold if you take it off.' Vanna gently lowers her hands.

'Who are you? I don't know you,' Luisa says as she grabs hold of Vanna's wrists.

'Please, Auntie. I won't be gone long.' Vanna frees her wrists and bends down to button up and smooth down the dressing gown.

It's when she comes out of the ladies' that she sees them. Ellie and Claire are standing at the door scanning the check-in hall. Ellie spots her first. She advances with her arms flailing while Claire runs behind her like she was her pet spaniel.

'You didn't bloody well think we'd let you get away with this?' Ellie says and grabs the handles of the wheelchair.

'Let go,' Vanna says and shoves her aside. 'Come on, Luisa, we're going through to the gate now.'

'You're doing no such bloody thing.' Ellie spreads her arms wide and tries to bar the way.

'Who are you?' Luisa retracts her neck into her shoulders as if Ellie is about to strike her.

'Luisa, it's me, Ellie, Eleonora. You know who I am, of course you do. I'm Clementino's daughter.' Ellie rests her hands on the arms of the wheelchair, her body looming over Luisa's tiny frame. 'Tell Vanna that you wish to stay here in Malta.'

'Are we going somewhere? I don't understand.' Luisa's eyes dart from Ellie to Vanna and from Vanna to Claire and back again. 'Who are you?' She leans forward and grabs Claire's hand. 'I know you. You're Sarita, aren't you? You're my baby sister. Who are these two women? Do you know them?'

'Luisa, *hanini*,' Vanna breaks in, 'Sarita is dead. This isn't Sarita. It's her daughter, Claire. You remember Claire, don't you? She and her father left Malta and never came back. Not like me and my father. We came back every summer. You must remember.'

Vanna can see tears welling up in Claire's eyes.

'She's right, Luisa, I'm Claire.' She strokes Luisa's arm.

Ah, Vanna thinks, suddenly Luisa has stopped being a leper.

'I don't know anybody called Claire. Where am I? What are all these people doing here? I want to go home.' Luisa makes a move to get out of the wheelchair, but she's too weak. 'You must take me home before something terrible happens, because something terrible is about to happen, but I can stop it, you know.' She struggles as Claire eases her back into the chair. 'Oh, please, please don't cry. I don't want anybody to cry. I can't stand tears. Tell me, please, what do you want me to do? But first of all make these women go away and take me home. Please.' She leans her cheek towards Claire's arm and rests it there.

Vanna can hardly believe her eyes, but there is Claire crouching down and putting her arms around Luisa. When Luisa's beret slides off, Claire, to Vanna's surprise, strokes her greasy hair.

'She can't board the plane now,' Ellie says triumphantly. 'You can board the plane, but Luisa isn't going with you.'

'Who are you?' Luisa asks her. 'Who are you?' She turns to Vanna again.

'You know me, of course you know me. I'm Vanna.'

'Vanna, oh yes, of course. I know you. I knew your father too. He let that girl die, didn't he?'

Claire

11 The Edge of Ourselves

At two o'clock this morning, I woke up with a jolt. It has always astonished me how the mind ticks over while we sleep. We go to bed with thoughts in a tangle and wake up with minds cleared. Although I'd been certain last night that I would never be able to penetrate the mystery of my mother's murder, now I felt the elation of someone on a journey of discovery and, though I couldn't remember dreaming, this seemed to be a carry-over from a dream. Sitting up in bed, I rolled my head from side to side. Surprisingly, the movement was smooth. Most mornings my hands, curled as I sleep into tight fists, are painful. But today I was able to limber them up without the joints aching. As I stretched my arms and legs, my body felt unfamiliarly weightless and, at the same time, muscular and strong. For the first time in years, I looked forward to the day ahead.

The French have an expression, *être bien dans sa peau*, to be comfortable in one's own skin. Whenever I hear it, I remember how I loved watching Yves pad naked around a room. Last night, he hadn't been in my thoughts at all, but now, on waking, I had a revelation that throughout my marriage I had lived continuously in fear, sometimes paralysing me, sometimes suppressed, but at no time wholly absent. I'd been anxious that Yves would not find me pretty or elegant enough, fearful that I would seem superficial to him, or worse, he would shrug his shoulders and walk away without deigning to reply to me.

Deep down, of course, my past experiences tell me that we cannot hold on to people we love just by being clever and beautiful. Nonetheless, I went on reasoning like the twelve-year-old child who had been unable to keep her mother alive. The itinerant existence of my teenage years had further conditioned me to an expectation of loss as my father and I formed and broke one attachment after another, not just to people but to places. My job as an interpreter may have seemed a logical outcome of our wanderings, but it is also a career with frequent comings and goings. A marriage based on frequent arrivals and departures was wholly in line with all that. In my happiest times, there was always that insistent voice in my head reminding me that nothing lasts.

This morning, however, I saw with visionary clarity that my marriage had lacked passion. This had weighed me down since well before Yves's departure. If he and I had seen each other daily, we might have quarrelled fiercely, but in making up we could have learned that compromises are rewarding. He would have become less peremptory. I might have spoken up for myself without feeling defensive. When he pointed out that I was in the wrong, I might have felt less devastated. In our long-distance phone calls, whenever an argument flared up, I would find an excuse to cut short the conversation. When I was shrill, he would say we would sort things out at the weekend, but we hardly ever did. I realised now that we had never known each other deeply, and I was just as responsible for that as he was. Alienated from my past and thus from myself, how could I live other than alienated from others?

Usually I'm slow to rouse myself out of sleep. First thing in the morning, I assiduously avoid looking into mirrors. But as I ambled past the full-length mirror next to the bathroom door, I glimpsed myself and stopped. In the bluish light of the vestibule lamp, the woman before me had pale skin, which although pocked by cellulite at the top of the arms and legs, was still soft to the touch. The face was too narrow, the brow not high enough, but the hair had a silky sheen. The bare feet were too bony, but the toes and heels were without calluses. As I stared, I began to relax. Removing my T-shirt, I slowly circled my nipples with the tips of my fingers then caressed the curve of my hips. Within seconds the concrete block that had pressed on my chest seemed to lift. After showering, I walked naked around the bedroom. The temperature was a comfortable twenty-three. Seated on the edge of the bed, I languidly massaged lotion into my arms, legs and feet. As I watched my reflection in the dressing-table mirror, I felt none of the hollowness that had dogged me for years. The search for my mother's killers had, over-night, turned me into a woman of action. From now on, I would look to no one to tell me how to act – 'bury the past,' my father had commanded – or how to look – 'you must learn,' Yves had decreed on matters of elegance and style.

Still not dressed, I set about pulling copies of newspaper articles I'd made from my briefcase and setting them out one by one on the floor of my hotel room. Then I re-shuffled them chronologically to form a storyboard. Until a couple of days ago, the sequence of events leading to my mother's death had been a jumble in my head. After my father and I left Malta, we never spoke of the disaster that had turned us into such rootless people. As the years went by, I thought of my mother less and less. Around the anniversary of her death, however, I always experienced a period of free-floating anxiety. At such times a word pronounced a certain way, the tilt of a woman's head, or the smells in a pharmacy could spring my mother back to life and leave me feeling vulnerable.

Stepping cautiously around the articles on the floor, I could see the events more clearly. The continuum was the conflict between Mintoff and the doctors, which had begun in the late 1950s. At the height of the turbulence, the connection between my family and Carmela Galea had also become troubled. Instead of greeting us children in her usual breezy way when we dropped by the pharmacy on cleaning day, she seemed sullen and resentful. Whenever my mother or aunts asked her to take care when moving precious furniture and objects, she would deliberately bang them down. The other day, Ellie reminded me of the time she and I were left to mind the shop for an hour while my mother went to an appointment in Sliema. When Carmela said she didn't feel well, Ellie felt her forehead and said she had a temperature.

Carmela got up and threw up in the doorway. We'd had to close the pharmacy for fifteen minutes. But she was not grateful. On the contrary, she said that it served us all right, which was bewildering. And then, a few days later, her brother, Tony, came to the pharmacy threatening my mother and aunts. The police arrested him after he smashed glass cabinets.

So why did my mother and my aunts ask to have the charges dropped? I thought the answer might be the key to my mother's murder. I would have to press Vanna and Ellie further, though whenever I've tried, both denied knowing any more. What if I were to set out the photocopies in the proper order before them? Perhaps that would jog their memories.

৵৵

Though it felt like hours, by the one working church clock at Balluta, it was only fifteen minutes. We were stuck behind the tailback, and the taxi couldn't overtake – the coast road is too narrow. I rolled the window right down, but that didn't clear the smell of cigarettes coming off the driver's clothes. Trapped between the stuffiness of the cab and the stench of petrol fumes from the backed-up traffic I shoved a couple of notes into the driver's hand and got out. On foot, reaching Lapsi Street would be much quicker. It looked as if it was about to rain, but the smell of iodine from the sea was invigorating.

By the time I reached Spinola, plump raindrops pinged on the pavement. Though I was wearing flat shoes, it was impossible to hurry up the steep slope from the roundabout on the cove to Lapsi Street. Both the narrow footpath and the sealed road were already as slippery as polished marble.

In one of my recurring nightmares, my father, who is in the wings of the stage I'm on, is shouting at me to hurry. Something terrible is about to happen. I must get off the stage and run home. I start to run and, in the nightmare, I am hurtling up this very street. There is Julian's bakery on the bend, and I cannot see past it. Every step forward pushes me further away from Julian's 'Come on, lift your feet!' My father is still shouting at me. 'Run! Watch out, it's going to explode! Run! No, don't run! Stay where you are!'

If courage is the greatest gift parents can give a child, I seem to have missed out on that too.

As I struggled up the hill, I had a very clear picture in my mind of the times my father would fix his gaze on a distant horizon and urge me on. 'Hurry! Pick up your feet. But never ever, look anyone in the eye!' This is what he used to say whenever former patients shook their fists at him from their windows or swore at him from passing cars or hissed as he jostled me past them on the pavement. Was it rage or fear that made his skin turn grey? I wasn't always sure.

'Go back to bed, Claire, it's nothing!' The night someone threw a rock at our living room window and smashed it, he was badly shaken 'There's no one prowling out there,' he barked at me, quickly banging the shutters closed downstairs then racing upstairs two steps at a time to fix the shutters on the first floor. I could tell he was afraid by the drops of sweat on his forehead, and his fear unnerved me.

Even more disconcerting, however, was the realisation that my disappointment in him for showing fear had not gone unnoticed. Fathers are supposed to be brave and this wasn't the first time I'd seen him afraid. Over the last year, envelopes filled with broken glass, or excrement, or both, had been pushed through our letterbox, and someone had scrawled obscene graffiti all over the walls of the surgery. Everything now seemed to throw my father into a panic. He grew increasingly jittery, and he bickered with my mother more and more.

Now, as I drew near my aunts' house, I could see that the solid outer front door was closed, as were all the shutters. Vanna prides herself on being an early riser. Even when there's an icy wind and it's threatening to rain, she throws the windows wide open first thing in the morning and drapes bedding on the sills. The two loaves wrapped in wax paper on the stone wall of the parapet told me the bread deliveryman had already come by. The paper was soggy. I reached up for the frayed rope of the doorbell. Nonna Rosa used to complain that the sound was as vulgar, but Nonno Giacomino said that's just how he liked it and, in a rare act of defiance, he refused to replace it. Then after he died, nothing was ever replaced or repaired.

I banged on the sitting room shutter. No reply. I peered through the slats. Inside there was no sign of anyone, no sound of movement.

'They've gone.' A voice from above my head startled me. Holding a green golf umbrella, Marian Debono, who has lived in the terraced house next door since the early 1950s, was peering over the railing of her first floor

256

balcony. 'The Wembley cab picked them up around 7.30. They didn't say goodbye.'

'Where's my other cousin?' I tried to shelter beneath the front door pediment, squinting upwards. By then my jacket and trousers were wet, and dripping strands of hair stuck to my face and forehead. 'Ellie, Eleonora, the tall one. She should be here. Do you know where she's gone?'

'She went for her usual run. And speak of the devil, there she is.'

Catching sight of me, Ellie broke into a sprint. 'Oh, shit!' At the bottom of the stairs leading to the parapet, she did a little war dance. 'Vanna's done a flit, hasn't she? I was only out half an hour.' Out of breath, she leaned forward and clutched her knees. 'Fuck you too,' she shouted over her shoulder as a driver tooted to get her off the middle of the road.

♥≈

The glass doors slid open automatically. Both of us spotted Vanna at the same time. She was standing by the car rental counter, her hands on a wheelchair in which Luisa sat crumpled like a wilted flower. Ellie shot forward, her wet shoes squeaking on the tiled floor. Her tracksuit looked dry, but my trousers and jacket were still damp and had begun to itch. We had run in the driving rain all the way to Paceville to find a taxi to take us to the airport.

'Come on, Luisa, you're coming home with us.' Ellie pushed Vanna aside and grabbed the wheelchair's handles.

'Oh, no you don't.' Vanna butted Ellie with her hip.

257

'Sorry, she's coming with us,' Ellie said as she pushed Vanna back, regaining control of the wheelchair.

A powerful jab from Vanna's elbow forced her to let go.

Around us, people looked up. It must have seemed comical, two grown women pushing and striking out at each other. But the sight of a frightened old woman in a wheelchair staved off any hilarity. Luisa was clutching both sides of her head and rocking back and forth. At first it sounded as if she was humming to herself. Within seconds, however, the hum had become an eerie wail and the rocking more frenetic. I tried to step between my cousins. On either side, both pushed me away. When Vanna raised her right arm, I thought she was going to hit me, but it was Ellie she lunged at. Ellie ducked. Panting hard, she kept her eyes fixed on Vanna's eyes and slowly circled her.

When we were children, the sheer force of her gaze could subdue Vanna. 'Go home, Vanna, Claire and I have things to do,' she would say. 'Like what?' Vanna would challenge.

'Like Russian.' Ellie would hook her arm round mine and we would march off.

When Vanna raised her right arm again Ellie sprang forward. Grasping Vanna's wrist, she twisted her arm behind her back, but Vanna broke loose easily. Shoving Ellie backwards, she prodded her right index finger repeatedly into Ellie's chest. It looked as if Ellie might lose her balance, but spreading her arms she steadied herself and pushed Vanna away.

'Make them stop!' With one arm still wrapped around her head and with her eyes tightly shut, Luisa tugged the hem of my jacket. 'Sarita, make them stop.'

'Sarita? I'm not Sarita,' I said crouching down to bring my face level with my aunt's. 'I'm Claire, remember me?'

'Claire? Claire?' Keeping her head hunkered down, she opened one watery red-rimmed eye and then snapped it shut again. 'I don't know you. I don't know anyone called Claire.'

By now a huddle of onlookers had gathered near the car rental counter. I noticed a young woman grabbing a small boy's hand and tugging him protectively close to her leg. An old woman dressed entirely in black crossed herself. A man grinned lasciviously and mumbled an obscenity in Maltese. Ellie scowled fiercely in his direction, then with her arms wide began circling Vanna once more. From behind the counter the car rental official stepped forward and took hold of the wheelchair. 'Better get this out of harm's way,' he said to me.

'Make Laura stop,' Luisa cried and, with her eyes still tightly closed, she tugged at my jacket. 'Fetch Clementino, he'll make them stop. Get Clementino or they'll blow up the pharmacy.' Her rocking made the wheelchair creak. 'Don't let them blow up the pharmacy!'

What was going on in Luisa's head? There was a low-pitched buzzing in my ears as I turned around and saw Vanna swerve away from Ellie. What happened next seemed to go in slow motion. Her flesh wobbling, Vanna hurled herself towards the car rental man and knocked him against the counter. In his attempt to stop himself from falling, he reached for the counter, knocking over a metal leaflet stand in the process. As he fell, the stand came crashing to the floor and leaflets wafted down all around him.

My voice was a jagged rock as I yelled for Vanna to stop. I coughed and then sprinted after Vanna now sailing ahead towards passport control with Luisa in the wheelchair. Ellie tried to stop her, but two security guards, who had come out of nowhere, barred her way. When she tried to barge past them, they herded her backwards. Shouting loudly, she tried once more to push past them, but they would not let her go. Torn between going to her aid and preventing Vanna from reaching the escalator, I opted for the latter.

'Come on, auntie, they've called our flight.' Vanna tugged at her skirt which, in the struggle with Ellie, had ruched up around her buttocks.

'Vanna, stop, can't you see Luisa's terrified? You don't think they're going to let you board with her in that state, do you?'

Vanna pretended not to hear me. As she pushed forward, I saw that her knee-high stockings had slid down around her ankles. What did that bring to mind? In that moment, I had a clear image of Vanna, aged of eleven, in the middle of the school playground, surrounded by half a dozen girls. With her back to a wall, she had slid to the ground and was sitting with her legs straight in front of her, like a Victorian rag doll.

'Your father's a scab,' Salvina Agius, the ringleader, taunted her.

'Go away, leave me alone!' Vanna kicked out as the girls loomed over her, their arms around each other's shoulders like rugby players in a scrum.

'Go away, leave me alone!' Salvina said, mimicking Vanna's whimpering.

'Help me, Claire,' Vanna wailed.

'Help me, Claire,' Salvina cried.

My feet were stuck to the ground. I couldn't deny that Uncle Joseph was a strike-breaker. While my father had been out of work for months, Vanna's father had completely ignored the orders of the Medical Association of Malta, and though by now there was little that my parents agreed on, both of them thought Uncle Joseph was a disgrace. One day, when my father had been taking tea with some of his colleagues at the Grand Hotel in Rabat, he'd seen Uncle Joseph in the lobby talking to some Libyan doctors. The government had granted these doctors licences to practise without bothering to consult the medical association. My father and his friends had made a big to-do about it, demanding to pay their bill though they hadn't even drunk their tea. As they swept across the hotel lobby, my father brushed past Uncle Joseph and hissed '*Vergogna*' at him, and something much worse than 'shame on you', which he wouldn't repeat in front of me.

'Leave me alone!' Vanna screamed as two girls took her arms and yanked her to her feet. She was red in the face and wheezing like an electric saw but doing her best not to cry. Still, I saw her bottom lip quiver. She must have fallen over or been pushed because her shins and knees were grazed, and her white socks had slid down to her ankles and were filthy. 'Go away, leave me alone,' she cried as she tried to punch her way out of the circle.

'Leave me alone! Leave me alone!' Salvina teased.

'Yes, you heard. Leave her alone.' Ellie barged through the barrier formed by Vanna's molesters. In no time, she had Salvina in a half-nelson. 'Come on, call the pack off!' She twisted Salvina's arm so hard it forced her to her knees. 'Okay, now, all of you, piss off!'

Uncle Clementino used to joke that Eleonora only had two modes of operating, which were actually two sides of the same coin: her Statue of Liberty mode and her Gorgon mode. Right now she was in Gorgon mode, her hair flying about her face, her eyes flashing with fury. My mother, who'd been present at Ellie's birth, said that of all the Toledano grandchildren the newly born Eleonora looked most like Nonna Rosa. Even when she was only one hour old she'd screamed the maternity ward down.

'Get going, all of you! *Issa ejja*! – clear off!' Ellie stood with her feet well apart and her arms spread-eagled to protect Vanna. Without looking back, the bullies straggled out of the school gate.

'Now, you go home too, Vanna,' Ellie said.

'Can't I come with you and Claire?'

'No you can't.' Ellie blocked Vanna's way. 'Your father's a strike-breaker, he's a traitor. Why would Claire and I want you to come with us? Go on, go on home!'

Watching Vanna waddle off all those years ago, I had felt sad for her. Her shoulders had dropped, her body was shrunken, exactly as she looked now in the check-in hall.

'Go on, stop this. Let me take Luisa home!' Ellie broke away from the airport security guards and parked herself in front of the wheelchair. Bending forward and bringing her face close to Luisa's, she spoke softly, trying not to scare her, but there was fear mixed with suspicion in Luisa's look. 'Do you want to go with Vanna or do you want to stay here in Malta?'

'Vanna?' Slowly but with her neck still retracted between her bony shoulders Luisa removed her arms from her head. 'Who's Vanna? I don't know any Vanna either. Where's Marguerita? Don't tell me. This terrible woman has kidnapped her,' she said and lashed out at Vanna, hitting her on the thigh.

'Stop, auntie, please stop! Calm down!' Tears welled up in Vanna's eyes. 'They're about to board our flight. We've got to go.'

'Tell this woman to leave us alone!' Luisa gripped my wrist and pulled me closer to her.

'Luisa, come on,' Ellie said and blocked the way. 'We're going back to Lapsi Street.'

'Laura?' Luisa frowned.

'No, I'm not Laura. I'm Ellie, Eleonora. Come on, let's go.'

'Please, Sarita, please!' Luisa drew her neck in even further. 'Take me home!' She tugged at my arm. 'Take me home. I want to go home!'

'You see, she doesn't want to board the plane.' Ellie took hold of the wheelchair again.

'You can't do that, you can't,' Vanna shouted as Ellie moved away.

But Ellie got no further than the glass doors. As they snapped open, two policemen in uniform stepped in and stopped her in her tracks.

'Would Mrs Weinberg and Miss Toledano please go to the departure gate where your flight is boarding ...'

Out of the corner of my eye, I could see Ellie waving her arms. When one of the policemen put a hand on her left arm, she shook it off. Then the second took her right arm. I could do nothing and anyway at that moment my attention was diverted by what was happening closer to me. Once more, it all seemed to take place in slow motion. Vanna was crumpling to the ground and sobbing. I bent down to help her, but she lashed out at me.

'Get away, get away from me!' She kicked her legs like that child in the fight in the school playground all those years ago. 'Go away!' A blow caught me on the shin. 'Leave me alone,' she howled as I tried again to pull her up. She was babbling now, and I wasn't sure if she was speaking English, Maltese, Hebrew or a combination of them all.

'They never loved me,' she said and hugged herself. 'They never loved me. You never loved me,' she cried and kicked her legs up and down.

'Come on, Vanna, please, get up. I think you've missed your flight. Let's take Luisa home.'

'Luisa doesn't know who I am,' she wailed.

'Let's go home,' I said as I smoothed her hair behind her ears. This time she didn't try to push me away.

'My father loved Malta, and he loved his family even though they treated him like a fool.' Vanna gulped in some air. 'And everyone was nasty to my mother because she was poor and had little education. I know you and Ellie thought I was stupid too. But who was it over all the years who kept the ties strong with the island and the family? What did anyone else care?'

All of a sudden, I felt a surge of tenderness for my cousin. To my surprise, my eyes began to prick with tears. 'Come on, *hanini*.'

Not since my mother's death had I used the Maltese word of endearment, and it felt strange saying it out loud. Even when we change language, the words of affection our mothers used remain the most spontaneous. But from the age of twelve I'd done my best to suppress spontaneity.

Many years ago I 'd realised that saying *chéri* to Yves was easier than saying the same thing in my mother tongue. I'd have felt too exposed if I'd called him *hanini*. What the French word conveyed was at a slight remove from the tenderness of the Maltese word.

'Look, you're going to make me cry.' I smiled as Vanna struggled to her feet. 'Hang on a minute, *hanini*.' I bent down and, gently patting her back with one hand, pulled up her stockings with the other.

❧

'I bet you'll never manage to get Luisa out of that filthy old dressing gown,' Vanna had said with a bruised smile, giving me a brisk hug. After the hysterical outburst at the airport, she had come quietly with me back to Lapsi Street to wait for a few days until the airline could find her a seat on a flight to Tel Aviv. Ellie was to leave the same day as Vanna. The commotion at the airport was not what had brought Ellie to the attention of the police. There had been a fire at one of the refugee camps. A few days before, someone had seen her talking across the barbed wire fence to one of the internees. In the end there was no proof that she had instigated the protest, but the advice from the police was to leave Malta as soon as possible.

265

'I guess my fate is always to be expelled from this bloody island,' she said. 'You go round thinking the world belongs to everyone, but there's always someone who'll remind you that you have no place on their patch of soil. So, Claire, *hanini*, this means that everything is in your hands now. You can't avoid it. You're the one who's going to have to decide now what's to be done with Luisa and Marguerita.'

Vanna had blamed Ellie for ruining her plans, but her distress ran deeper. 'The rest of the family always blamed my father for the death of Carmela Galea, but they all failed her, every one of them. If anything, my father was least at fault. He did try to help. Uncle Clementino, Luisa, Marguerita and your father and mother too, Claire, what did they do? Nothing, until it was too late. Your mother was on duty at the pharmacy when Tony Galea came asking for help. Carmela was bleeding. Your father was the Galeas' family doctor, but he wasn't seeing patients. So he was the traitor, not my father. No, don't look so hurt! Refusing to treat the sick and poor must have made him enemies. And, no, I don't know what was wrong with Carmela. It always sounded like a miscarriage, but my father never spoke to me about that night, though I did catch bits and pieces when he argued with my mother. I remember Tony banging on the door of our house around midnight, throwing stones at the closed shutters. He wasn't alone. Clementino and Luisa were with him. Apparently Tony had gone to find Clementino and the two of them had come here to collect Luisa. Ellie, you must remember this. You and Danny were staying at our place that night. The commotion outside woke us both, though Danny went on sleeping like a log. The last clear memory I have of that night, a memory which is truly my own and not something pieced together over the years from overheard snatches of whispered conversations between my parents, was my father hurrying down the street with Tony, Luisa and Uncle Clementino scampering behind him. I remember too that for several days afterwards all the grown-ups were in a terrible state.'

'Carmela bled to death,' I said. 'Let me show you the newspaper article I found. I've worked out a sequence of events, and it's why I came round so early the day you tried to leave with Luisa, to show you, and Ellie.'

'If your father had refused to treat Carmela, Claire, wouldn't that have given Tony Galea a good excuse to send a letter-bomb to him?' Ellie said. 'On the other hand, if your father had botched an abortion, Vanna, I imagine her family would have been out gunning for him. Anyway, we can't prove a thing. We're no further on than the police were decades ago.'

'Well, what about your father?' Vanna said, pushing away a plate of half-eaten food. Briefly, Ellie and I exchanged glances, in astonishment.

'What about my father?' Ellie took the plate and scraped everything onto hers. All the food on our plates was cold now. None of us was hungry.

'Uncle Clementino and Carmela had been lovers. Nonna Rosa always said.' Vanna folded her arms across the platform of her breasts.

'Nonna Rosa? Jeezus, we all know what a vivid imagination she had, especially when it came to sexual indiscretions.' Ellie said.

'She was so puritanical,' I said.

'Precisely.' Ellie picked up our plates and strode into the kitchen. 'The thing about Puritans is they're constantly thinking about sex, ostensibly to avoid its pitfalls.' She scraped the remaining food into the dustbin. 'I don't think we'll ever know who sent the bomb. Even if it was Tony Galea, how do we know who he intended to kill, Uncle Joseph or Uncle Albert? All the grown-ups were involved in Carmela's death in some way, didn't Vanna say that? They were all responsible, even Sarita, because she had turned Tony away. No wonder the family fell to pieces afterwards. The burden of guilt was too much for any of them to bear. The Sins of our Fathers …'

'My father was a saint,' Vanna said as she sprang up, knocking her chair over. 'I won't have you speaking in this nasty way about him. You don't know how he suffered.'

'Yeah, yeah, we all suffered.' Ellie stepped over the fallen chair.

'But not as much as we did,' Vanna said. 'You should have seen where we lived when we first got to Israel.'

'You should have seen what happened to us when my father ditched us …'

'Stop it, just stop it,' I said and slapped my palm on the table. 'It wasn't your mother who died. It was mine, my mother.' As I spoke, there was tightness in my chest. 'It was my mother.' The pain was so sharp it felt as if my lungs might burst.

'Oh shit,' Ellie said, 'don't start crying. Don't bloody well start crying.'

'Shut up!' Vanna walked around to my side of the table. 'See what you've done?' She wrapped her arms around me. 'You've really and truly upset her. You're always upsetting everyone. You may be some big deal freedom fighter, but what about the people close to you? Do you care that you hurt their feelings?'

'You're such a self-righteous bitch,' Ellie said.

'Stop it, the two of you.' I started rummaging in my bag for a tissue. In the past, my father had always coaxed me out of my tears. A year after my mother's murder, he had gone through our house and removed all the pictures of her, declaring that he had mourned enough and it was time to get on with his life. Time for me to get on with mine too. His tone wasn't harsh, but I remember hoping against hope that he would put his arms around me as he spoke.

As an adult I have never cried about anything. Not when Yves declared our marriage over. Not when I learned he had a son. Now, I couldn't stop myself. Vanna's body was so soft and warm. When she too began to sob, I started to wail.

'Shit!' Ellie said. 'I'm glad to be going home on Thursday,' and stomped out of the front door.

❧

From the end of the corridor I can hear the ragged bleating of women and men congregated in the chapel at evening mass. There is a faint whiff of urine in the nursing home which no amount of scented air fresheners, detergents and carpet cleaners can mask. Above the head of Marguerita's bed, on a dark wooden crucifix,

269

speckles of blood made of wax drip down the sinewy legs of the Christ figure and woodcarver has skilfully shaped the excrescences on his callused feet. I'm reminded of a photograph of Rudolf Nureyev's feet. On the face of it, they were ugly, almost deformed, but in black and white the photographer had turned them into a work of art.

It's not impossible to see beauty in the real thing, I say to myself, as I bend over Marguerita's feet, which I have propped up on my lap. The toenails are bent claws, thick and brittle, and some kind of fungal infection has turned them black. It must be months since anybody cut them. I bite my bottom lip. The thing is to concentrate while clipping, not to think too much. Marguerita sits up in her chair like a queen, one leg in plaster still, her left arm in a sling, holding up a book that she seems genuinely absorbed in, not saying a word. It's as if she believes what I'm doing is her long-withheld due.

As I tend to her poor old feet, I think again of the hostage who said that his time in captivity had taken him to the very edge of himself. The words sounded beautiful, strangely evoking an image of the earth as seen by an astronaut floating in space. I longed to experience what he had experienced which, as he went on to explain, was a life enhanced by disaster rather than blighted by it. His attitude to his suffering had made him more generous towards others and kinder towards himself. I, on the other hand, had suppressed a catastrophe that might have led me to a more expansive view of the world. Once, I would have thought myself incapable of touching deformed feet let alone washing them, but this is what I've been doing since Ellie's and Vanna's departure, and I feel no disgust.

I'm the one in charge now, and so I must deal with the situation. I'm not unhappy. On the contrary, I continue to wake up each morning looking forward to the day ahead. Marguerita will be able to walk again very soon, and I will be at Lapsi Street when she returns. As a freelance worker, I can take as much time off work as I like.

I'm in no hurry to go back to the low skies of Brussels.

The End

About the Author

Born in Malta and brought up in Israel and Australia, Aline P'nina Tayar is the author of a memoir, *How Shall We Sing?: A Mediterranean Journey Through a Jewish Family* (Pan Macmillan/Picador). Her home is in Bath but her work as a conference interpreter takes her frequently to Brussels. *Island of Dreams* was short-listed for the Outbound Best Novel Prize 2011 and was runner-up for the Harry Bowling Prize 2012.

Made in the USA
Charleston, SC
05 October 2012